FOWL PLAY

~~~

by
Monique MacDonald & Carla Howatt

By the Book Publishing
404, 11716-100 Ave, Edmonton, AB T5K 2G3 Canada

First Edition 2024

Acknowledgments

We would like to acknowledge and thank our fantastic beta readers, Alexandria MacDonald, Tanya Holm, Jennifer Mulder, and Fiona Beland-Quest for their valuable comments and recommendations. Harlan Coben for his interesting and encouraging seminar. And because he said he'd mention us if we mentioned him. And last but not least, we would like to acknowledge our wonderful families. Especially our husbands, Larry and Don. Without their support, cheerleading, and never-ending patience, this book might never have seen the light of day.

Monique's Dedication

To my husband Larry, for always supporting every single one of my ambitious and not-so-ambitious projects and for encouraging me to write, no matter what. To my daughters, Ali and Naomi, for pushing me beyond my fears and trepidations, and showing me what courage and taking chances are all about. To my grandson, Bash, for filling up the missing pieces of my heart. To my angel parents, for leaving Egypt and starting from scratch to give your future family a better life, and for believing in me, even when I didn't believe in myself. And finally, to Mémé Liane, for teaching me the magic of the written word. I miss you.

~~~

Carla's Dedication

To Penny and Derek, your love is an inspiration and a balm to this Momma's soul. To Adam, I hope you would be proud. To Mackenzie, you are the unexpected addition that I didn't know my life needed. And to Mum and Dad, my role models and the two people who showed me what unconditional love looks like.

Prologue

The late spring humidity, mixed with the airlessness of the enclosed space was slowly suffocating the lone woman inside the box. The rasping sound of her labored breathing was the only thing breaking the deafening silence. The hopelessness of it all was slowly eating away at her sanity.

How long would they keep her here? Could she dare to move her numb limbs or would she risk dislodging the straw-like tube precariously hanging between her lips? Blindfolded, hands and feet tightly bound, she tried to stay flat on her back. If the straw slipped out of her mouth, she feared there would be no way to retrieve it. It was her only lifeline to water. Being unable to see meant she couldn't be certain where the source of water was located. The woman only knew that she could suck through the straw to quench her thirst. Having not eaten in days, she knew that continuing to drink water was important, not only as a thirst quencher but as a means of survival.

Why was she here? What was going to happen to her? She couldn't remember having done anything to anyone to deserve this kind of extreme treatment. She had no enemies she could recall. Her heart began to race, and she started to count out loud, focusing on the sound of her voice and the numbers she was reciting. The therapist she'd been seeing for the last few years had taught her this calming technique back when she had been prone to panic attacks. She needed to stay calm. But damn, how could she? Her eyes were tightly covered, she had no idea where she was being held nor who her captors were. "No," she told herself. "Don't let your mind go there". Deep breaths. In and out. In and out. In and...

Wait, what was that? She stilled herself and listened intently. There it was again, the sound of distant footsteps coming towards her. Someone was here. Maybe her situation wasn't completely hopeless. Maybe she would be rescued and see her family again.

"Oh God, help me."

"Help! Help! I'm over here!" she screamed. "Someone help me!"

She didn't know how thick the enclosure she was imprisoned in was, or what it would take for someone to hear her, but this might be her last chance. She screamed as loud as she could.

"HELP!!!"

As she drew a breath to yell once more, she heard the footsteps come nearer. They had heard her! A rush of relief washed over her.

"I'm here, I'm here," she began to shout. The footsteps paused by her head.

"Let me out, oh God, please let me out!" she whimpered.

She heard an odd sound that caused her to freeze. It was quiet at first, almost imperceptible. Then it grew louder and louder. It painfully jolted her. Laughter. Haunting laughter now echoed in the room. Followed by a quiet, eerie voice, slowly whispering in her ear.

"I don't think so."

Chapter 1

Whose bright idea was it to stick a bottle of beer, upside down, in a Margarita? Why hadn't she stopped at two? It'd been her friends' wedding anniversary last night and everyone else was already on their third drink. She had to catch up, right? She was a responsible adult, so how could it hurt? Well, it did. Damned Bulldogs. Damned Tequila shots. She didn't recover as fast as she used to. Now that she had to concentrate on work, those Mexican ghosts from last night's binge had decided to haunt her. Just great.

She hadn't made up her mind about what she wanted her starting bid to be. A tag hanging off a bag at the side of the storage unit was distracting her. Because she didn't recognise the store logo on it, she presumed it came from somewhere expensive. It looked fancy. Gold lettering on a shiny black label. Her taste ran more towards New To You, Goodwill, and other second-hand shops or, if feeling particularly flush, Reitmans and Winners. Damn it, this hangover made it difficult to decipher the writing on it from a distance.

MacDonald & Howatt

The eye-catching tag dangled from a large bag that looked to be full of clothing. That bag was precariously sitting on top of two bins placed on an old Tall Boy dresser and looked dangerously close to falling on top of the people bidding below it. The group was quite the motley assortment, from a tattooed guy with spiked hair to a bleached blonde with a red-lipsticked mouth who couldn't stop snapping her gum in rhythm with the overhead fan. They stood around, watching the auctioneer set up and prepare for the morning's auction. He yawned, not seeming to be in any rush, slowly sipping coffee out of a Tim Hortons paper cup. It was obvious that this wasn't his first auction; he had the worn, bored look of someone who'd 'been there and done that' many times over.

The group shifted from side to side, as they waited for things to get started. They had to get up early this morning for this particular auction and were anxiously waiting for it to begin. None more so than Maddy Whitman. Standing away from the group, she was leaning up against the unit opposite the one that was first up for auction, enjoying the feeling of the cool metal against her back. She'd been up far too late and the tequila felt like it was oozing out of her pores. Gawd, when would she ever learn not to drink so much the night before an early workday? Especially before one involving an auction.

Trying to steady her stomach, she was taking deep, slow breaths when the bidding finally began. A man with hair sticking straight up in the air, molded into dangerous-looking spikes, came out of the gate decisively by bidding $50. The bleached blonde jumped in with $60. Maddy wondered what they could see up there that she'd missed. She had been on the auction house's

2

website last night to see what was up for auction, but nothing had stood out. While the bidding was certainly not big bucks, it was a bit much for a locker that only had a stack of bags full of used clothing, a piece of furniture, and two plastic containers with the word "Decorations" scrawled across on pieces of masking tape stuck on them. One could never tell how these auctions would go. Who knows, maybe Spikey had found a new buyer for used clothes that she didn't know about.

In the end, it was just the two of them bidding and Spikey walked away with the unit's contents for $65 smackeroos. Soon, the flock of human sheep followed behind the auctioneer as he moved on to the next unit. Unlike TV shows that portrayed storage auctions as lively affairs, these were, in reality, more subdued and uneventful; full of hungover people who scrounge through other people's castoffs to earn a living. Maddy didn't even bother trying to stifle the yawn that took over her entire face, her green eyes squeezing shut.

"What's the matter princess, late night?"

Maddy opened her left eye mid-squint to see who dared to speak to her this early in the morning. She blinked quickly to clear her vision and saw a short man with a bad comb-over looking up at her. He looked like he could be Danny DeVito's twin nephew Squiggy.

"Um, yeah," she said, inching away from him. What was it about storage yards that brought out the Lothario in some guys?

"What's a pretty girl like you doing in a place like this?" he pestered, trailing behind her.

"Hoping to buy some peace and quiet," Maddy scowled as she pushed herself away from the wall, quickly walking towards the group that was peering into the unit. There were so many people at these things sometimes that it was tough to get a good look. That's the reason why she liked to check the auctions online first, hoping to weed through some of the more obvious duds. There was one unit in particular today that she was quite interested in. She damn well wasn't going to let Squiggy here make her miss it.

"Ha!" said 'Mister can't-take-a-hint' as he slithered behind her, "Anyone ever tell ya you're quite funny?"

She was desperately trying to see around a large man wearing a Budweiser ball cap and was not having much luck at all. Every time she moved to one side, he'd shift from one foot to the other, blocking her view. And when he wasn't moving, an annoying woman, probably his wife, stepped out in front.

"Dude, I'm busy." Turning sideways, she snuck between Mr. Budweiser and his Missus. Unfortunately, just as she did, he shifted right as his wife went left. Maddy was almost sandwiched between them.

"Excuse me, s'cuuuse me," she muttered as she pushed her way forward. Mrs. Budweiser frowned, crossed her arms over her ample bosom, and stood her ground. Maddy contemplated putting to use a tight angle tackle she'd been taught years ago in high school Phys. Ed. but thought better of it. There was probably something against using physical violence in the auction participation forms she'd signed. Instead, she made a quick deke to the right, slipping past Mrs. Budweiser's other side, all the while looking over her left shoulder and smiling sweetly at the couple. Maddy was quite pleased with herself. Not even a bottle of tequila could hamper her stealth moves.

Unfortunately, it wasn't the locker she'd been waiting for, so all her smooth moves were wasted. The dismal contents of that locker brought in a measly $50, and the group went shuffling en masse to the next unit.

Bingo! This was the one. The unit wasn't full but looked promising. At first glance, an old couch piled high with plastic bins and boxes, a dresser, and a toolbox were what most people might notice in the unit. But, buying storage lockers was part knowledge and understanding of the market, part gut instinct, and, lastly, a whole whack of luck. Maddy preferred not to rely on that last one. She made sure to keep herself educated and only then, would she allow herself to follow her intuition. What she saw in that particular unit was not an old couch, but a couch of quality. She could tell it wasn't one of the myriad of couches found in local furniture store chains. Through the clear plastic boxes, she could discern what looked like photo albums that had very thick pages. She knew from experience that these were less apt to be photos and more likely to be collector's cards or coins.

Bidding began at $25 for the unit's content. Maddy waited patiently to see who else might be interested. An older, mustachioed gentleman wearing suspenders and a cowboy hat, opened the bidding. It was quickly upped when Spikey jumped in. They bid it up to $125 before they slowed down. Maddy could almost see the tips on Spikey's hair start trembling in anticipation. She'd noticed during previous auctions that he seemed to get as much excitement in the bidding process as in the winning itself. She couldn't fault him for that. She felt the exact same way.

It looked like Suspender Man had decided this bid was too pricey for what he thought he saw in there.

"We're at $125. $125... Do I hear $150? $150? Going once..."

"$175!" Maddy interjected with the confidence of an experienced no-nonsense bidder.

A murmur ran through the crowd as they sensed bidding excitement happening. Spikey frowned at Maddy, annoyed that he hadn't walked away with it for $125. She gave him her most serene smile. No one would have guessed it by how calm she looked, but her heart was pounding faster and faster in her chest. The adrenaline from the auction was rushing through her body. This was the best part. She'd learned to look relaxed and confident when bidding; not desperate and hungry so her competitors could tell she was worried. She looked for all the world like she had the money and didn't really care how much she ended up paying for the unit's contents. It was hers and the rest were just a bunch of unimportant details.

Spikey didn't say a word, just nodded his head, turned, and walked away. The auctioneer finished up the bidding and the unit was all hers.

~~~

After Maddy settled the $175 plus service fee she owed, she took the key Marty, the auctioneer, had turned over to her. Lifting the garage-style door up, she walked into the unit. What she was most interested in finding out was if she'd been right about the sports cards and coin collections but refused to let herself dig into that box until she'd done all the hard labor. It would be her reward tonight once she had gone through everything else.

Pulling out her cell phone from her back pocket, she called one of her best friends for some help.

"Hey Rick, ole buddy, whatcha doin'?"

"Probably helping you move something somewhere," was the laughing response.

"Awesome! I'm at the Triple A."

"Give me about 20 minutes and I'll pop on over."

Rick Nasser and Maddy had been friends since high school. He'd been a plump and awkward guy with a slight Arabic accent, definitely a late bloomer. He didn't fit with any of the 'in' crowds. Maddy was a shy and sad teenager who kept to herself. They both sat in the back of French class. Two loners. He loved to joke around. Maddy rarely smiled. So Rick made it his mission to make her smile. He succeeded most of the time and still made her laugh like nobody's business to this day.

Maddy spent the next half hour rooting through some of the bags and boxes that were near the back of the unit. A bunch of jeans, some with sewn-on patches, a cute winter hat, a couple of coats, and various other pieces of clothing. She considered them a bonus as no one had been able to see them when they were bidding. That was the thing with bidding on a storage unit, you were bidding only on what you could see from the outside, and no one was allowed inside the unit. You couldn't move or touch anything. Sometimes this worked against her, other times, like today, it worked to her advantage.

By the time she'd made it through the third bag, she realized most of them were indeed full of clothes. Not necessarily a bad thing as, like the couch, the clothes were a bit dated but still of high quality. There were lots of vintage stores that would pay decently for the right clothing. In fact, if she's lucky enough, these bags might just pay for the whole locker. All it would take was for one piece to be a rare find or all the rage right now.

She heard the sound of Rick's truck before she saw it. He had replaced his truck's mid pipe with an x-pipe to make sure you heard it coming, much to his family's displeasure. And that was intentional. Rick didn't want his wife nor his almost ready for their learner's license daughters to 'borrow' his vehicle. All three hated the loud muffler. Rick wasn't into loud trucks but a guy's gotta do what a guy's gotta do to protect his beloved ride.

"How much we got this time, Mads?" Rick asked, standing by the unit's door. Sweeping one hand through his thick black hair, he scratched the back of his head. He then placed both of his hands on his hips and stuck out his lower lip as he surveyed its contents, nodding. He always did that when he looked things over, Maddy thought. He could be checking out a truck, bottles of beer, or his hot wife. Made no difference.

"Not much," Maddy smiled, he was so predictable. "Mainly the couch, desk, and tool chest, the rest are just boxes and bags."

"Sweet," he said, seeming pleased that it wasn't too much this time. He never knew what he was going to find when Maddy called him for help, like the time she had moved a two-headed wooden goat. One thing's for sure, it was never boring. He did an exaggerated stretch and flexed his biceps to show off his muscles.

Maddy bit her lip, trying not to laugh at him. "Ready now, strong man?"

"Whaaat? A guy's gotta stretch and warm up before doing any heavy lifting. I can't go and injure myself now, I have a wife and two daughters to think about," he grinned and winked. Those dimples of his could melt any woman's heart. Good thing Maddy wasn't any woman. She knew him much too well for them to have any effect on her.

He riffled through the steel chest for a few minutes, holding each tool, switching them from one hand to the other, and weighing them. Nothing seemed to impress him.

"They're in pretty good shape but just your average quality tools."

"Rick…"

"Yeah?"

"What do you usually say in Arabic when you want us to get started?"

" 'Yalla', why?"

"Yalla Rick! YALLA!" "Alright, alright," he laughed.

They took the things off the couch so they could move it onto the back of the truck first. It was a solid couch that left them huffing and puffing by the time they had it safely positioned in the truck's box. Next came the tool chest and the dresser, then followed all the rest of the heavy items.

"Sofa, so good! Eh, Mads?"

Maddy groaned trying hard to hold back a smile. "Hey c'mon, admit it, it was begging to be said." "Mmmhmm, let's get this over and done with so we can get the show on the road, Mister Nasser!"

9

They topped off the truck with the boxes and then wedged the bags in wherever they could find a spare inch of space.

"There, that must be record time, eh?" Rick looked at the truck, feeling satisfied with a job well done.

"Definitely," Maddy agreed.

They high-fived each other and jumped into the cab of his truck. Rick grabbed two towels and handed Maddy one to wipe her hands. For a body shop mechanic, he was quite particular about keeping his hands impeccably clean. Maddy was pretty sure it was a direct result of living with three females.

"Alright habibi, give me directions to our destination."

"Turn left here," she instructed him.

"Here? But that's away from the exit," he pointed, frowning.

"I know, trust me."

"Trust you?" He raised an eyebrow. "Famous last words, Ms. Whitman!"

They hadn't gone further than 20 feet when she told him to stop. She then jumped out of the truck. Rick got out behind her, trying to catch up. Walking to the storage unit only two doors down from the one she'd just won in the auction, she pulled a key out of her jeans' pocket, inserted it in the lock, and rolled open the door.

"Let's try to get as much of it as possible into one corner," she instructed a confused-looking Rick.

"Ummm... we're moving it two doors down? Why?" "Oh, didn't I tell you? I decided it was time to hang up my shingle, get legit, and have an office," Maddy explained.

"In a storage unit?" "Yeah, and?"

"Of course, a storage unit, why not?" He waved her in. "You know it would've been easier, and a lot less work for us, if we'd just carried everything over, right?"

Maddy grinned, "And where would the fun be in that? Good thing you warmed up, eh?"

Rick swept his hand through his hair again and began pulling bags off the truck. After knowing Maddy all these years, not much she could do surprised him anymore. She reminded him of his eldest sister in Egypt, Mona. That's probably why he chose her as his 'adopted sister'. And like his sister, her reasoning escaped him. The process of unloading was identical to what they'd done just a few moments ago, only in reverse order. Off came the bags and boxes, then the dresser and tool chest, and finally the couch.

"Sofa, so…" "Don't say it, Rick!"

"You're no fun as a grown-up, you know that?"

By the time the contents were all moved again, they were both covered in sweat and trying hard to catch their breath. Rick reached into his truck and pulled out a plastic bottle of water, the one-liter kind you buy at a 7-Eleven, and took a long, deep swig. Maddy reached out a hand for him to pass it to her, but he pulled it away, holding it close to his chest.

"Nope, didn't you say plastic water bottles weren't good for your health? That they leach chemicals into your water or something like that? I wouldn't want to be responsible for you having babies with gills! I'd never hear the end of it. Nope, not gonna happen," Rick declared half-jokingly. "Tasha would have my head if she knew that I'd let you do something that went against your beliefs."

11

"Knock it off Rick and hand over that bottle NOW!" Maddy demanded grumpily. Her body was dehydrated not only from last night but also from this move. If she didn't get some water in her, Rick was going to hear some language come out of her mouth that would've made him question his choice of having her as one of his twins' godmothers.

"And leave Tasha out of it. We both know your wife would take my side. She always does."

"That's only because you know more of my deep dark secrets than she does, so she needs to stay on your good side."

Tasha and Rick had met at Julio's Barrio on Whyte Avenue where Maddy had insisted on celebrating her eighteenth birthday 'Mexican style.' She'd gotten drunk, started dancing around with one of their huge sombreros on her head, and bumped into Tasha spilling her beer all over Tasha's white top, which resulted in it becoming see-through. Maddy, drunkenly mortified, started wiping Tasha's top with every napkin in sight, including those that had salsa on them. White became pink. Tasha just stood there. Rick ran over, threw Maddy over his shoulder, and started apologizing to the most gorgeous woman he'd ever seen while Maddy kicked at him. People started hooting and hollering. Maddy kicked harder. The manager asked them to leave. Tasha told the manager that all was fine, they were all old friends 'Just messing around.'

"In that case," the manager said. "You can leave with them."

So, she did.

Outside Julio's, Tasha eyed them up and down and began to laugh uproariously. She then demanded that

Rick make it up to her by taking her out on a date and buying her a new top. He did both and the rest, as they say, is history. Maddy's still adamant that Tasha had planned the whole 'bumping into her' incident so she could meet Rick.

"What are you smiling about?" Rick asked Maddy suspiciously.

"Nothing. Can't a girl smile in satisfaction after a good day at work?" she replied, handing the bottle back to him. Thirst quenched and body rested, she headed into the unit again and picked up the box that'd been set aside earlier while they were unloading.

"Whatcha doing with that?" Rick wanted to know. "I saw some stuff in there that I thought might be interesting. I want to take it home and slowly go through it," she answered. "Thanks for the help. I'll bring some beer when I come over next. It's time for me to get home and wash up before I start attracting junkyard dogs or something."

She began walking towards her car and stopped, looked him over, and added, "Speaking of which, you'd better take a shower too or Tasha will have my head if you stink up the furniture."

Rick smirked, "Tasha loves me all sweaty and smelly. Pheromones and stuff, don't cha know?" "Too much information, Rick."

"Nah, when you're single, you live vicariously through me, admit it."

"Say goodnight, Gracie," Maddy laughed.

"Goodnight Gracie!" Rick shouted as he revved the truck's engine.

Chapter 2

Nu-mis-ma-tism'. Maddy had looked up coin collecting on the internet. She knew it had an official name, of course it would, didn't everything fancy? But for some reason, she couldn't remember it. She didn't know much about 'numismatism', and she blamed her stepfather for that. PopPop, her kind and silly 'step' grandfather, loved collecting coins and displaying them in albums that had little individual pockets for each coin. One day, he'd given her a shiny new gold-colored Canadian one-dollar coin. He told her it was nicknamed the 'Loonie' because of the loon minted on it. It had come in a tiny blue square envelope. '1987 was the very first year Canada's one- dollar coin was minted,' he'd proudly explained. That was the year they switched from the one-dollar green paper bill to a coin. She was to keep it safe and never play with it. 'Several years from now,' he added, 'this coin would be worth a lot more than its face value, maybe even a hundred bucks!' That didn't sit well with her stepfather who turned red in the face and got upset at PopPop. He yelled at him to stop putting fantasies in a little girl's head. No child living under his roof was going to have any false hopes as he had had as a kid. Besides, "Money is meant to be spent on things you need," he spewed. "It's not meant to buy coins you can't spend. Besides, nobody in their right mind would want to pay more than a dollar for a dollar!" Maddy was being raised to be a realist. Period. Her stepfather had been one nasty piece of work.

Maddy remembered running to her room and hiding the coin in her special ballerina glass music box, another gift from PopPop. She didn't care what her stepfather thought, she loved PopPop and she loved her new 'Loonie' coin. She turned the key on the music box, sat back, and watched the ballerina in her mesh pink tutu twirl and twirl while she dreamt of how rich she would be one day all because of her sweet PopPop and his gift. A few weeks later, her coin had disappeared. She searched everywhere for it; in her night table, behind her curtains, and under her old second-hand bunk bed. She even tore off the My Little Pony sheets, just in case she'd forgotten to put it back and fallen asleep holding it or something. Maybe it had gotten lost in the folds. She even looked in her piggy bank, thinking that perhaps her mom had accidentally put it in there. It was nowhere to be found. Maddy was heartbroken. When she finally asked if he had seen her coin, her stepfather replied that her mother had been short a dollar for the laundromat, and he didn't feel like leaving the house just to get her a single Loonie. He remembered her useless coin and just 'borrowed' it. At least it'd been useful for something, he said, adding that she shouldn't worry, he'd pay her back, eventually. Then he laughed at her while taking a swig of beer.

He never did pay her back. Maddy added that to the long list of things he owed her. She got even though by dumping half of his bottle of Vodka and replacing it with water. PopPop had taught her that trick, along with a bunch of others that had come in handy over the years They'd had such a loving relationship, PopPop and her stepdad. Yeah, great memories.

And now, here she was, a couple of decades later, all grown up and living on her own. After looking through the first album of coins, she found herself staring in disbelief at a one-dollar 1987 Canadian Loonie preserved in a clear protective sleeve, laying right there on top of a pile of miscellaneous coins and jewelry. She picked up the Loonie and thought wistfully of PopPop. Thanks to him, she knew it could be worth something. As for the other coins? She had no idea, but she knew exactly who might.

Plopping herself down on her cherry red armchair, feet on the coffee table, she pulled out her cell phone and started texting, '*Hey Ash! Whatcha up to?*'

Getting her friends involved when she found cool stuff in a locker was the best part. It was more fun to share the excitement of unique finds with them. Maddy counted herself lucky that they loved what she did for a living and were more than happy to help her. It was no wonder they'd been friends for so long.

Ashley Mueller was her other best friend. Maddy, Rick, and Ashley had been inseparable from almost the moment they met in high school. She loved jewelry and all things shiny. Maddy, on the other hand, preferred things cozy and demure. She was pretty sure that Ashley would know about the bling and, hopefully, about the coins.

Less than two minutes later, Ashley called. "It's Friday night, what do you think I'm doing?"

"Damn, you've got plans?" Maddy's excitement diminished some. She should have guessed she'd be busy. Her friend was blonde, smart, and beautiful inside and out. Ever since Ashley had started online dating, she was rarely home on weekends. Maddy's weekends were mostly spent with Netflix and chilled wine.

"Not a single one. I needed a Friday night for myself. Shocking, I know. I was hoping you'd call for some girlfriend time. I have a bottle of Tawny Port begging to be opened. It's looking for some dark chocolate to keep it company. You wouldn't happen to have any, would you?" she asked knowing full well that Maddy would have a cupboardful of all types of chocolate.

"If you bring that port over, I promise it won't be lonely," Maddy laughed. "Just no tequila tonight." Then adding, "Oh, and I just bought the contents of another storage locker in an auction. This one's the motherlode of all lockers. You'll love this, it contains jewelry!"

"Did you say jewelry?"

'Click'

"Ash? Hello? Ash?" Maddy looked at her phone, shaking her head. Apparently, Ashley was in a hurry to see the bling and had immediately hung up.

~ ~ ~

Ashley had a hell of a long workweek. Most Friday nights, she'd have been out on a date. Being back on the dating scene had at first been exciting. Now? It was like playing a game of roulette. You never knew what you would end up with. But she wasn't going to stop. She wasn't looking for Mister Right. She was after Mr. Fun.

She'd had too much seriousness and heartbreak for a lifetime. She was finally being true to herself, living the life she'd always dreamed of living. This meant that she was going to explore all her options, and that included dating, a lot of it. Sometimes even going out several nights a week. This week though, she was exhausted.

She'd been traveling, meeting clients, and going to antique auctions. What she craved was some downtime with her best friend, not having to be 'on' with a stranger on a date. She could always count on Maddy to provide a much-needed distraction.

"There's gotta be over a hundred coins! Do you know anything about them, Mads?" Ashley was spreading the coins around the table.

"Not a single thing. I haven't won bids on any lockers that had coins before," Maddy replied.

"Once or twice, I found loose change in couches and la-z-boy chairs, but they've never been worth much. I just got rid of them online or bought myself a coffee. What about you? I was kind of hoping you might."

"Sorry hon, coins aren't my thing. The only thing I know is if they are silver or gold, they're worth, at the very least, the weight and value of the metal they're made of. Other than that, I'd say that if any of these are old or rare, then they might be worth something."

"I guess I better start researching then," Maddy said, her shoulders slumping.

"I'll lend you a hand. Two heads and lots of port will get faster results," Ashley assured her as she poured more of that dark burgundy deliciousness into their larger- than-reasonable stemless glasses. "The jewelry," she added. "Now that's worth a bit. These pieces are incredible." She started shifting the jewelry around, admiring each piece. "Diamond studs, a diamond ring, a pearl choker and matching bracelet, a large sapphire ring, a man's gold school ring, a ruby tie clip, emerald cufflinks..." She picked up the diamond ring and twirled it in the light, making it sparkle. "Most here are a bit dated but still resalable." She put the ring down and admired the choker, running the smooth pearls between her fingers. "You found all this in a storage locker?"

"Yup"

"An abandoned storage locker?"

"Yeah, that's why the locker ended up in an auction for abandoned lockers."

"Smarty-pants, it's just that it makes no sense whatsoever. I mean, look at that man's ring." She put it on her finger and held it up. "That's one big honking piece of jewelry. It's heavy, lots of gold was used to make it."

"I know, right? The price of gold has been on the rise. That, by itself, should make it worth something."

Ashley took out her cell phone, "Okay, I'm sending you the name and address of a place on 124th Street that buys jewelry and coins. It's called Bernard's Antiques and Collectibles. Only take a few of these pieces. See what they'll give you for them first before you bring them the rest. Bob, the owner, is usually pretty fair when it comes to jewelry. Coins, they're not interested in unless they're rare."

Maddy smiled, she knew Ashley would be able to help with some of these things. She had graduated from the University of Alberta with a degree in Art History, then traveled the world to learn about antiques and interior design. She had years of experience as an antiques and estate buyer and now she was working downtown for an import/export business. The cherry on top was that she knew lots of people too. When possible, she'd connect Maddy with folks who liked unique items. Unfortunately, unique items didn't show up in abandoned lockers often enough. That's why Ashley had encouraged Maddy to expand her professional horizon and get a Business Management certificate from NAIT, one of the local colleges. This certificate had been the first step in what Maddy called her future 'big plan'.

"What about all those hockey cards in the albums? Have you ever dealt with any Ash?"

"Nope. You know who you should ask?"

"Who?"

"Rick. He used to collect them all through high school, remember?"

"Oh yeah! He sold them to help buy his first truck. He got A LOT of money for some of them too." Maddy was hopeful that maybe some of those cards could be valuable.

"Do you have any more chocolate, or should we get something delivered? Researching coins is going to work up my appetite and I can't work if I'm hungry."

Ashley looked like one of those women who never ate, but in reality had a very healthy appetite. Maddy had no idea how she did it. If she wasn't such a nice person, Maddy would hate her.

"Sure," Maddy said, "Will pineapple pizza with extra ham and cheese and some double chocolate brownies from Pietro's Pizza do?"

"Oh, how you know me, girlfriend," Ashley answered with a sly smile. "Now, let's get started on sorting this treasure of yours. Separate them by country of origin first and... Hey, wait a minute! What's that big bulky thing in the bottom of the box?

"Big bulky thing? What are you talking about? I didn't notice anything." Surprised, Maddy reached for the bin to take a closer look.

"Here, let me get it out for you," Ashley pulled a bulky rolled-up purple towel. She carefully unrolled it, jumped up, and screamed as she tossed the towel and its contents on Maddy's prized second-hand green leather couch.

"What is it?" Maddy asked as she instinctively jumped away in horror, fearing it was some gruesome object. "Is it a shrunken amputated hand? A Voodoo doll? No, wait, is it a stuffed tarantula like last time? No, don't tell me! I don't even want to know. Just throw it out!"

Ashley, shaken up, started mumbling "Bad juju. Very, very bad juju! You need to get rid of that thing, like, right now." She backed away from the couch and stood as far as possible from the ominous object.

"What the hell IS it?" Maddy walked over and lifted the corner of the towel to peek at the horror hidden beneath. She pulled the towel completely off and stood staring at it, then looked up at Ashley in disbelief. "For crying out loud, Ash! It's just a stone Mexican mask."

"It's not JUST a mask, it's a bad omen Aztec mask. And look, it's covered in blood!" Ashley then lowered her voice to a whisper, "You have to get rid of it or it'll bring us all bad luck."

"Okay, okay, I'll put it away, and try to sell it with the coins tomorrow," Maddy assured her. "But you have to promise to settle down."

Ashley thought about it for a moment, looking unsure. Lifting her chin up stubbornly, she replied "Only if you put it in a box, in your guest room closet. In the far corner. With it facing away from us. BUT you MUST get rid of it tomorrow. There's blood on that thing!

"There's no blood on it," Maddy laughed. "It's probably just some ketchup, or paint that someone spilled on the mask's base. I'll wipe it off."

"NO!" Ashley yelled "Don't do anything else to it. No more interacting with the Demon from Mazatlán."

"Demon from Mazatlán?" asked an incredulous Maddy. "And you know where it's from, how?"

"You know I know things. It's important in my profession… as a buyer… to be knowledgeable about stuff like that"

"Ash?"

"Yes?"

Maddy slowly raised an eyebrow while inspecting the mask a little more closely.

"It's important in your profession, you say?"

"It absolutely is!" She gave Maddy a side look, "Why are you asking me like that?"

Maddy turned the mask upside down, pointing directly to the sticker on the bottom of the base that read 'Made in Mazatlán'.

"Whatever. It sounded good," her friend replied with a shrug, then she bashfully added, "I saw it when you flipped it over to look at the blood. Come on," she laughed. "Admit you were impressed."

"Just a little and only for a split second. Here," she said, tossing her cell to her. "Order the pizza while I put this wee little demon to bed... don't worry, it will be in the farthest corner of the closet."

"With its head turned away from us," Ashley reminded her.

Maddy nodded, "With its head turned as far away from us as humanly possible. I might even blindfold it with a scarf. Then can we start doing some research, Ms. Chicken Little?"

Chapter 3

A shley left once Maddy had assured her, several times over, that she would take care of the mask and get it out of their lives. Pinky swear.

She was always amused whenever Ashley showed her superstitious side. She was such a complex woman, Maddy grinned thinking of her friend's unique kookiness. She wasn't ready for bed yet, still feeling some of the excitement buzz she got from sorting through an interesting batch of items from the locker purchases. She often thought storage locker auctions were the adult equivalent of treasure hunts. Sometimes the things she found were valuable, sometimes they were junk, and other times they were interesting to her but not worth much moneywise. Like the love letters she'd recently found in an estate sale. They were tucked into a box of old crystal, yellowed with age, and obviously forgotten about. She had set them aside to read on a rainy day but decided that tonight they would be a good distraction.

She dug the letters out and made herself comfortable on the couch, spreading them around her. Maddy was surprised to find that only one or two of them had ever been opened. That wasn't the usual state of the correspondence she ran across in auction sales. They were typically letters or notes that had been opened and thrown in with a bunch of other items one tended to forget about, but they usually were opened.

She separated the letters into two piles; one pile for opened letters, and another for the ones that weren't. She would start by reading the ones that weren't sealed.

Dear Brigitte,

Hi, I can't believe it's already been a week since we were together. I haven't been able to think of anything but you. Can you please let me know if you got there okay and if everything's fine? Even if you never want to hear from me again, please let me know. Not hearing from you really sucks. I tried to call you; did you get my message? Your father wasn't happy I phoned so I'm not sure if he let you know. You're everything to me and I can't stand to think that our time together meant so little to you. It meant everything to me...

Maddy, hopelessly romantic, got caught up in the emotions conveyed in the letter, even though many years had passed since they were written. The date on the first one was April 25, 1971. The last opened letter was a few months later and had grown desperate.

Brigitte, Please, let me know if you're ok! Why won't you talk to me? If you've found another dude, just be honest and tell me. I can't keep this up, not knowing what's happening. Don't leave me hanging. The sweet girl I knew wouldn't act this way; I just don't understand. Man is my heart ever aching for you. Please don't break it...

It was obvious that Brigitte, the object of his affection, didn't reciprocate his love as she'd only opened a handful of his letters. Seemed like a pretty crummy thing to do to someone who was obviously head over heels for her. She sat staring at the letters, lost in thought. She did some quick calculations and realized that the person who had received these letters was quite likely still alive. She picked up an envelope and read the name on it "Brigitte Schell".

"Well, Brigitte, I think now is as good a time as ever to find out if you and Mr...." she looked at the return address "...Robert Ozinski, ever worked things out."

Maddy grabbed her laptop and began searching for the letters' author. She couldn't find any profile on Facebook that fit his age and nationality, so she moved on to LinkedIn. She'd skipped over TikTok thinking that, given his age, it was unlikely she'd find him there.

On LinkedIn, she struck paydirt. Robert Ozinski, a retired mechanical engineer, had a profile that seemed promising. She sent him a message, asking if he was the same Robert Ozinski who had written to a certain Brigitte Schell in the early 1970s.

She should probably just mind her own business, but what would be the fun in that? She needed a hobby other than researching coins and demon masks. This would be perfect.

Chapter 4

'Keys, coins, jewelry, wallet, the Demon from Mazatlán,' Maddy mentally checked off the items on her list of things she needed to bring with her as she walked out of her apartment. She then made sure that her door was double-locked. Living downtown in a loft with underground parking she had to take precautions, you never knew who might slip in behind an unsuspecting neighbor. Edmonton might have a small-town feel and friendliness to Maddy, but it was still a big city. Carrying her treasures, Maddy decided to take the stairs instead of the elevator for a change. Unlike Ashley's metabolism, her's was uber- slow. Last night's trifecta of pizza, chocolate, and port needed to be burnt off, one way or another. The gym was not an option. She would leave that kind of torture to Rick and Tasha. Working out exhilarated them. Weirdos. Not her. No way. Today, she would make it her goal to only use stairs. As she was trying to convince herself that doing so would be more than enough exercise for her, she noticed that the garage was still dimly lit. She'd have to remind the management about replacing those burnt-out light bulbs, again.

"Damn," she mumbled as she watched her keys drop to the floor.

Oh well, bending down to pick them up should also count as exercise she figured. Just as Maddy was grabbing hold of her keys, two hooded figures rammed into her, violently knocking her down onto her butt. She barely held onto her bags as they slid past her and through the door that led to the staircase.

"Oh, for frig's sake!" Maddy exclaimed, picking herself up from the concrete floor and dusting her behind. Luckily she was fine, other than a bruised dignity.

She angrily walked towards her car. This was not how she had expected her day to start.

"What. The. Hell?" she cried out to the empty garage, stopping dead in her tracks. "Aw, man! Those two hooded dipshidiots broke into my car."

She ran to Bugsy, her VW Beetle. They hadn't even bothered to shut the door! She stood there in shock, staring at her empty glove compartment. Every last bit of its contents had been strewn all over the car floor, some were even tossed out on the ground. She made her way around the vehicle and peered into the open trunk. Spare tire, blankets, jerry can, booster cables, first aid kit, candle, empty coffee can for said candle, reusable shopping bags, and granola bars. Nothing had been taken. It was a mess, but at least everything was there and accounted for. She placed the things she was carrying on top of the disaster, grabbed a granola bar, and slammed the trunk shut. She picked up all the stuff that was spread on the ground and car floor and shoved them back into the glove compartment. Swearing under her breath, she unwrapped the bar and started munching on it. "Bunch of punks." Angrily she took another bite out of her granola bar. "Ha! Jokes on you. You got nothing but some loose change and my old cell phone!" she grumbled, tearing chunks out of the bar, and bumping the door shut with her hip. She suddenly stopped mid-chew, realizing that she needed her old cell phone after all; it had lots of old photos she'd never uploaded onto the cloud and even some saved passwords. "Damn it! Now I have to go to the stupid police station and make a report."

Pulling out of the garage and onto the street, she switched her phone to hands-free and asked it to dial the one person she always called when needing to vent, Ashley. "You won't believe what happened to me! Some jerks broke into my car and stole my old cell phone."

"Talus Balls!" Ashley exclaimed. "Told you that that demon mask was bad juju. Get rid of it, pronto!"

"That's what I was on my way to do, Ash. Now, I've to go to the stupid police station to do a stupid police report first." Maddy signaled to turn in the direction of the downtown police station.

"Nope. Maddy, listen to me. You must get rid of it first. Then you can go and check out the cutie patootie cops."

"That's them!"

"Who??"

"The assholes who shoved me and broke into my car, that's who!" Maddy slammed on her brakes, screeching to a halt, almost causing an accident. "I'd recognize their hoodies anywhere. They're running the other way down the street." Cars started honking. The guy behind her flipped her the bird as he drove by. Who did he think he was, Mr. High and Mighty in his Tesla? Maddy, angry and yelling at everyone, decided on the spot to chase the black hooded thieves. "Bunch of friggin nimrods! Damn! Ashley, I'm turning the car around. I'm gonna show them who they're messing with."

"Maddy? Maddy! What the hell are you doing? I'm hearing lots of honking and swearing from you!!"

"I'm chasing those bastards. I'm gonna get them. There.... No! Bastards! They just ran around the corner on 116th Street. They're going towards the stairs by LeMarchand Mansion. I just need to run through this red light.... carefully.... No cars... and..."

"S T O P!!!!!!" Ashley hollered through the phone. "STOP right now!" Ashley heard Maddy breathing heavily and mumbling unintelligently. "Maddy?"

"Yes."

"What are you doing?"

"I'm by LeMarchand Mansion" "You're not following them, are you?"

"NO! I'm not following them. I'm parked in the lot between the Mansion and the park."

"Good! ... Maddy?" "Yes?"

"Take a deep breath..."

Ashley waited until she heard Maddy inhale and exhale. She did so quite loudly, obviously for Ashley's benefit

"All good, Mads?"

"No! Yes! But not happy about any of this. I

would've gone after them but they were running pretty fast down those monster stairs and I'm wearing my new pumps. I can't run worth a damn in heels."

"The yellow ones from Goodwill?" "Yeah."

"Those are too cute to wreck over an old cell phone and a shove."

"Yeah, there's that too." Maddy hated giving up but it would be useless to try and catch up to them. They would be long gone down any one of the many River Valley trails. She started the car up again, backed it out of the parking lot, and turned it around towards the main avenue.

"Now forget about those hooded thieves and go get rid of that mask."

"Ash, come on!" "You promised Mads!

"Fine! I'm just on Jasper and 116th now. You said that Bernard's was on 124th Street?"

"Yes. Trust me, we'll be better off without that thing.

And Mads…" "Yes, Ashley?" "Thank you."

~~~

Pulling into the parking lot on 124th Street, Maddy turned her car's engine off, leaned her head back, and closed her eyes. Her adrenalin was finally wearing off, leaving her tired and shaky.

'*Come on Maddy, get it together,*' she thought, reaching into her purse and pulling out her cell.

No new texts, but there was one new LinkedIn notification! She was tickled pink to see that it was an update from Robert Ozinski. He was happy she'd connected with him and most definitely remembered the letters. He left his phone number. She couldn't wait to talk to him to find out what happened. She dialed him up right away. Bernard's could wait.

"Hi, Robert? This is Maddy." "Well, that was fast!"

"Yeah, I believe in dealing with things as they happen," Maddy said, laughing.

"So you found my letters to Brigitte, did you? I've often wondered what happened to her. It was quite a shock to hear about her after all these years."

"I bet it was. I wasn't sure what to do with them, I usually try to return personal things to their owners, but this was an estate sale."

"Well that's odd, I wonder why they were kept? She didn't acknowledge any of my letters, and wouldn't take my calls. I'm surprised she cared enough to keep them," he mused. "And you say some of them were never opened?"

"Well, umm… no, they weren't open when I got them," Maddy stammered, suddenly feeling like a voyeur for breaking the seal on the long-closed envelopes.

"Not to worry, I'm okay with you reading them. We were young and in love. I wasn't afraid to tell her either. I'd just turned 18 and thought I had found the woman of my dreams," he reflected, his voice growing quieter as he reminisced. "You said 'Estate Sale', is she dead?"

"No, well, I don't know. I don't have the name of the estate's owner," Maddy replied, feeling a bit bad for not knowing. "What happened between you two, if I may ask?"

"Her family moved away. Her dad was in the military and got stationed in Alberta. My heart was broken but I intended to work until I had enough money to go out West. By then she'd be done with high school and we'd get married. That never happened."

"That's so sad," Maddy said.

"I guess you could say that, but it was so long ago, and we were young. I've thought about her over the years and often wondered what she might have been up to," he confessed. "You never really get over your first love."

They sat there in silence for a minute, both reflecting on his last comment, when an idea hit Maddy. Might be a bit crazy but why the heck not?

"Why don't I try finding her? Maybe she's still alive and well. Then we can ask her ourselves, erm... What I meant is that you could ask her why she didn't answer the letters."

"Oh, I don't know... It's been so many years, she probably wouldn't even remember me."

"I bet you she would! You even said so yourself, you never get over your first love."

"Ha ha, aren't you the clever one," Robert chuckled. "For all we know, she could be dead."

"Come on Robert, you make it sound like she's ancient now. She'd be, what, 65?"

"Yeah, but she could still be dead," he insisted. "You did find the letters in an estate sale after all."

"Sure, but she could also be alive and could die next week. You'd have missed out on your chance to ask her why she ghosted you," Maddy insisted while in the back of her mind, she wondered why she was not only volunteering to find his long-lost love but pushing the issue. It wasn't like she didn't have other things preoccupying her these days. She'd always been a sucker for a good love story.

"Why don't you send me all the information you have and I'll see what I can find out?" Maddy asked. "Then you can decide if you want to approach her or what you want to do."

"You're a persistent young lady, aren't you?" Robert laughed again.

"Yes, sir, I sure am."

They hung up with Robert promising to search through some of his old papers and see if he could find any clues that might help Maddy track down his Brigitte. Now she had to keep her promise to Ashley and go to Bernard's to try to get rid of that demon mask.

Chapter 5

"So, you're saying these coins aren't worth much?"

Maddy was pretty disappointed with this dealer so far. After friendly introductions and telling him that he'd come highly recommended by one of his 'best' customers, her very good friend Ashley, he'd only offered her half the coin's value. She and Ashley had looked them up online. They were worth more, according to eBay and Coin Value Checker anyway.

"No, that's not exactly what I said," Bernard's owner, Bob, clarified. The guy must have been as old as some of his antiques; gray-haired, horned-rimmed glasses, a well- worn cardigan, and a bit of a hunched back made him fit right in with all the old treasures in his shop.

"Please sit down, you may be here for a while," he gestured to the armchair in front of his desk. "The bad news is that they're not rare coins. The good news is that they're collectibles, he emphasized the word 'collectibles' using his fingers to make air quotes. Who does that anymore? Maddy thought, taking a seat.

"Unfortunately," Bob added, "I already have a dozen or more of these coins in similar condition in that display case right over there," he pointed to a glass display case lined with blue satin. "I can buy them from you but only at today's market price for silver." He took out a calculator and tapped in some numbers then turned it around and showed it to her. "I'm not interested in the non-silver ones. They're not worth much. Take those pennies for example. They barely have any copper in them."

Maddy tilted her head and wrinkled her nose, "Aren't all pennies made of copper?"

Bob shook his head, picked up a penny, and started twirling it on the desk. "That's a very common misconception. They used to be made of copper. Any Canadian one-cent penny minted after 1997 is 94 percent steel, 4.5 percent copper plating, and 1.5 percent nickel."

"Are you serious?" she asked, leaning forward. "Absolutely serious, Maddy." Gesturing towards the pennies, he added, "They aren't worth a penny." Bob started laughing at his own joke. "Every time I say this, I crack myself up. Look, I'm truly sorry. I'll buy the silver coins off you," he gave her one of those grandfatherly looks that reminded her of PopPop. "But not the pennies nor the coins from other countries. There's not much demand for them in my shop. They're not in mint state either, some have too many scratches or have lost their luster. I don't buy anything less than in an MS-65 condition. Those would have a lot fewer scratches and scuff marks than yours," he pointed at one scratched-up coin. "You're better off selling them on Kijiji or

Facebook on some of those collector's group pages. They'll probably bid against each other for some of them. These are more for people wanting coins from different countries, or kids just starting up. It's not worth my time, but it might be worth yours."

"Thanks for the advice, Bob. I'll think about it. Might be the best option for me."

"I'm willing to take that 1987 Loonie off your hands though," he said, reaching for the gold-colored coin.

"Nah," she slid it away from him. "I'm not sure about that one yet." Suddenly feeling sentimental, she put the shiny Loonie in her purse.

"No worries," Bob looked at her and smiled. "That's a special coin. I would keep it too. Do you have anything else in that bag of yours that might interest me?"

"A few pieces of jewelry. I'm not sure if they're 'old- old' or just vintage," Maddy handed him the pearls, diamond ring, and some other pieces.

"Let me go get my tools. I'll be back lickety-split." Bob shuffled away, at a not-so-lickety-split pace, to the back of the shop and disappeared behind a set of heavy, burgundy-colored, velvet curtains.

Maddy sat there contemplating what to do with the other coins and the ones still at home. Online made sense but it was time-consuming and dealing with a bunch of collectors looking for a bargain was never any fun. She could try other collectible shops, but Ashley had assured her of this guy's honesty, other shop owners would probably not give her much more. She should have brought some of the coins that had been in sleeves, not loose like the ones she had shown Bob. They were probably in better condition too. Oh well. Maybe next time.

"Sorry, I can't find all of my tools," Bob said, quickly poking his head out from behind the curtains.

"No worries," Maddy replied, but he was already gone.

Half a second later, Bob's head popped out again, "My son's looking for his tools." His head disappeared once more.

Maddy laughed at his whack-a-mole impression.

Two seconds later, Bernard's owner's floating head stuck out one more time and added "He'll just be another minute," and swoosh, like a magic trick, he was gone.

Ashley had been right, Bob seemed honest enough. A bit odd, but a decent old gentleman. She looked down at the coins on the counter, dollars, quarters, and some nickels. It was a good thing Ashley told her not to bring all the silver coins. She might be able to sell those online for more money after all. And if she couldn't, well, there was always Bob here who would buy them for the price of the silver.

Speaking of the devil, Bob reappeared, this time there was a bounce to his shuffle. "Turns out my son, Niko, had borrowed my loupe. I keep telling him that tools are special and should be treated like babies. You can't just leave them lying around. I don't know about that boy of mine. But I'm not giving up, not yet. I'll make a good appraiser out of him yet. Have to if he plans to take over my business one day. Everyone needs to retire eventually!"

He should be retired now, Maddy thought to herself, all that lickety-split shuffling had left him breathless. Niko his son better smarten up and learn fast.

"What's a loupe?" Maddy asked. Might as well learn all she could. This knowledge could be beneficial for her business.

"Oh, so glad you asked, young lady!"

Uh oh, Bob seemed a bit too happy she'd asked that question. Damn, that meant she would get more than a short, to-the-point answer. She leaned back in the chair and decided it'd be best to get comfy.

"Loupes are extremely important in my line of work, you know," he told her as he lovingly took out a small lens from a leather case. He unfolded it and slipped one of his index fingers into the metal ring opposite the glass. "They help us see details in the smallest of stones, like a tiny diamond," he straightened himself up in his chair.

Maddy leaned forward, this could be interesting stuff after all.

Bob brought the loupe up to his eye, pressing his thumb against his cheek. He took an old ring out of a drawer with his other hand. "With this tool, I can see tiny cracks and imperfections. You should always inspect a stone before buying any piece of jewelry or selling it for a matter of fact. This way you know its worth."

Maddy nodded. This was certainly a useful little tool. She must get herself one of those loupe thingies.

"Here, have a look at this old diamond ring," he handed her the loupe and ring. "I keep it as a reminder for Niko to never buy a piece without looking at it through a loupe. He lost us money on this one."

Maddy slipped the loupe onto her index finger just like she saw Bob do and brought it up to her eye to inspect the diamond.

"Do you see that line in the stone?" he asked her.

"No…" She squinted and looked harder. "Look on the right upper corner", he said.

"I see it! I see it!" Maddy jumped in her chair, excited to have found it.

"That, Maddy, is a crack. It reduces the value of the ring," Bob told her as he took the ring and loupe from her.

"Other things that affect the worth of a diamond are its color and clarity," Bob put the loupe back on his index finger.

He took the bag of jewelry that Maddy extended towards him and picked out the diamond ring.

"You have to look at a stone from different angles," He moved the ring left and right, steadily looking at it. "No cracks, very little wear."

Bob moved the loupe away from his eye and set the ring down. "Let's take a look at the remainder of your treasures."

After a few minutes, Bob placed all the jewelry aside except for the school ring. "You have some very nice vintage pieces here. That sapphire ring is quite stunning and in very good condition. The pearls are lovely. Not as popular as they were a few decades ago but there's still some interest in them. I'll buy all of them except for that school ring. Nobody would buy it from me. It only has sentimental value to the original owner."

"But what about the stone?" Maddy asked.

"The stone is synthetic like most school rings. The gold is real. It could be melted but I don't buy gold jewelry to melt, just the silver. Try selling it online too. I wouldn't hold my breath there though. You could also try those folks who advertise that they buy gold. Just be careful, they usually try to buy low."

"Well, that's a disappointment. I was hoping it would be worth more considering its size. Too bad the stone isn't real. Hmm, how about this Mexican mask?" she asked, taking the demon mask, still wrapped in the purple towel, out of her shopping bag, and handed it to him, hoping that she might get rid of it.

Bob unwrapped the demon mask, looked at it, turned it around, ho-hummed, bobbed his head from side to side, and handed it back to Maddy.

"These are a dime a dozen, painted stone masks on a marble or granite base, made for tourists. I don't know why people buy these and bring them back as souvenirs. They're heavy and not even worth the price that those gullible folks are suckered into paying for them."

Maddy wound the towel back around the mask and put it away. Maybe she'll go to the Goodwill store on Whyte Avenue and drop it off after her stop at the police station.

"Sorry," Bob felt bad that she'd be stuck with the thing. "This is a knockoff, they sell on the internet for between fifty and seventy dollars. If it was made of semi-precious stones or Mother of Pearl, then you could sell it for more, maybe even for four or five hundred dollars. You might want to wash off the blood on the base though, before trying to sell it. That's a bit of a turn-off." 'Here we go again with the blood', thought Maddy. What's with people and their wild imaginations?

After negotiating a bit with him for a higher price on the jewelry, Maddy put the money from the sale, the unsold coins, and the school ring into her purse.

"Thanks, Bob! I'll definitely come back if I find anything else that might interest you."

"You're welcome, young lady." Bob waved as he shuffled away. "Be sure to tell your friends about Bernard's Antiques and Collectibles!" he added, doing a final disappearing act behind the magic velvet curtains.

Chapter 6

S itting at the intersection, waiting for the lights to change, Maddy drummed her fingers impatiently on the steering wheel, they were taking longer than usual to turn green today. While she liked living in her downtown loft, she could do without the annoying, time-wasting traffic. The police station was only a few minutes away as the crow flies, but she'd made the mistake of driving there by way of the Ice District. 'Can't get more Canadian than that,' she thought to herself, 'nicknaming an area because the NHL hockey arena is there.' This part of town was always busy, next to the arena, there was also an all- year-round outdoor entertainment square. Add to that, a huge museum, music hall, art gallery, central library, shopping malls, and City Hall. They were all within a two- block radius of each other making this a very high-traffic zone.

To make matters worse, everybody seemed to have decided to converge on Churchill Square to attend one of Edmonton's many festivals. Lucky her.

As her car slowly inched forward, Maddy's thoughts turned to the contents of the storage locker she purchased yesterday. Something about the unknown possibilities that came from a new storage locker auction win always excited her; not knowing what she would find, wondering about the stories behind the objects. Take that demon mask, for example. 'Seriously, could someone, anyone, take it?' She mentally begged all the Mexican gods she could think of.

She had no idea how this cheap travel memento ended up in a box filled with high-end jewelry and coins. Whose was it and could that be blood on the base? If it was, did the blood come from someone having a bloody nose during a tour of Chichen Itza? Maddy had always been fascinated by other people's stories, imagining that they'd led much more interesting lives than she had. Her thoughts briefly landed on her family and quickly steered her thoughts elsewhere. Some thoughts were better left buried.

She finally pulled into the police station and walked up the stairs to the entrance. Carrying her purse over her shoulder and the bag that held the mask in both hands, she pushed one of the large double doors open, stopping to take in the scene before her. A police officer sitting behind the front desk was watching another officer in the lobby patiently explaining to someone that, no, they couldn't turn themselves in for littering in order to get a bed to sleep in tonight. However, he would be more than happy to drive them to a place that could help with some food and lodging. The man argued with him and seemed quite indignant that the officer would think he needed charity.

Maddy skirted around them and approached the counter. "Can I help you Ma'am?" asked the officer sitting at the desk.

"Umm... is Detective Kyle O'Brady in?" she asked, looking around as though she expected Ashley's friend Kyle to appear.

"Detective O'Brady is not in today. He'll be in on Sunday," he informed her.

"Okay, Officer..?" She leaned over the counter to read the name tag pinned to his uniform, "Stan Kowalchuk?"

"Can I help you instead?" Officer Kowalchuk asked, a long-suffering look on his face. It was obvious he had more important things to do than serve the public.

"I was hoping to chat with Kyle about something that's come up."

'Something?' Can you please elaborate?"

"My car was broken into," she decided to lead with the obvious crime first. She didn't want to start out talking about the Demon from Mazatlán with this seemingly bored and uninterested officer. For some reason, his lackluster response made her immediately distrust him.

"Okay, fill out this report, sign it, and bring it back," he slid a form and a pen towards her.

She walked over to the side counter and began writing a description of this morning's events from the moment when she entered her parkade. Skipping the fact she'd followed the criminals, fearing the police would think that it was a stupid move on her part. Because, let's be honest, it had been. Maybe she'd have included it if

45

she'd been only dealing with Kyle. She had met Kyle through Ashley, who had known him for a few years. Maddy now considered him her friend too. She wasn't sure if he'd want to be as close of a friend to her if it hadn't been for Ashley. It was a not-so-well-kept secret that Kyle had a major crush on Maddy's best friend. They'd finally gone out on a few dates last year but Ashley had decided to put the brakes on as he was getting much too serious for her liking. She'd just gotten back on the dating scene and still had a lot of wild oats to sow but Kyle, on the other hand, was ready to settle down and have babies.

Taking the report form up to the counter, she handed it over to Officer Kowalchuk. Unfortunately, Maddy knew she'd have to bring up the mask to this officer. She had to keep her promise to Ashley to get rid of it. To be honest, she was more than willing to let it go; that demon from Mazatlán kind of gave her the heebie-jeebies. Kowalchuk glanced down at the form and looked at it long enough to see that all the required areas had been filled. Time-stamped it, then placed it on top of a large pile of papers in the in-tray beside him.

"Thank you. Here's your file reference number, an officer will be in touch."

"Okay, um, there's one more thing," Maddy said hesitantly.

"Yes? What is it?" he appeared a bit annoyed that she wasn't getting on her way.

"Well, it isn't a crime exactly," she began.

"I'm afraid that's pretty much all we deal with here. If you need a social worker or a counselor, here's the number you can call," he cut her off, handing her a card with various community outreach phone numbers listed on it.

Now he was just starting to annoy her. She looked closer and noted his slightly unclean hair, with the front of it a tad bit longer than required for an officer. She got the feeling he was the type of person who liked to take rules as a suggestion. His just-within-the-regulations hair length, and the less-than-enthusiastic way he handled desk duty, made Maddy think that he felt to be a bit too good for the position he was holding. Great. Just what this world needed, another entitled, misogynistic male.

She stood up a bit straighter, made prolonged eye contact with him, and spoke in a firm voice. Maddy believed that these types of men only acknowledged strength and confidence, otherwise, they walked all over you.

"I recently purchased the contents of a storage unit and found an item in it that was covered in blood," she informed him. "I've brought it in so you can take a look at it."

At the word blood, the officer sat up in his chair and leaned forward. Things weren't looking so boring anymore now, were they?

"What kind of object? Do you have it in your possession?"

Maddy reached down and pulled the mask out of her bag. She placed it on the counter with a thud. The officer looked at it closely, trying to hide his interest.

"The blood is here," Maddy explained as she turned the mask around slightly and pointed.

"These spots here? How do you know it's blood?" Officer Kowalchuk asked. It was obvious he was disappointed in the mask, Maddy guessed he had hoped for a dripping knife or something exciting like that.

"I don't, but more than one person has identified it as blood," she informed him, trying to cover her embarrassment. It was only a small amount; she didn't know for sure if it was blood, but here she was in a police station with the spotted mask. He wouldn't be out of line in thinking she was being a bit over-the-top to bring it in. But she'd promised Ashley, so she was going through with it.

"What d'you want me to do with this?" he asked, looking almost amused.

"Could you please see that Kyle gets it?" There wasn't enough reason to test the blood or anything, but this way she'd be able to say to Ashley that she'd got rid of the mask. It would be Kyle's problem after that.

"Sure thing," he responded, looking slightly amused. His smirk showed what he thought about her concerns. She placed the mask back in her bag and handed it to him. He moved it off to the side, continuing to sit there, looking at her, his hands clasped in front of him.

"Anything else, ma'am?

"Nope, that's it," Maddy said. "Guess I'll be going now."

"Have a nice day," he responded in a dismissive tone that implied he'd rather say 'Don't let the door hit you on the way out,' but due to the police station's PR policy, he couldn't.

Maddy left the police station wondering how she could get the last half hour of her life back.

Chapter 7

"Well, at least I got rid of that demon mask," Maddy grumbled. That took more effort than it should have. Ashley would finally stop nagging her. It was such a beautiful day out that Maddy lowered Bugsy's convertible top.

She'd bought Bugsy at a car auction. The price had been so ridiculously low that she couldn't resist it. Nobody wanted the beat-up VW. They didn't know Edmonton's best body shop owner, but Maddy did. Rick and his crew worked their magic and Bugsy was reborn. There's nothing better than driving along the Yellowhead Freeway with your car top down and feeling the wind blow through your hair. Edmonton's weather was so nice when there was no snow. Other than the odd bug hitting you on the forehead, this was as close to Nirvana as you could get. The never-ending construction appeared to be on hold, thankfully making her trip to the storage lot much faster than usual. She turned off the freeway and took the next road a bit slower, no need to get another speeding ticket to add to her collection. Pulling up to the gate, she punched in the code. It creaked as it opened at a snail's pace, finally swinging wide enough to let her through, then closing just as painfully slow behind her.

'I swear Shirley uses that gate to notify her of all the comings and goings of unit renters so she can stop them for the latest gossip,' Maddy thought as she parked Bugsy by her storage locker.

Rolling up the unit's door, she caught sight of a second box she'd purchased at yesterday's auction, sitting next to her desk. She had an odd nagging feeling about what had recently transpired. Call it intuition or sixth sense, but finding such a large amount of silver coins, valuable jewelry, and a "Demon" mask which, she hated to admit, possibly had blood on it, wasn't the common treasure trove she'd come upon in the local storage locker auctions. That was stuff you saw on TV, not what you were likely to find in Edmonton, Alberta. To top it off, she didn't trust that condescending Officer Kowalchuk. She wished Kyle had been there. He would have handled Bugsy's violation with much more professionalism and seriousness than Kowalchuk.

Grabbing the box, she placed it on her desk, reflecting on how her day had gone so far. Nope, nothing made sense. Maybe this box would contain a clue that could enlighten her about the owner and even perhaps about why they would leave valuable items in a locker instead of in a safety deposit box. What she found instead were odds and ends that made no rhyme or reason: three single shoes without their matching pair, three bundles of what seemed to be hair extensions tied with bright bows, a single red glove, a scarf, and some smaller, nonsensical stuff.

"*I might as well take this home and go through it there,*" she thought. She took the box and one of the clothing bags and placed them in Bugsy's trunk. Seeing the mess in the trunk from this morning reminded her that she'd need to clean it all up once she got home.

To add more joy to her day, that slimy guy from the auction was now lurking by the lot's office. Why the heck was he carrying Shirley's dog, Engelbert, in his arms?

"Hey, Maddy! How goes it? It's Maddy, right? Atchoo! Sorry." He sniffled and waved a couple of fingers in her direction.

Maddy walked around her car and took a few steps towards him, trying to figure out what was up with this guy and Engelbert. Shirley never let 'Bert' out of her sight, let alone allow anybody to carry her precious 'poochie pooch'.

"Bet you're here to pick up your stuff from yesterday's auction, eh?" added Mr. Slimy.

"Hello erm… sorry, I didn't catch your name."

"Oh yeah, my apologies. Guess I never did introduce myself. Rod Henry here, at your service ma'am," Rod bowed, almost dropping Bert. "I'm Shirley's nephew. I'm the new manager of this bea-u-ti-ful storage facility. So, if you ever need help with anything. And I do mean ANYthing, just you holler my name and I'll come running."

"Ah okay, thanks Rod, I'll be sure to keep it in mind."

She then looked at Engelbert and couldn't help cooing, "Hi little Bertie Bert!".

Hearing his name, Engelbert immediately wiggled out of Rod's arms and ran over toward Maddy who bent down to pick him up.

Bert, ecstatic to have been freed from captivity, started eagerly licking her face.

"Stop it, Bert. Stop it!" Maddy laughed. "Can you please come get the little mutt?" she called out to Rod. "Sorry, can't. Gotta stay by the office. I'm expecting a very important call."

"Oookay then, I'll bring him over to you." Maddy wasn't impressed with this guy. He seemed to have no respect for the people who rented the lockers. Great. Now she had Slimy Rod to deal with every time she used her storage 'office'. She'd have to talk with Shirley about these new arrangements. Maddy lived by the adage 'Never trust a man with two first names.'

"Here you go. Try not to let him run off again." She handed Bert over to Rod, aka Squiggy, and cautioned him, "The little mongrel could get run over."

"He's not a mongrel. He's an Alberta Special. Atchoo!

Damn allergies.

"Isn't that the same thing?"

"Not according to Aunt Shirley. Atchoo! Sorry. An Alberta Special is a dog who has parents of different breeds, but they're purebred or something like that." Sniffling some more, Rod continued his explanation, "A mongrel is of... what did Aunt Shirley say? Oh yeah, a mongrel is of unknown origins." Rod stood very tall, well, as tall as his five-foot-something height allowed him to. Holding Bert at arm's length, he appeared quite proud of himself.

"Rod, she made that up. Look at him. He has an overbite and patches of missing fur. He might be cute, but he's a mongrel. Be it, what did you call him? An Alberta Special? Or even a Heinz 57, he's still a mongrel." "I can't believe she lied to me! I've been telling everyone that he's one of them designer mixed breeds!

I'm so embarrassed, I could just... Hey Maddy, who's that going in your locker? Did you bring a friend?"

"What are you talking about?" Maddy looked confused at the sudden change in conversation.

"Are they single?" Rod eagerly added.

"What do you mean? Where?" Maddy turned around just in time to see come out of her locker a black hooded person wearing sunglasses. They looked suspiciously like one of the thieves from earlier. Looking around, appearing to check that nobody was nearby, they tried her car door.

"Not again!" Maddy yelled. Starting to run, she suddenly remembered the cute yellow pumps she was wearing and slowed down enough to remove them. "Hey, you! Get away from my car! I just can't anymore with you dipshidiots!" She then started running at full speed, pumps in hand. 'How many chases can one go on in a single day?' she asked herself. This time there were no stairs, no Ashley, and no shoes on her feet to stop her.

Startled, the hooded figure looked up and saw a very angry Maddy bulldozing towards them, waving shoes. Caught in the act, they took off to the end of the row of lockers and turned the corner.

Maddy ran up to the corner and saw them standing at the far end of the neighboring lockers, hooking one finger towards her, taunting her to follow.

"The nerve! Just you wait, I'm going to make you pay for today." She was steaming mad and shaking. "I've had it with you!" she shouted, continuing her pursuit.

The figure had once again taken off. Maddy rounded the corner at the end of that second row and caught sight of a partial shadow entering a locker. "Gotcha sucker! You're dead meat," she muttered with a victorious grin on her face.

Slowing down, she inched her way closer to the locker, then realized that she was still holding her pumps. She placed them just outside the door, then quietly entered the locker.

There was just too much stuff piled in the locker to see anything. Thinking that the wannabe thief had to be hiding behind one of those stacks of boxes, she figured she needed to use the element of surprise. If only it wasn't so difficult to see. Turning around to flip the light switch on and hopefully blind them, she suddenly felt her head explode into a million pieces, stars bursting all around her, images of yellow shoes encircling her head. Then, total darkness engulfed her.

Chapter 8

A thin band of light pierced the bottom of her eyes for a few seconds before it all went black again.

Then the light band returned, this time a bit wider. She could almost make something out in the distance before everything darkened once more.

She lay there for a moment, breathing deeply before forcibly trying to open her eyes. The back of her head began throbbing incessantly and painfully. 'Oh yeah, stars.' The last thing she remembered was seeing stars. That pain in the butt thief must have come from behind and hit her on the head. Slowly rising onto her elbows, she let the pounding in her head adjust to her changed position. Once it had settled, she was able to stand and slowly make her way over to the storage unit's door. She jiggled the knob, trying to lift the door, and realized it was locked. She banged on it twice but then had to stop to hold her aching head between her hands. After a few minutes had passed, she gave the door one more hit and shouted "Help!" as loud as she could.

She wasn't sure how often she could keep banging and yelling, it caused her head to pulsate, threatening to erupt like Mount Vesuvius.

Relief flooded over her at the sound of footsteps outside. She took another deep breath and shouted "Help! In here!" one more time.

The footsteps came closer which meant that she'd been heard. They stopped, not too far, then sounded like they were receding, walking in the opposite direction from the door. Maddy choked back a sob. She didn't have it in her to bang and shout anymore. If this person hadn't heard her already, more yelling and banging wasn't going to help at this point. She leaned against the wall next to the door and closed her eyes. She hadn't prayed since she was a kid. Now she silently prayed, asking PopPop to please send some help, any kind of help.

Without warning, the door rolled up and piercing sunlight hit her face, causing sharp, stabbing pain to shoot out behind her eyes as she squinted, trying to block out the glare.

"Oh, thank you! Thank you!" It took all Maddy had not to sob, "I heard you walk away and thought you were leaving me!"

"How on earth did you get yourself locked in here?" a male voice asked.

Unable to do more than squint, she could barely make out the silhouette of the voice's owner. The silhouette appeared to have sticks coming out of their head. Maddy started to give her head a shake, thinking she was imagining things but then a wave of searing pain warned her not to. Eyes focusing a bit better, and she realized who it was. Those weren't sticks, they were hair.

56

"I left because I had to find a way to get you out," Spikey explained, nodding towards Rod, who she hadn't noticed was standing next to him. Rod held a large hoop full of keys in his hand, twirling them and looking confused to see Maddy in there.

"How d'you get locked in?" Rod asked.

"Someone hit me over the head and locked me in," Maddy explained.

"Why?" both men asked at once, sounding both incredulous and a tad shocked.

"Wish I knew! I saw the people who'd been in my locker and was trying to get into my car so I followed them in here, and then 'BANG!' I saw stars," Maddy began to look around the unit, hoping she might be able to find an answer.

"You better get that head looked at princess," Rod said. "You do know that Triple-A isn't responsible for what happens inside the units, right?"

"Don't worry Rod, I'm not going to sue your sweet Aunt Shirley," Maddy reassured him while gingerly rubbing her head.

"Good, 'cause she's in Hawaii."

"Hawaii?!" Maddy exclaimed, automatically jerking her head up to look at Rod. The sudden movement caused pain to shoot through her head, making her wince. "Yeah, she eloped over two weeks ago, I thought everyone around here knew," Rod said. "Why d'you think I've been hanging around here with her yappy mutt? It sure ain't 'cause it's good for my health."

Come to think of it, Maddy hadn't seen Shirley around in quite some time... But eloped? Good for Shirley!

"Who did she elope with? I didn't even know she had a boyfriend," she asked.

"Someone she met online when she was bidding against him for a Vandor Betty Boop Hula Dance bobblehead," Rod said casually.

"Did she know him for long? Seems very sudden," Maddy remarked.

"Yeah, it does. But she did end up getting that bobblehead," Rod smiled, seeming to think that was all that mattered.

"Maybe so, but that's kind of a drastic way to go about getting it."

"Well, it was a rare Vandor Betty Boop Hula Dancer bobblehead," he said with the insistence that can only come from an avid collector.

Maddy looked over at Spikey, he simply shrugged his shoulders as though to say, "What can you do?" He seemed like a fairly laid-back guy who didn't let a whole lot faze him.

"Alrighty then, thanks for helping me out. I'd better go lock up my own unit and get home," Maddy told them. "Are you sure you're okay to drive?" Spikey asked. "And shouldn't you maybe call the cops, you were assaulted. That's not a normal thing."

"I don't know, I need to think about it. I couldn't even pick the person out of a lineup; I didn't get that good of a look at them. I'm not sure it would do any good."

"Yeah, maybe. But if you need a ride home just let me know. My name's Zane, by the way. I'm just finishing up a unit here, then I'll be heading out myself."

"Thanks." Remembering that she'd taken her shoes off, she looked around but couldn't find them. "Hey, one more thing," she asked. "Have you seen my shoes?"

"This one?" Rod pointed to a single yellow pump behind her.

"That's one of them but where's the other?"

"Are you sure you had two?" asked Zane, looking around.

"No, I hobbled here on one shoe. Of course, I'm sure I had two of them!"

"I'll go and look in the lost and found bin in the office, Cinderella." Rod handed her the pump and left.

After thanking Zane once more, Maddy went back to her unit and saw that she'd left the door wide open. Entering very slowly, she turned on the light. This head-bonking experience had now made her a bit leery of walking into any darkened space.

Looking around, she noticed that someone had rifled through her belongings. The bags of clothes that had been neatly stacked in the corner were tossed around on the floor, and some of the papers that had been neatly organized on her makeshift desk were now scattered around the unit. She stood at the doorway, uneasily surveying the mess. She wasn't sure if she should clean up or report it to Rod. In the end, she decided to shut and lock the unit, and and then head home. Bending down to tidy up was not a particularly inviting option given that her head was still throbbing badly. She'd deal with the mess some other time, just like the one in her car. When in doubt, put off and ignore.

~ ~ ~

Finally in her loft, she gingerly sat herself down on the couch and sighed. What a day for the history books it had been, a car break-in, an eccentric store owner, a snarky policeman, a bloody 'demon' mask, and being bonked on the head in a storage unit, locked away, and then saved by Spikey and Squiggy.

If there was ever a time that called for an evening of watching TV, this was it. She grabbed the remote control and hit the power button. She was in the middle of a popular mini-series and was overdue to get caught up. There was nothing worse than being halfway through a series only to hear spoilers because she wasn't quick enough to finish it.

She pointed the remote at the giant red N on her screen and clicked. A page came up asking for her login and password. "*What the heck?*" she thought, it should've logged in automatically. Irritated, she entered her old boyfriend Chad's email address and password. Maddy considered the use of his account the least he could do for the time she lost dating him. Time she'd never get back. Kind of like payment 'in lieu' of something.

"What?!" she yelled at the TV as a 'wrong password' message popped up on the screen. Taking her time and making sure she had the right password, she entered it a second time. The same message appeared.

"Are you kidding me?" she exclaimed. "Are you friggin' kidding me right now?!"

As if her day hadn't been trying enough. Now she didn't even have access to her Netflix account! Why now? And then it dawned on her, Chad had probably changed his password. Why did this damn guy have the audacity to think he could do this to her? The insult stung to the core. As if it wasn't bad enough that she'd wasted her time on him, now he was changing his passwords too?

Fuming, she sat on the couch considering her options. Her head was still aching, but all she could think of was how outrageous it was that he'd behave so childishly. What was she supposed to do now? He didn't honestly think she should be paying for her own, did he? What a ridiculous thing that would be when he had a perfectly good account she could use. It was no skin off his nose that she was watching on the guest account.

When she finally got tired of sitting on the couch angry and feeling sorry for herself, she reached over and grabbed her phone.

"Hey, Ash, do you know what that dumbass did?"
"Um, who?"

"Dumb ass, you know, DUMB ass!" Maddy insisted, surprised that she had to explain herself.

"Oh! DUMB ass!" Ash exclaimed as realization hit her. "It's been so long since you mentioned DUMB ass Chad that I'd forgotten all about him."

Ashley had never thought much of Chad. He was one of those extra clingy, to the almost icky extent, type of guy. He wanted to go everywhere with Maddy. They couldn't even have a girls' night out alone without him wanting to be there, not just with them but right there sitting in between them. Ten to one he had been a mama's boy. She was quite relieved when Maddy gave him the old heave-ho.

"What did dumbass Chad do now?"

"Oh, it's low, real low. This time he's gone below what stands as simple, human decency," Maddy fumed.

"He isn't getting married, is he?" Ashley whispered. "The DUMB ass isn't getting married, is he?"

"No, of course not. No one would want to marry him," Maddy said, ignoring the fact that there had been a time, not that long ago, when she'd given it serious consideration herself. "It's worse than that."

"Worse than that?"

"Yes, much worse, it's unbelievable," Maddy rested her head on the back of her couch and ran her hands over her eyes. "I knew he was a jerk but even I wouldn't have thought that he'd stoop to doing that."

"What? What did he do?" Ashley couldn't take the suspense any longer. "Tell me!"

"He changed his Netflix password!" Maddy stated in a tone that spoke to the sheer incredulity of his actions.

"Netflix password?"

"Yeah, he changed it," Maddy confirmed, "Can you imagine? The nerve!"

"He changed his Netflix password, that's what's got your panties all in a knot?"

"Well of course it does! What am I supposed to do now? I'm only halfway through the series that stars what's his name, the one where he shows his butt," Maddy whined.

"Well, now that you've mentioned that a butt scene's involved," Ashley replied, dripping with sarcasm. "You do know that you can sign up for your very own Netflix account like a grown woman, right?"

"Of course, I know Ash-ley! I'm not stoo-pid," Maddy pushed back. "It's the principle of the matter. Who the hell does he think he is?"

"Umm, I don't know, let's see, maybe the owner of the account? The guy who actually pays for it?"

There was silence at the other end of the phone as Ashley's statement hung between them. The tension grew as Maddy let the words sink in until she finally spoke.

"You've been friends for a lot of years Ashley Mueller, like, forever," Maddy said quietly. "I can't believe you don't know me better than that. This is not about whose account it is or who pays for what. This is about him having no consideration for my feelings, just like when we were dating. This is about him owing me some respect."

"Of course," Ashley acquiesced. "It's the principle of it all."

"Exactly."

"So, what are you going to do?"

"I need to give it some thought," Maddy answered. "I need to come up with a plan. While I do that, can you do me a favor? Could you ask around and see if he has a girlfriend?"

"I don't think I want to know why you want that info, but okay, I will," Ashley said reluctantly. "Do you want to use my account until you figure things out? I don't mind."

"That's kind of you Ash, I knew you'd understand," Maddy sighed as she felt the indignation slowly drain out of her body. "It is just the icing on the top of the cake after a lousy day, first that damn mask, then getting bonked on the head, stuffed in a storage unit, and left to die, it was just too much."

"Ash? Why aren't you saying anything? Ash, are you there? Ash?" The line had gone dead. This hanging up without a word was becoming annoying.

Chapter 9

Adjusting the ice pack on her head, all cozied up in her NAIT sweats, and feeling sorry for herself, Maddy reached for the special stash of Jacek chocolates she kept hidden for days like today. Days that were crappy from beginning to end. Other than her stop at Bernard's, everything else had been one gong show after another. To add insult to injury, dumb ass Chad had the audacity to change his Netflix password on her. Dumb Ass with a capital D and A. She needed a drink. If only someone would bring her a glass so she wouldn't have to get up from this comfy old couch. She loved her couch from the Goodwill secondhand store, it was already broken in, all soft, with no stiff pillows poking you in the wrong places. This reminded her that she hadn't been shopping there in a while, and she needed some Goodwill retail therapy soon. It was most definitely one of her favorite shops. It had everything, furniture, clothes, shoes... Shoes! How could she have forgotten about her missing yellow pump? Rod hadn't found it in the Lost and Found box. Damn, that black hooded thief!

She'd just about talked herself into getting up to pour a couple of drams of scotch when her cell rang. Someone was downstairs buzzing to be let in. Who the hell would dare show up at this god-awful time? Unimpressed, she answered.

"Hello?"

"Let us in. NOW!" demanded two very familiar voices.

"What are you guys doing here?"

"You better buzz us in right now if you know what's good for you!" Ashley's voice reverberated through the phone.

Maddy buzzed them up.

Great, Ashley must have called Rick right after she had hung up.

They knocked. She slowly went to the door, cursing them under her breath with every painful step she took. She could see them through the peephole, standing in front of her loft's door, they didn't look happy. Great. That's all she needed to add to this day from Hades.

"Come in," she opened the door and stepped back. "But keep your voices down. I have a pounding migraine and can't deal with any noises or arguments right now. I just want to watch my Netflix in peace." She shuffled towards the kitchen to get her drink.

"And don't you dare turn any more lights on," she added, glaring at Rick who was reaching for the light switch.

"Sit down!" Ashley told Maddy as she took her by the arm, half walking, half dragging her to the couch.

Maddy gave her a death stare. She was not in the mood for a lecture. She needed to come up with a quick way to distract them.

"Rick, did Ash tell you that Chad had the nerve to change his Netflix password on me? Can you believe it? How dare he?! After we almost got engaged and all. That's low, even for him, right?"

"He what? That's so immature. What kind of man does that? Half a man, not even that. Where's his pride? I would never…"

"Rick!" Ashley stopped him before he got any further into his Middle Eastern bravado speech. "At the moment, it's the least of our worries. Maddy got hit on the head by some maniac. That's what we're here for, not some ridiculous password."

"Oh, yeah, right. Good try," Rick gave Maddy a disappointed squinty look. "What the hell happened to you today?" he asked, walking to the fridge to grab a beer.

"You don't have to use your dad's voice with me." Maddy cradled her head, looking at him between her fingers.

Rick, leaned on the fridge door and raised an eyebrow at her.

"Fine. Some thief wannabe lured me into a locker and bonked me on the head with who knows what. Could you grab me a beer too, please?" She figured she might as well have him bring her one. It'd save her from getting up again.

"What kind?"

"Grab me a Campio IPA," she answered.

Rick grabbed another can, walked to the couch, and reached over Maddy to hand it to Ashley. She then proceeded to open it and take a long, slow sip before setting it down next to her, all the while looking at Maddy. Rick took his regular spot on an oversized lime-colored leather bean bag, across from them.

They both stared at Maddy. She was not impressed with them, not in the least.

"You've got some nerve, Rick Nasser! That's MY beer. Why did you give her MY beer? Why are you staring at me, and why are you here, interrupting my Netflix evening?" she demanded, arms crossed.

"First of all, you got hit on the head and probably have a concussion. So, no beer for you! Ash, care to answer the rest of her questions?"

"Oh, I'd love to," she turned towards Maddy reaching for her hand, trying to somewhat soften her tone, "Look, this is serious. Your car was broken into this morning. This afternoon you were hit on the head. Add to all that the bloody demon mask from Mazatlán, and we've got some very suspicious business happening here." Ashley picked up the ice pack off the table and handed it back to Maddy. "Please start from the beginning, Mads. What happened at the lot before you were hit?"

"Not much. I was talking to Rod, Shirley's nephew. Remember Shirley?"

"The old lady in a muumuu who's always flirting with me when I help you move stuff?" asked Ashley.

"She flirts with you too? Man, I thought she and I had something special going on," Rick said winking at Ashley. She gave him a dirty look and threw a pillow at him, "Don't interrupt."

68

Maddy went on, picking up from where she'd left off, "Shirley's gone..."

"God rest her soul" Rick crossed himself. Ashley and Maddy both looked at him.

"Whaaat? It's a Lebanese thing." He gestured with his hands. "You know I've got to show some respect. Continue, Shirley's gone..." Rick crossed himself again.

"Yeah, Shirley's gone... to Hawaii! She's gotten married and now Rod's running the show."

"Oh, so she's "muumuu'ved" to Hawaii."

Ashley threw another pillow at Rick who ducked and laughed, quite pleased with himself and the picture of Shirley in a muumuu he imagined.

"Rick, can I at least get a can of diet soda? I'm parched and I think that I might be dehydrated."

Bowing at her, Rick rolled off the bean bag.

"And since you're up, could you please bring us the cookie jar too? I bought some cookies today when I was on 124th Street." Maddy knew how to change his mood. "Cookies from a bakery? You're sure well-stocked today." While Rick was busy fulfilling her request, she continued with her story.

"Anyway, we saw a hooded figure trying to get into my car, so I chased them. Then when they got to an open unit, they waved me toward them,"

"Wait, so that person gestured you to follow them? And you did? Oh, Maddy," Ashley bemoaned.

"Yeah, it was weird. That person was dressed the same way as this morning's two nincompoops, black jeans, and similar black hoodies. I figured it was related to Bugsy's break-in and I wanted answers. When I came to, I was locked in that unit. If it wasn't for Zane walking by, I'd probably still be in there."

"Zane? Who's Zane?" Ashley asked.

"He's the guy who was bidding against me for the locker," Maddy answered.

"And he just happened to be walking by, eh?" Rick mumbled, his mouth full of London Fog cookie crumbs. Ashley stood up and started pacing. She took another sip of beer, then walked towards the box Maddy had brought back from the locker that afternoon. "Is that another box of stuff from the same unit?"

"Yes. Please stop pacing. You're making me dizzy and worsening my headache."

Dragging the box back to the couch, Ashley sat down and started taking things out. Rick moved the bean bag closer, taking a look at the contents that were being spread out on the table.

"There's some pretty weird stuff in here," Ashley remarked. Making a face she pulled out the hair extensions and held them at arm's length. Placing all three on the table, she dug back into the box.

"What the heck?" Ashley started pulling out one shoe after the other, "There's one black patent high heel, one bright fuchsia ballerina flat, and one blue Hoka runner." She lined the three single shoes up on the floor in front of the coffee table.

Rick picked up the ballerina flat, examined it and then looked in the box, "There's only one of each?"

"Yeah, and they aren't even the same size," Maddy replied. "They're quite dirty too. The black one's heel is almost falling off like someone got it caught in a manhole cover. I should put my lonely yellow pump next to these so it can have company."

"What are you talking about?" Ashley asked, pulling a long green silk scarf out of the box. It had a dark, blackish stain on it.

"I took my shoes off so I could run after him... or her," Maddy explained. "Then I put them outside the storage unit door so I wouldn't accidentally drop them and make noise. I wanted to sneak up on the bum. After I was let out and we were leaving, I could only find one of my yellow pumps."

Rick and Ashley looked at each other, then at Maddy. The realization of what this meant slowly dawned on her. Was her missing pump tied to these shoes somehow? Ashley stood up and started pacing again, "Oh no. Oh no, no, no. I told you that the Demon from Mazatlán was bad juju!"

Maddy wasn't convinced.

"Do you guys honestly think this box belongs to the person who knocked me out and took my shoe?"

It was Rick's turn to get up and pace, "None of this makes any sense to me," he said, "Why would someone go to so much trouble for a few odd shoes?"

Maddy moved the ice pack to the back of her head, "I don't know. Let's look at the rest of the stuff. There must be more to this. Hopefully, the answer lies somewhere in this box." Holding the ice pack with one hand, she lifted a hair extension off the table with the other and inspected it closely. It was made up of a handful of black hair and tied with a red satin bow.

Ashley picked up another extension, this one was a mess of blond hair and had a pink ribbon around it.

Rick ran his hand through his own hair and looked back and forth between the two hair extensions and the one tied in a green Christmas ribbon still laying on the table. "Ladies, I don't know much about women's hair and stuff, but Tasha bought some extensions a few years ago, remember when she worked at that salon, and they practiced on her? She ended up with that awful haircut?" "Oh yeah, that was quite an unfortunate choice of hairstyle," agreed Ashley.

"She looked like one of those long-haired chihuahuas," laughed Maddy.

"Yeah, well, don't ever tell her that. Anyway, those extensions were glued together, and she put them on like a backward headband or something. These here are loose hair tied with ribbons. I don't think these are extensions." "Oh my God!" Ashley exclaimed in shock, tossing the one she was holding back onto the table.

Maddy looked closer to the bundle she was holding, then slowly put it down. "These are not extensions. I… I think this is real hair," she felt around her head and let out a sigh of relief. "Mine's still all here."

She then picked up the green scarf that Ashley had pulled out of the box, taking a closer look at it. "Guys, this dark stain looks like blood."

Ashley sat back next to Maddy and stared at the scarf, "Could this be the same blood as was on the demon mask's base?"

"How should I know? Blood is blood!" She placed the scarf next to the 'not extensions' hair, put down the ice pack, and started digging deeper into the box.

"Mads, you better stop digging in that box." Rick warned, "These look very suspicious. Tasha and the girls are always watching those true crime shows on TV…"

"Those CSI ones give me nightmares. Do they watch those?" asked Ashley.

"Yeah," he sighed. "These things here, they almost look like they could be crime trophies lunatics always collect on those shows." Rick leaned forward, examining the hair extensions, "Let me rephrase this, they DO look like a serial killer's trophies!"

Blood drained from Ashley's face. "Maddy, you need to take this to the police. Like, now. We can't be playing detective."

"Ash is right, Mads. Like I said, this is very serious stuff."

"No way, not until we know for sure," Maddy kept looking through the box, "That Officer Kowalchuk, he didn't take me seriously enough the first time around. We need irrefutable proof or else they won't follow up."

"And how are you going to get that proof?" Rick knelt by the box to help Maddy sort.

"I'll figure something out. And don't worry about me, I'm a big girl. I swear not to take any unnecessary risks, I'll just poke around a bit," Maddy promised.

"Fine, but only if you let us help too, right Rick? We have to find something that could lead us to the owner of this box." Ashley said.

After half an hour of looking at all its contents, all three sat back, dejected. The box had completely been emptied and they had found nothing.

"I give up," Maddy stood up angrily and kicked the box away from them. She walked to the freezer to get another ice pack, then grabbed two more beers and a Diet Sprite from the fridge. Once back on the couch, she put the pack on her head, lied down, and closed her eyes.

Ashley and Rick watched her silently while munching on some more cookies.

"We can't give up guys. There's some kook out there that has it in for Maddy and we need to put a stop to it," Ashley went to retrieve the box. "Would those TV detectives give up so easily? I don't think so. And neither will we. There must be some clue we missed. Let's look at everything with fresh eyes tomorrow."

Maddy groaned. "Go home guys. I need to pass out now."

Ashley started packing all the creepy trophies away, "I'm not leaving you alone tonight, not after having just been attacked by a potential murdering maniac out on the loose. Especially with you having a concussion."

"I have a possible concussion. Nobody has officially diagnosed me. And besides, don't you have a late date night with Bill or Will, or something like that?"

"It's William. I'll cancel it. He's boring anyway. All he talks about is his collection of military men. You know those little green plastic toy soldiers. I mean seriously, it's ridiculous."

Rick rose suddenly and grabbed the box out of Ashley's arms. "Look, there's a label on the box!"

"Let me see! Let me see!" In her excitement, Maddy forgot about her head and jumped up. "Oh no, the room is spinning."

"Potential concussion you say?" Ashley tsked as she guided Maddy back down onto the couch.

"Look," Rick brought the box over and showed them the label. "There's no name but there's a delivery address." He smiled, raising his shoulders, "That's still a good starting point, right?"

"Right! That's a southside address, isn't it?" Ashley pointed out. "That's nowhere near your storage lot."

"How about I drive by to check it out? I should be getting on my way home anyway. My cell has vibrated several times tonight, pretty sure it's Tasha," he said, looking at his phone. "Yup, it's her. She's worried about you. I'll call her back from the car to update her while I go take a look at that place."

"Are you sure?" Maddy didn't want him going there alone. "Maybe we should all go together?"

"Nah, don't worry. I won't go in. I'm only going to look at it from the car, see if there's any sign of life or anything, okay?" He bent down and gave Maddy a hug.

These two women had come to mean the world to him. He couldn't help but feel protective. They had seen so much hurt and been dealt some poor cards as far as families were concerned. He felt somewhat guilty because he'd hit the jackpot with his large and loving Middle Eastern family. Maddy and Ashley, on the other hand, had missed out on that. Rick made up for it and they'd become part of his.

"Okay, thanks. Please hug Tasha and the girls for me." Maddy said, then added, "I'll call Kyle at the police station in the morning, he's supposed to be in on Sundays this month. I'll see if he can get me a name to go with that address. Probably will have to mention Ashley's name or something to get him to help." She gave Ashley a side glance.

"Oh no, you're not! You have to stop taking advantage of his feelings for me. You're giving him false hope. I'm not ready for a serious relationship and you know it! You might think he's perfect in every way, but not for me, not right now. I want to have fun, Mads, check out all the other cute little fishies in the sea and whatnot. Using my name will just make him think that I put you up to it."

"Ash, she doesn't have a choice this time," Rick reasoned. "You want her to ask that useless cop she met this morning?"

Ashley sighed. "Aren't you supposed to be leaving or something?"

"Yeah, yeah, I'm going."

Ashley walked him to the door and whispered, "Call me right away if you spot anything weird or unusual. I don't want her dealing with any more excitement tonight."

"I will. Be sure to double lock the door behind me and don't let her buzz anyone in. This whole mess has me very worried."

"You don't have to worry, Rick. Trust me. Nobody's going to get past me tonight. I've been taking some self- defense refresher courses and I'm itching to practice on someone."

"I'd rather you didn't. This person is likely very dangerous." It was her turn to get a hug as he was leaving the loft. "Remember to check up on her every few hours, okay?"

"I know, I know, and ask her her name and if she knows where she is."

"She's going to be mighty pissed at you tomorrow morning."

"Yeah, well her head will be too sore for her to yell at me, so there's that at least." Ashley closed the door and double-locked it behind him. "Goodnight Rick, you can go home now," she added, knowing full well that he would be standing behind the door, making sure she had followed his instructions to a T.

Returning to the couch, she helped Maddy up and walked her to her bedroom. "I'm going to sleep on the couch tonight instead of your guest room so that I'm closer to you and can keep an eye and ear on the front door too."

"Thanks, Ash, you're truly a gem, you know?"

"Yeah, I know. Try to remember that in the morning.

Nighty-night now." "G'night."

~ ~ ~

At two in the morning, Ashley's phone alarm came on playing "Fur Elise", waking her up with a start. It took her a few seconds to remember where she was. Exhausted, she shuffled, half asleep, to Maddy's room to check in on her.

"Wake up, come on, wake up Maddy." "Five more minutes Mom, please." "Do you know what your name is?"

"Go away, Ash!" Maddy mumbled, turning her back to Ashley.

"Tell me and I will go away. Come on, Maddy." Ugh, Ashley just wanted to go back to bed herself.

"MADDY! Now please don't wake me again. You've checked on me three times already. I. Am. Fine."

"Perfect, I'll check on you later." Ashley hadn't finished her sentence when she heard Maddy snoring. Must be nice to be able to just pass out like that.

Rick was right, she would be majorly ticked off at Ashley in the morning. At least she knew Maddy was okay. Good thing Ashley could work from home this week, she'd need to crash as soon as she got there.

Boy was she thirsty. Tomorrow, she would look for her extra humidifier and bring it over here. This place was too dry. She'd warned Maddy about loft living. Those high ceilings with all those pipes and vents exposed made this place feel like a desert. She barefooted her way towards the kitchen sink, turned the tap on and reached for a glass in the cupboard. Ashley had to admit that this place had a nice kitchen. Too bad it was wasted on Maddy.

Walking back to the couch, she heard a rattling noise. Stopping dead in her tracks, she tried to focus on where the sound was coming from. Then she heard it again. Someone was rattling the knob on the loft's front door, trying to open it. Warily, she approached the door and peeked through the peephole. All she could see was what looked like a black hood. They tried turning the doorknob again. Spooked, Ashley grabbed the baseball bat Maddy kept by the door 'in case of emergency' and stood by the closet, on the righthand side of the door. Using her deepest voice, she snarled a warning to the wannabe intruder, "We have a gun and it's loaded. I won't hesitate to shoot you through this door if you keep trying to get in. My friend is on her cell right now calling the cops. You'd better leave and never come back again. Got it?"

After a couple of minutes that seemed like an eternity, Ashley crept to the door and looked through the peephole. The hooded figure appeared to be gone. She went back to the couch but didn't lie down.

"Damn you, Demon from Mazatlán!" There'd be no sleeping tonight.

Chapter 10

Waking up in the morning, Maddy's head still hurt like the dickens but was at a manageable level compared to the previous night. She was surprised to see Ashley sound asleep on the couch, clutching her 'in case of' baseball bat as though the outcome of the World Series depended on her. Maddy made a fresh pot of coffee and waved a cup of it under Ashley's nose to wake her.

"Huh?" Ashley sat up straight, pulling her arms back, ready to hit a home run.

"Whoa!" Maddy backed away, barely avoiding scalding herself with the coffee. "Easy does it, slugger!"

Ashley looked around the loft, her eyes glazed and unable to focus. It took a few moments for her to shake the sleep away and come to life. By that time Maddy was sitting across from her, frowning. She'd never known Ashley to be so reactive or slow to wake up.

"What's with the baseball bat, Ash?"

"Oh, I just wanted to protect us," Ashley explained. "From what?"

"Someone tried to get in last night, I didn't know if they were going to come back or not."

"Why on earth didn't you wake me up and tell me?" Maddy stared at Ashley. "You could have been hurt! I wouldn't have even known!"

"As you can see, nothing bad happened to me. I wanted to make sure you got the rest you needed, your brain needed some mending."

That comment brought a smile and a look of question on Maddy's face.

"You know what I mean," Ashley laughed. "Anyway, how are you feeling today?"

"My head still hurts but nowhere near as bad as yesterday, so I think my brain was able to mend a bit," Maddy pushed Ashley's coffee cup, which had been placed on the coffee table for safety's sake, towards her. "Drink up, it sounds like you had a pretty long night and could use some caffeine."

Ashley gratefully gulped down her cup of much-needed caffeine, gave her friend a lecture on personal safety, and then bade Maddy farewell after making her promise that she'd check in with her later in the day.

She finished her cup of coffee and showered. Feeling a bit more alive, Maddy figured that she was well enough to leave her loft. She headed out the door to see if she could discover anything further about the owner of last night's unusual box. Hungry for some breakfast, she stopped on her way for a toasted bagel with extra butter at the corner coffee shop, making a mental note that she needed to pick up a few items at the grocery store on her way back. She then hopped on a bus that took her within a short walking distance from the police station. Maddy hoped Kyle would be able to help her with the address

MacDonald & Howatt

they'd found on the box. While sipping her coffee this morning, Maddy had done a quick online search to see if she might get a hit on that address but came out empty-handed. All she knew was where it was. She didn't know who lived there, owned, or rented it, or anything else. Rick hadn't called her yet; he was probably busy at work doing some overtime, and she preferred not to bother him after last night.

Kyle was busy so she didn't stay long after he ran the address, wrote it down on a slip of paper, and slid it across his desk to her. A name. Jason Thomas. Along the bottom of the paper Kyle had scribbled "I'll look into this more when I have time."

"You owe me," he told her jokingly. "We can discuss repayment at another date. And please don't tell anyone or I could get into trouble."

She knew he would have been happy to chat with her, but she wanted to respect his time and position. Wouldn't do him or her any good to wear out her welcome.

She wasn't happy that even this small excursion was bringing back her headache, so she headed home. Ashley was right, she did need to take it easy. Groceries could wait.

Back at her loft, the couch beckoned her, so she crawled up on it with her laptop. Wrapping herself in a throw, she began doing an online search for Jason Thomas. Nothing came up in the databases she'd accessed, so she headed over to Facebook. You could always count on social media, the land of oversharing.

She did a search for his profile on Facebook but couldn't find any that could logically match her Jason Thomas. They were either located too far away, seemed

82

like a fake profile, or were ridiculously young - wasn't there a minimum age in order to join Facebook? She was pretty sure it wasn't nine years old.

Maddy already belonged to some of the groups in the local area, so she went on those pages. First, she did a search in each group for his name, thinking she might strike it rich, hoping to find that he had posted or commented on something. No such luck. She joined the Edmonton Lost and Found page, the Alberta Missing Reports, and Edmonton's "Ask Here" groups. She would have finished her search much sooner if finding out who the top 25 richest people in Hollywood hadn't been such a tempting rabbit hole.

She posted messages in the groups where it was allowed to do so, and even in some where it wasn't. You never knew who might see it before an administrator removed her post. She asked if anyone knew Jason Thomas and if they did, could they please contact her? Once she had exhausted all the groups she could think of, Maddy began a search of a different kind, researching Robert's long-lost love, Brigitte.

It was hard to hide in this digital world nowadays, and while Maddy was no private investigator, she did have a few tricks up her sleeve; an online search tool. While it wasn't always up-to-date or even 100% reliable, it was cheap and might be able to, at the very least, point her in the right direction.

Grabbing a diet Coke from her fridge and a bag of ketchup chips from her snack cupboard, she flipped on the television for some background noise. As it turned out, she had barely begun her search when she struck paydirt. Apparently, Brigitte Schell was all about Facebook. At least, she was 99% certain it was Brigitte. Robert had emailed her a picture he had of Brigitte.

Although it was somewhat old, it wasn't difficult to see the beautiful young lady from the photograph in the smiling face of the older woman's profile.

As Maddy flipped through the pictures and posts, she thought that maybe she could be wrong, a likeness isn't a confirmation. Then she saw what appeared to be another old picture of Brigitte. It didn't take long for her to realize that it wasn't old, it was a much more recent photo but the resemblance was uncanny. But the teenager in it was much too young to be Brigitte's daughter. Maddy clicked on the name of the person tagged in the photograph. She found herself on a profile with no posts showing. More security conscious than Brigitte, this person's profile was locked up tight. But her profile picture still showed. Clicking to enlarge it, Maddy gazed at the family picture in front of her. It was a picture of three women, three generations. The pieces fell into place. This young woman wasn't Brigitte, she was her granddaughter! The resemblance between these women was unmistakable.

Maddy was pleased she had found Brigitte so easily, but she also found the photos a bit jarring. She had been reading the letters of a young man, professing his love for a beautiful young girl. Now, she almost felt as though she had entered a time machine. The years unfolded before her as she saw Brigitte as a 65-year-old woman, her daughter, appearing to be around her mid-forties, and then her granddaughter. Young, and with her whole life stretched out before her. She took a moment to sit back in her chair and wondered what would be different if Brigitte had answered Robert's letters. Would she still have this beautiful granddaughter, this happy-looking family? Maddy laughed quietly to herself. Wasn't she feeling introspective tonight?

If anyone should know that the way a family looks to the outside world has no real bearing on actual reality, it was Maddy. She clicked back to the family picture and noticed that there was no Mr. Brigitte. Was she a widow? Or a divorcee?

Done with wondering, she clicked on "Message." She asked Brigitte some identifying questions, such as the high school she went to and her parents' names to confirm that she had the right person. Although she was almost positive, she didn't want to freak the woman out by jumping right into things. She simply told her that she had come across some property that might belong to her.

Setting her laptop aside and leaning back on the couch, she closed her eyes for a short catnap.

Moments later, she was jolted out of Ryan Reynolds' embrace, the warm white sand surrounding them disappeared, and she was back on her lumpy couch.

"Damn it!" she groaned. Her dream was just getting good! It then dawned on her that the Facebook notification bell was what had woken her, snatching her rudely from her soul mate's arms. Pulling the laptop toward her, she looked to find out if the notification was in response to one of her posts. It was.

"Check your DMs" was all it said. It had been posted by a certain Sally WWB. Whenever she saw a comment like that, it reminded her of her grandma, phoning her to tell her she'd sent her an email. It always seemed to defeat the purpose of sending the email in the first place, she could just talk to her on the phone. But Grandma insisted on 'getting with the times.'

Sally WWB had sent Maddy a message telling her that, although she didn't know Jason personally, she was friends with his sister. Not exactly a home run, but something to go on. Maddy would take it. After exchanging pleasantries with Sally, she explained that she was looking for Jason because his name had been drawn in a contest he'd entered. Sally agreed to give Maddy the name and contact information of his sister.

"Well, that was too easy," Maddy mumbled to herself as she triumphantly looked down at the sister's name scribbled on her notepad next to Jason's. It always amazed her how easily people were willing to divulge information on social media. To read the headlines in the papers, you'd think that the average Joe worried about their financial safety and having their personal information stolen due to huge online privacy issues. In reality, Maddy had found that folks tended to willingly overshare, thinking nothing of voluntarily giving away their personal info to be allowed to play games and fill questionnaires that told you what kind of faery princess you would be or how opinionated you were.

Done with her mental rant, she dialed Jason's sister's phone number. After a few rings, a woman answered.

"Hello?"

"Hi, Rhonda? I received your name from Sally," Maddy began as she paced her loft.

"Sally? Your cousin Stephanie's friend?" she explained.

"Oh yes, yes, they've been friends since high school," she confirmed.

"Anyway, I'm trying to locate your brother, Jason, I have some information about his storage locker." She asked and then waited for a response.

"Rhonda?" There was only silence at the end of the phone. Maddy looked at her phone, wondering if they had been cut off.

For several seconds, all Maddy could hear was the slight sound of breathing at the other end of the phone.

"Jason's dead," Rhonda said quietly.

Maddy stayed silent for a while, giving his sister some room to emotionally recover. It was obvious that asking about her brother had upset Rhonda. She wanted to respect her emotions.

Eventually, Maddy spoke.

"I'm so very sorry to hear that Rhonda, I had no idea." "It's okay, you had no way of knowing.

It's just that question coming out of the blue like that, took me aback."

"I can imagine," Maddy said. "How old was he?"

"He was 38," Rhonda said, sniffling slightly. "He was so young."

"Yes, that is still young," Maddy agreed. "Was he married?"

"He was, but they weren't together when he died," she said. "They weren't on very good terms."

"Do you keep in touch with her?" Maddy knew she was pressing her luck and that the grieving sister might begin to ask questions soon.

"She showed up at his funeral, but I haven't heard from her since," Rhonda explained. "I don't know if she's even still around."

"Would it be possible to get her name and maybe the last phone number you have for her?" Maddy asked. "I just want to ask her about the storage locker."

"Sure, her name is Lauren, just a sec, I'll grab her number."

Maddy crossed her fingers, hoping that she would get the phone number before Rhonda had enough time to wonder why she wanted the ex-wife's phone number and what was up with her dead brother's storage locker.

"I don't know if this is still her phone number, but she only had a cell phone, so I assume it is," Rhonda explained after rattling off the numbers. "Nowadays people don't change their phone numbers as much, do they?"

"No, they usually don't," Maddy agreed. "Thank you for your time and I'm truly sorry to hear about your brother."

"Thanks, you surprised me at first, but honestly, it's nice to hear someone say his name again," Rhonda said sadly.

They hung up and Maddy plopped down on the couch, gazing unseeing at the phone in her hand. While she had a phone number to follow up on, the conversation with Rhonda had taken the wind out of her sails a bit. She shouldn't have been surprised; the locker had been abandoned after all. After a few minutes, she took a deep breath and started to punch the ex-wife's number on her cell.

"Hi, can I please speak to Lauren?" Maddy asked the woman who answered.

"You're speaking to her."

"Oh, hi, my name's Maddy, I received your name and phone number from your former sister-in-law," she began.

"WOW! I didn't think she'd remember my number," Lauren said with a small chuckle. "What's this all about?" "I was looking for Jason, to talk to him about a storage locker he abandoned," Maddy began to explain.

"Really? I didn't know he had a storage locker," Lauren responded, sounding a bit taken aback. "What was in it?"

"There were a number of small items," Maddy hedged, not wanting to get into the particulars just yet. "How long had you guys been split before he died?"

"Hard to pinpoint a date, we were on and off near the end. We kept breaking up and then missing each other and getting back together. You get the idea. I'm not convinced we wouldn't still be at it today if he had lived," Lauren mused.

This meant she might know something about the items that were in the storage unit, Maddy thought. She might not have known about the unit itself, but maybe she could explain some of the stuff they had found in it. "Hey, would you like to meet for coffee?" Maddy asked.

"That would be great," Lauren responded. "I like talking about Jason and don't get to do that much anymore."

They set a time for later that afternoon at a coffee shop just across from Maddy's place.

Chapter 11

Maddy easily knew who Lauren was the moment she walked into the coffee shop. She was the only woman who opened the door and immediately scanned the tables as though she was looking for someone. Maddy lifted her cup and nodded when their eyes met. Lauren smiled and then gestured that she would be getting herself a coffee.

There's a feeling one gets when they see someone for the first time. You know right away whether you'll be getting along or not. She had that feeling about Lauren. She thought that they would hit it off quite well. For one, Lauren seemed to have the same fashion sense as Maddy, casual yet leaning towards country chic. Lauren wore a pair of well-cut jeans and a cute lace top with a brown leather belt around her slim waist. Maddy had to remember to ask her where she had found those gorgeous cream-colored cowboy boots, they finished off her outfit quite nicely.

While waiting for Lauren, she nibbled on a white chocolate raspberry scone and surveyed the room. Some people she recognized as regulars in the neighborhood, others were complete strangers. That's what downtown city living was like. Even those you considered regulars might only be known to you as 'old man with a beard' or 'frazzled young mom.' They smiled and nodded in recognition when they passed on the street, but names were never exchanged. On the one hand, Maddy thought this was a bit sad, yet on the other, she quite liked the semi-anonymity it gave her. If she didn't want to talk to anyone, she didn't have to. And no one got into her business. Not that she had that much business for others to get into these days. In fact, she wasn't sure she remembered exactly when was the last time that she had any business at all. Probably not since Chad. Dumb-Ass-Netflix-Stealing Chad.

"Hi, I'm Lauren." The woman approached her with a coffee in one hand and the other outstretched for a handshake.

"Hi Lauren, Maddy, thanks for meeting me here."

"No problem, I was looking for a diversion from my work anyway."

"What kind of work do you do?" Maddy politely asked.

"I'm self-employed," Lauren answered with a smile. "I do research for a bunch of different clients, anything from prospective business purchases to the effects of asbestos on pet budgies."

Maddy laughed along with Lauren at the absurdity of the last topic.

"So, Jason and a storage locker," Lauren cut through the small talk and went straight to the topic at hand. Maddy liked that.

"Yes, you do research for a living, I buy stuff in abandoned storage lockers and estate sales," Maddy lifted her mug of hot coffee towards her mouth and blew on it. "Recently I purchased the content of a storage locker and your ex-husband's name was on a box of stuff." She figured there was no need to tell her the whole story.

"I don't know anything about a storage locker, but that doesn't mean much, Jason did a lot of things he didn't tell me about," Lauren said with a derisive snort.

Maddy frowned and I leaned closer in a show of interest, keeping silent so Lauren would explain without her needing to probe.

"Jason wasn't exactly an up-front and honest kind of guy," Lauren continued. "One of the main reasons why we were on again-off again was because he had a hard time sticking to one woman if you know what I mean."

It was pretty hard not to know what she meant. "What did you find in it? Skimpy lingerie? Home movies?" Lauren seemed more amused at the thought than upset.

"No, just some shoes and stuff," Maddy responded. She didn't want to outright lie to the woman, but she also wasn't going to reveal all about the locker's content until she had a better read on her. Maddy wasn't naive.

It was Lauren's turn to look quizzically at Maddy. "There was what appeared to be a souvenir mask and a few odds and ends that I thought might be of sentimental value to someone," Maddy explained. "Whenever I come across stuff in units that aren't valuable but appear to be very personal, I try to get it back to the rightful owners."

"That's very kind of you," Lauren said. "But there's nothing that Jason might have had in a secret storage locker that I would want, so do with it what you will."

Maddy nodded understandingly. She was familiar with bitter feelings after a breakup, she could totally relate to what Lauren was and wasn't saying.

"Jason and I had a complicated marriage," Lauren began with absolutely no prompting. "I was so in love, and he was so absolutely perfect. He doted on me and made all my dreams come true."

As she was speaking, Lauren leaned back in her chair and stared across the room, her eyes looking dreamy, Maddy knew she was going back to a happier time and place.

"It was so romantic and idyllic... until it wasn't."

They sat in silence for a while. Maddy somewhat felt a bond with the woman. She could totally relate. "I know exactly what you mean, I had this boyfriend who just locked me out of his Netflix account..."

Chapter 12

Maddy's coffee visit with Lauren made her realize that it was time to stop worrying about things that weren't even a real issue and to start focusing on the important things.

She fired a message off to Ashley to see if she wanted to come over for a visit. She tempted her with the love letters and a bottle of Chianti. If truth be known, she just wanted some company.

~~~

"This is so sweet and so sad all at the same time!" Ashley exclaimed as she set down the last of Robert's love letters and took a sip of Chianti. "So much unrequited love. It breaks my heart."

"Right? And what's up with this Brigitte that she couldn't even answer one of his letters? He took the time to write to her, many times! He was worried. A simple

'It's over' wouldn't have killed her. It would have put his mind at ease."

"So, why do you want to find Brigitte, Maddy? Do you think she's going to want to tell you why she was so heartless, even if it was years ago?"

"I don't know, I just feel like it would be the right thing to do."

"But what do you want the outcome to be? Chances are she says "thanks" and she dumps the letters into next week's trash," Ashley, the ever oh-so-practical one, pointed out.

"I guess you're right, but it's just that I feel like I don't want those poor letters to just sit there unopened and, I don't know, just lost to time," Maddy tried to explain something she wasn't sure she quite understood herself.

"And anyway, I told Robert I would try and find her," Maddy stated. "I can't back out now. The balls in her court now that I've reached out to her."

They sat in companionable silence for a while, each sipping from their glass of chianti, lost in thought.

"Did you find anything on that weird box's address?" Ashley asked, breaking the silence.

"Yeah, I talked to Kyle, the guy who lived there's name is Jason Thomas."

"And... anything else? "The guy's dead."

"Oh. Well, that explains the abandoned locker." "Yeah. I met his ex-wife to see if I could find out more

about him. She's quite nice. We hit it off right away. That Jason guy was a real jerk. Cheated on her." Maddy frowned.

"I hate guys like that," Ashley said. "Why stay married if you want to cheat? Just leave."

"Right? I've stopped trying to figure relationships out. Get this, turns out that they still had a thing for each other. They kept hooking up."

"Sounds like she was a sucker for punishment."

"No kidding. Anyway, she didn't know anything about the locker nor the mask, so we aren't any further ahead."

"Hopefully Kyle will come up with some answers for us."

"I hope so. I also hope he doesn't think this means I'm interested in dating him again." Ashley added, giving Maddy a not-so-thinly veiled look.

Chapter 13

C an you throw some extra Feta cheese on there please, and some Kalamata olives too? Maddy stared up at the expansive menu board hanging behind the counter of Pietro's Pizzeria. It had a rotating screen that tempted you with a variety of Italian dishes. She could never resist adding something else to her pizza order. "And a side of chicken wings with Fire of Hell sauce, please." The hotter the wings, the better. Her mouth was already starting to water just at the thought of those juicy, straight-from-hell hot wings.

After paying for her food, she sat down on the bench by the window to wait. Scrolling through her phone, she visited Facebook and deleted her posts asking about Jason. She wasn't sure what she was going to do about that whole situation now. Rick had called to let her know that the house at the address they'd found on the box was a dead end, pun fully intended of course. There were no lights on and it looked abandoned. Maddy didn't know what to do next or even if there were any other options available to her.

"Why even bother? It's much ado about nothing," she said out loud, convincing herself that she was buying into some overreacting group hysteria from Ashley and Rick. The person sitting next to her on the bench gave Maddy a side look and slid down the bench, putting as much room as possible between them. She smiled meekly at the woman hoping to reassure her that, although she was in the habit of speaking out loud, she was just as sane as the next person.

Startled out of her musings when her name was called, she jumped up and went to grab her food. An idea had been percolating in the back of her mind on exactly how she might be able to trick Chad into giving her his new password.

When she returned home, she threw the pizza box down on the coffee table and grabbed a Diet Coke from the fridge. Sitting down, she tapped on Chad's name in her contacts. Maddy could tell he knew who was at the other end of the line by his cautious 'Hello'.

"Hi! It's Maddy," she made herself sound upbeat and happy.

"Hi…" Chad responded hesitantly. "How are you?"

"I'm great, was just sitting here thinking about you and the good old days," she said.

"The good old days?" He sounded skeptical. "Well, yeah, we had some good times, didn't we?" "I guess so."

There was a lull in the conversation, as though neither of them was quite sure what to say next. Maddy decided it was best to just take the bull by the horns and get to the point.

"I was wondering if you were busy tonight, maybe I could come over for some wine and watch a movie?"

There was silence at the other end of the phone. Maddy waited expectantly, wishing he would just answer already. She wasn't used to having to appear so needy. She could almost hear the cogs and gears in his brain click into place.

"Oh! Wine and a movie!" Chad sounded like he was hitting his head with the palm of his hand. He had finally clued into what he thought she was suggesting.

"Yeah, sure, I'd love some wine and a movie."

Maddy rolled her eyes, he was still as daft as ever. "I can be ready in an hour?" she suggested.

"Yeah, perfect! I'll get the wine ready," Chad replied. "And the movie, don't forget the movie," she reminded him.

~ ~ ~

She jumped out of her car, and was almost at Chad's front door, her finger inches from the doorbell when the door flew open.

She stepped back, a bit surprised by his speedy appearance.

"Hi! Come in, come in," he said, grinning from ear to ear like a horny teenager.

Chad hadn't changed a bit. It was obvious that he had cleaned himself up for the evening. His pale blonde hair was neatly combed and looked a bit damp from a recent shower, his beige t-shirt was freshly pressed as were his crisp blue slacks. A strong scent of Axe trailed behind him as he led her into his living room.

The room was fairly basic and with a neglected air that Maddy always felt implied that Chad was waiting for someone to magically appear and tell him what his personal style was. If she liked leather, he purchased a leather couch. Suede? A beige suede chair magically appeared the next day. That was part of the problem she had with him when they were dating. It wasn't that he was doing it to please her, it was that he found his identity through her. He seemed to be waiting for a woman to come along and create the perfect life. It had made her feel claustrophobic, as though he was relying on her for something she simply wasn't able to give. She wanted to be with someone who was fully formed and mature. A guy who knew what he liked and what he didn't, not someone who felt they were incomplete unless they were with someone.

"Have a seat and get comfortable, I'll go get the wine." Maddy took her place in the middle of the leather couch and immediately reached for the remote control that was sitting in the middle of the coffee table. She aimed it at the big screen television hanging on the wall and turned it on. It was one of those smart TVs and she barely remembered how to get to the Netflix account. She was fumbling with the buttons when Chad came into the room holding two wine glasses and an open bottle of wine.

"I have a Malbec, I know that's your favorite," he said with a smile, "I even uncorked it to let it breathe like your friend Ashley always did."

"Oh, thank you," she smiled back at him, groaning inside. Wait until she tells Ashley about the wine.

"I see you're getting right into the movie part of the evening, huh?"

"No, no, I was just going to see what was on while you got the wine." She placed the remote back on the table, turning towards him as he sat beside her on the couch. He poured her a generous glass and handed it to her. After setting the bottle down on the table, he raised his glass as though to toast. Maddy raised her glass to his, a bit uncertain as to what he felt was toast-worthy.

"To good times," he said, winking at her.

"To good times," she repeated after him, clinking her glass against his.

"So, what have you been up to these days?" he asked, leaning back and stretching his arm along the back of the couch, just behind her shoulders. "Managing to keep out of trouble?" His hand had slowly inched its way closer to Maddy's shoulder.

"Oh, you know me, nothing new or unusual. My life's pretty boring."

"Hardly! I've always found you to be an interesting person. I don't know anyone else who makes a living buying and selling other people's abandoned junk."

"Well, that's all in a day's work for me." She sipped her wine, trying to ignore his "junk" remark, and wondering how she was going to make small talk long enough to make this work.

"What about you?"

"Oh, things are moving along, I received a promotion at work a couple of weeks ago," he said proudly. "I'm in charge of some really big client files now."

"Congratulations, that's great!" She hoped that she sounded excited enough.

"Yeah, at the rate things are going, I may even get my own office soon," he punctuated this statement by raising his glass in a mock salute and taking a swig.

"Oh wow, an office," she said, forcing a smile. All this fake smiling was starting to hurt her face.

"I know, you don't care much about those types of things, but believe me, they're important in the business world."

Maddy's smile tightened as she was once again reminded why they weren't a good match. He had his career precisely mapped out for himself. He had little imagination outside of the corporate world. Although he lived in a townhouse just bordering the downtown area, she knew from past conversations that his long-range plan was to build some equity in it so he could eventually reach what he saw as the quintessential sign of success; moving to a stereotypical, whitewashed suburban town, one of the bastions of Alberta middle-class that bordered Edmonton.

"Have you seen any good shows lately?" she asked, hoping to change the topic.

"Not really, I went to see that superheroes one that was out a couple of months back, but you know how I hate to go to the movies alone," as he said the last bit, he reached out and traced a circle on the top of her shoulder.

"Oh yeah, right," Maddy said. "Can I use your washroom?"

"Of course, you don't need to ask," he replied, "I'm sure you remember where it is."

She walked down the hallway towards the small half bath that was just off the living room. Getting that darn password was going to be harder than she thought. Going back to a relationship was never a good idea, even if it was for a short period of time. A very short period in this case. Only hours long, hopefully.

By the time she returned to the living room, Chad had finished his glass of wine and had poured himself a healthy helping of what was left in the bottle. He must be nervous to be drinking this fast. Good, she thought. Time to get this done. Enough messing around, she decided. Maddy grabbed her wine glass, tipped her head back, and downed the remaining wine.

"Hey, hey, easy does it, we don't want you getting tipsy and doing something you might regret," Chad said, leering at her.

"Don't you worry about me, I know exactly what I'm doing," Maddy smiled. "Do you have more wine?"

"I'm sorry, I don't, I wasn't expecting company tonight, but I have some diet coke if you would like some?"

"That would be lovely."

As soon as Chad left for the kitchen, Maddy grabbed the remote, chose Netflix, and quickly signed him out of his account. She plopped down on the couch just as he returned with her pop.

"I'm afraid your Netflix is signed out," Maddy explained, the remote still in her hand.

"That's odd," Chad made a move as though he was going to take the remote from her hand.

"Oh, you know how technology is," Maddy said, pulling the remote towards her. "Why don't I just log on again."

She pointed the remote towards the television and clicked on the appropriate buttons until she needed the password.

"Is it still the same one?" she asked innocently. "I think I still remember it…"

"No, I changed it the other day," he answered. "Do you want me to put it in, I know how much you hate doing passwords on the TV."

"Oh, I'm fine, what's the new one?" She waited expectantly.

"Capital 'A'- n-d-r-e-w-s, capital 'C', the hashtag symbol, and the letter one," he explained.

"Okay, so AndrewsC#1," she recited as she set up the account. "That's an easy one to remember."

"Yeah, you know me, I hate trying to remember passwords, although Netflix is one you don't have to remember all that often. Usually, once you are logged in, you stay logged in."

"Then why did you change it?" It was hard for Maddy not to sound like she was accusing him of something.

"A weird thing happened, someone tried to get into the account from an unknown location, so I needed to change it. It was time to update it anyway," he said.

Maddy felt oddly deflated and maybe even a little disappointed that the password change had nothing to do with her.

"Oh!" It suddenly dawned on her that it could have been those stupid thieves who took her cell phone. *"I bet they were probably the ones who tried to log in using the password and Netflix info I had saved on my phone's notepad. Dipshidiots, complicating everything,"* she thought to herself.

She was flipping wordlessly through the movie selections. She'd only planned the evening right up until she had the new password, not considering how she would handle the 'chill' part of the Netflix and chill evening.

They settled on watching a new western starring Hollywood's latest heartthrob. It was a bit violent by Maddy's standards, but she didn't plan on being there until the end. Or did she? She briefly considered staying and indulging in a little 'chill' just for old times' sake. A girl did have needs... No, wait! What was she thinking??? She could hear Ashley's voice in the back of her mind, admonishing her. She couldn't get involved with Chad again, not even for one night. Chad looked over at her quizzically. That's when she realized she'd given her head a shake. Oh boy, this was going to be harder than she thought.

"Everything okay?" Chad asked as he moved closer to her, reached out, and moved her hair back and away from her face, resting his hand on her neck. A shiver went through her. It had been so long. Sex had always been awesome between the two of them... No! Stop it, Maddy. That wouldn't be fair to him, she knew she wasn't interested in him anymore today than the day they had broken up.

She pulled away from him and abruptly stood up, almost knocking over the last of his Malbec all over his shirt.

"I'm sorry Chad, I don't know if it's the wine or what, but my stomach is really acting up," she explained. She grabbed her purse and tripped over the shoes she'd left at the front door. Good thing too, she was about to take off without them. She couldn't afford to lose another pair.

Slipping them on, she added "Thanks for everything and congratulations on your promotion!"

Chad stood up, thoroughly confused. Poor guy had no idea what was going on.

"Umm thanks?" he said, uncertain about what brought on the sudden change of mood, "Maddy, may I call you? Can we have a rain cheque?"

"Erm, I, erm… Oh, Gawd! I gotta go, gonna puke." And with that, Maddy slammed the door and ran to her car. This most definitely did not rank as one of her most graceful exits.

Chapter 14

Monday mornings were usually dead as far as storage auctions went. Today was an exception. There were a few very promising lockers that showed up on one storage facility's website. The owners of the storage lot had to do some emergency renovations due to a burst pipe and wanted all of them auctioned off, emptied, and moved by the end of the day. Also unusual was the demand for such a quick turnaround. Buyers are given 48 hours at least, not this "end of day" parameter.

While munching on an avocado and bacon burger she'd picked up at Starvin' Marvin's, Maddy made an inventory list of the items found in the unit she'd walked away with this morning. Zane had also been there and had won the second locker. No fuss, no crazy bidding wars, it had been quite uneventful. She liked furniture, especially old furniture that could tell stories. Zane, apparently, did not. He seemed to avoid bidding on any locker that had more than just the odd piece of furniture, whatever the reason. Maddy was quite fine with this. He was her fiercest competitor when it came to bidding wars lately. Sometimes, he wouldn't bid on a locker until the very end. Then, bang! He'd swoop in and bid a much higher amount than anyone expected. He seemed to have learned from her at the last auction. And that's when Maddy knew that he must have spied a valuable item, but she wasn't interested in the unit, not today. She won that locker at a pretty low bid.

Rick had stopped after work to help her move the pieces. This time the move had been further away than just one row of lockers, which pleased him to no end. This storage lot was located in the northwest part of the city in an industrial area. It was hidden behind some big, smoky, cement factory. There had been a lot of heavy furniture lifting involved in this move and she was quite grateful for Rick's help. He didn't mind, and Maddy always suspected that it gave him an excuse to get away from his house and the three strong-headed females who resided there. He'd left Maddy's with a case of beer under his arm and a few bucks for his effort and gas. He always made a big fuss about taking money but, in the end, he always accepted the cash knowing she didn't like charity. Maddy appreciated this, as she did have some pride after all. Rick usually treated Tasha out for dinner on the days he helped Maddy. Not that he needed to make it up to her or anything like that, Tasha wasn't the jealous type, she loved Maddy and didn't mind one bit. It was easier for him to be away from home after work hours if his wife knew there would be something in it for her.

They had transported the furniture and a couple of boxes to her 'office' locker at the Triple A lot. There was one certain piece that she had fallen in love with, an old hope chest, so she had Rick bring that one back to her loft. Occasionally, if she liked an item that she'd come across at an auction a lot, Maddy would keep it. This was one of those times. It was quite beautiful, made of carved walnut wood with a cedar lining. The chest would be perfect to store her linens. Loft living didn't offer much storage space. Hers had two bedrooms, which was unique. In truth, they were more like two cubed spaces divided by walls, each with a door but no ceiling. They had been added by the previous owner to give some semblance of privacy. Maddy was grateful for this as it allowed her to have a friend spend the night on a proper bed in a proper guest room instead of the living room couch. The only other walled "rooms" in her loft were the bathroom which, thankfully, had a ceiling, and the laundry closet where her washer and dryer, hot water tank, and furnace were hidden. They both also had doors. But that was it. No real storage spaces. She had been slowly adding storage pieces over the last couple of years. Too slowly.

She finished her supper, cleared the dishes, poured herself a glass of milk, and grabbed two cookies from her Cookie Monster cookie jar before settling down to start a second inventory list. This one would be of the contents found in the chest. These antique pieces often hid lovely mementos. She was looking forward to an evening of imagining what these treasured keepsakes' owners' lives might have been like. She enjoyed making up stories about them. The more romantic, the better. Since she was experiencing a rut in the romance department these days, might as well dream about someone else's.

As she opened the chest, the scent of cedar escaped, enveloping her like a hug from the past. She loved that scent. It reminded her of her late grandma's cedar closet where she stored her wool clothes and winter coats. She stretched back on the couch and dunked her chocolate chip cookie in the milk, leaving the London Fog one for later. Maddy enjoyed the occasional quiet evenings like tonight's. Finishing the last bite of cookie, she licked the chocolate from her fingers, put the glass down, and got up to half-push half-drag the chest closer to the armchair. Pen in hand she took the items out one by one. A dried carnation corsage in what appeared to be its original box from the florist, a couple of souvenir postcards from Vancouver, Banff, and Miramichi, a few old yearbooks, a pretty quilt, some swim meet medals, an old teddy bear that had been shown a lot of loving, some comic books, movie stubs, a tablecloth, and some other miscellaneous linens. She should probably keep the tablecloth. It would look nice on her glass table and save it from getting scratched. Look at her adulting and all, she thought. Owning a tablecloth, that's definitely a sign of maturity.

Maddy was drawn out of her reverie by a loud noise at her door like someone dropping a box or something. She didn't remember ordering anything from Amazon recently. She got up and went to investigate, making sure that her baseball bat was nearby. Looking through the peephole, she couldn't see anyone. She figured that it was probably okay to open the door. To be on the safe side, she grabbed her bat, then slowly and quietly slid the security chain into place and unlocked the deadbolts. She opened the door just enough to peek through. Nobody there. Lowering her gaze to the floor, she spied a large Amazon shipping box. Maybe someone had sent her a gift? She wouldn't put it past Ashley to send her something special to cheer her up. She shut the door, put the bat down, and slid the chain off to open the door and get the package. Bending down to pick up the box, she discovered it was quite heavy. Maddy chose instead to push it in with her feet and closed the door behind her.

"Well, that's weird," she thought. The box was not taped shut. The flaps had been closed crisscrossed with one half of each under the other. She opened the box and almost fainted. She staggered back, feeling bile rising in her throat. She turned around and ran straight to the bathroom where she promptly threw up her dinner.

Grabbing her cell phone and, keeping as much distance between herself and the box as possible, she speed-dialed Ashley.

"Hi, Mads! So how did it go with Chad? Did you get his Netflix password? Please tell me that you didn't have to do THE DEED to get it Miss 'It's The Principle of the Matter.'"

"He's, he's... he's dead."

"Chad's dead??? What did you do???" No, don't tell me. I don't want to be charged as an accessory after the fact."

"N...N...Not Ch... Ch...Chad," she hiccupped. "Then who's dead? Oh God no, Maddy! Please, tell me you didn't kill anyone!"

"I...I... didn't k...kill him, or it could be her," she tried to get a grip of herself. "I didn't look. I DON'T KNOW HOW TO TELL IF IT'S A HE OR A SHE!!!"

Maddy blurted out between sobs. "Where are you right now?" "Home."

"Don't move, I'm just leaving a work dinner downtown, I'll be there in ten minutes."

"Okay."

Ashley must have driven at a lunatic speed because she was ringing from downstairs in less than the promised ten minutes. Maddy buzzed the lobby door open. Letting herself into the loft, Ashley found Maddy standing by the kitchen sink, clutching the cell phone to her chest. "Stay away from that box!" Maddy, having calmed down some, warned Ashley as she walked by the Amazon package.

"What the hell is wrong with you, Mads?" "There's a body in that box! It's dead."

"In THAT box? A dead body's in THERE?" Ashley turned around to look at the box. "Oh honey, there's no way that a whole dead body is in that box. Even cut up in pieces."

"It's not cut up in pieces," Maddy said, shivering at the thought.

Ashley bent down to open the box and see its 'dead' content herself.

"No! Please don't open it!"

"Honey, I have to look inside to figure out what you're so upset about," she lifted the flaps and peeked in. "Oh, Sweet Baby Jesus!" Ashley let the flaps fall back down. It was her turn to gag.

"I told you not to open it," Maddy said.

"Dear God! This is a Rick problem. There's no bloody way in hell that I'm getting anywhere near that thing again," Ashley responded.

"What are we going to do, Ash?" Maddy asked her. "First, I'm getting us a stiff drink. You call Rick while

I pour the Scotch." Thinking better of it, she changed her mind. "No, forget it. You do the pouring;

I'll do the calling. You might give the poor guy a heart attack."

While Maddy got the drinks, Ashley dialed Rick's cell. Rick and Tasha had been scheduling a weekly date night since the twins were four months old. It was something Rick's mom had insisted on. She'd sat them both down and told them that to keep a marriage 'hot and healthy', they needed to have 'alone' time out of the house and in the bedroom. That had been quite the awkward conversation. Discussing their love life with Mama Leila was not something they had ever wanted to, nor repeat, ever again. Turns out Mama knew best. They looked forward to those date nights. And Mama was a more than willing babysitter. They suspected that their love life hadn'tbeen her first concern. She wanted time with her granddaughters.

As a result, Rick was in a particularly good mood this evening when he answered Ashley's call especially since tonight's date had been covered by Maddy's locker move money.

"Hey there Ashley Go Bashley! What's up Habibi? FYI you're on speakerphone. I'm on a hot date with my baby mama!"

"I've told you not to call me your baby mama. The girls are almost 13 for cripe sake," Tasha laughed at Rick. "Ashley, darling, what can we do for you?"

"Tasha, this is serious. I know it's your date night but could you guys please come to Maddy's place right away? It's an emergency."

"Say no more, we're on our way Amica. Rick, babe, make a U-turn right here."

Chapter 15

"**M**adonna Mia!**" exclaimed Tasha, bending down carefully so as to not spill out of her sexy "date night" outfit while at the same time attempting to look in the Amazon box.

Rick approached his wife, looked in, and immediately crossed himself.

"For crying out loud, Rick!" Tasha smacked him across the head.

"Whaaat? Rick asked, rubbing his head.

"It's a goose. You don't cross yourself over a dead Canada Goose!" Taking control of the situation, she motioned to Maddy and Ashley, who were standing as far as humanly possible from the goose, to go sit on the couch. "Rick, babe, sit down too, please," Tasha circled the box. "Let me see if I've got this right. Someone just dropped a goose with a broken neck?"

"Yeah…. Who would do something like this?" Maddy asked, obviously still shaken up. "I brought the box in, opened it up, and then ran to the bathroom to throw up," Maddy repeated the whole story to them.

"So basically, you saw the dead Cobra Chicken and literally whoofed your cookies?" Rick smirked as he picked up Maddy's second cookie from the table and dunked it in the glass of milk.

"Not the right time, Rick!" Ashley gave him a nasty look and grabbed the cookie out of his hand, setting it back down on the table.

"Sorry, I couldn't help myself. No more jokes," Rick turned towards Maddy "Everything's going to be okay. We're all here with you now." Putting his arm around her shoulders, he added, "Nobody is going to do anything to you with us here."

"Ash, you were right to call us. This IS serious," Tasha walked to the kitchen counter and grabbed the bottle of Scotch and two more tumblers. "Do you mind, Maddy?" "Have atter. I think we all need a drink right about now," Maddy said, lifting her glass up for a refill as Tasha poured out three scotches, neat. "Who, in their right mind would attempt to grab a mean Canada Goose, let alone be able to catch one? And then break their neck and slip a noose around it!"

"Those geese are nasty mothers," Rick rose and went to look at the dead goose one more time, rubbed his chin, and shook his head. "Whoever caught it is a psychopath. A very bruised psychopath."

"Here you go, Bella," Tasha refilled Ashley's glass and handed it back to her.

"Thanks. What should we do guys?" Ashley grabbed the quilt from the couch and threw it over the box. "Do we look for any clues on this box? Do we ask Maddy's building manager to look at the security camera footage? We can't just stay here and wait, can we?"

"I know I definitely can't just sit here and do nothing," Maddy took a sip of scotch, then started putting all the items from the hope chest back into it. "This was a senseless act of animal cruelty and whoever did this must pay! Killing an animal to scare me is beyond criminal. This is sick," she slammed the lid shut and looked at her friends who were nodding in agreement. They all became pensive, trying to come up with some kind of solution.

Tasha was the first to speak up. "Look, Maddy, I agree that this psycho needs to pay for all the nasty things they've done, Mia. But I don't think we should be the ones going after them."

"As usual, ladies, my wife's right. I'll gather up a few of the guys from work, we'll check the security camera footage, and…"

"No 'ands' Rick," Tasha cut in, "What I meant was that it's time to get the police involved. There's the weird 'trophy' stuff and bloody mask, the person trying to break in here the other night, and now this."

"And don't forget Maddy getting whacked on the head and locked up in that storage unit," threw in Ashley. "Che cosa?!" Tasha angrily looked at Rick, "Why did you neglect to tell me this?"

"I didn't want to worry you, Habibi. We had things under control."

"Don't you 'Habibi' me! You call a dead fowl, delivered in an Amazon box, having "things under control'?"

"Yes…. No…. Okay…. Maybe? I don't know! Ladies, you can jump in here at any time… Please?"

116

"Tasha," Maddy said. "I called Ash's cop friend and had him investigate stuff. We couldn't just go to them with no real proof, they would have dismissed me, and I'd still be getting dead bird deliveries anyway."

"You guys wanted real proof that you're in danger, Maddy? Now you have it," Tasha nudged the goose box with her foot. "It's time to go to the police and tell them everything. And we bring this, this…" gesturing towards the goose. "Dead Snake Chicken with us."

The three friends knew that Tasha was right and that they'd better agree to do what she wanted. Her Italian accent was coming out strong and that meant only one thing, she was getting angry. An angry Tasha was not something any of them wanted to face. That would be worse than dealing with an angry Cobra Chicken.

"Alright, we'll go to the station but only after I call Kyle and ask him to meet us there," Maddy took her cell phone out of her pocket, "That other officer is good for nothing. He hadn't even sent the mask to be processed when I checked in with Kyle!"

"Maddy, this time when you call him, please, please don't mention me," Ashley implored.

"Hi Kyle, it's me, Maddy. Look, something happened tonight, I absolutely need to meet you at the station right away," she put her cell phone on speaker.

"Hey Maddy, look, I'd love to help out, but I just got home and I'm bushed. One of the officers at the night desk can help you. They're just as qualified as me."

"Please Kyle, Ashley and I won't keep you long. I just don't trust the other officers the way I trust you."

"Ashley's there with you?"

Maddy had his attention now. And Ashley's.

"Yeah, she's driving me to the station. She'd be so disappointed if you weren't there to meet us. Ash was just mentioning how it's been so long since she last saw you." "Don't you dare pimp me out!" Ashley hissed. She picked up her scotch and tossed it back, glaring at Maddy. "What did you say? I didn't quite make it out. Did you say something about a pimp?"

"Oh, no, no, it's nothing," Maddy gave Ashley a wide- eyed look, "it's just the television in the background."

"Okay, give me half an hour and I'll be there to meet her, I mean you, the both of you."

"Thanks, Kyle. See you soon."

If looks could kill, Maddy would have been pulverized by Ashley's death stare.

Chapter 16

Police stations in the evening can be filled with odd characters, Edmonton's Downtown Division was no exception. There were ladies in various states of undress, unhoused folks, drunks, and tonight, Maddy and her not-so-merry group of friends. One in NAIT sweats, two in sexy clothing, and Rick, looking sharp in a fitted suit.

All four of them, and the dead goose-in-a-box, were standing at the reception desk asking for Kyle O'Brady. The night officer on duty looked Tasha and Ashley up and down, smiled, and then gave Rick a conspiratorial wink. That did not go over very well.

"What are you smiling at? This is my wife and these are my best friends. I expect you to show some respect!" "Right, right. Take it easy buddy. I didn't mean to disrespect your, erm, 'wife' and lady friends here. Let me call the detective down. Why don't you just go on over there, take a seat on those benches, and wait, okay?"

Tasha took Rick by the arm and quickly guided him towards the benches, "It's okay, Rick. Let's just do what the nice officer suggested and wait calmly for Kyle."

"He's certainly not a 'nice' officer and I don't like the way he looked at you and Ash, as if you were some kind of... of... you know!" He gave a long side-eye look at the desk officer.

"I know amore mio, but we don't want to make a scene in a police station, do we now? And we three ladies are more than capable of standing up for ourselves, remember? We don't need protection."

"I can't help it, Tash. It just gets under my skin when people look at you and all they see are hot women and jump to conclusions. It grates on me."

"Come on, Rick, we appreciate your concern but we're fine. Tasha's right, Kyle will soon be down. Why don't you go and sit down here, next to Ash, and cool down some, okay?" Maddy pointed to the empty spot next to Ashley, who scooted over and patted the bench for him to join her.

He grudgingly acquiesced.

About ten minutes later, or what seemed more like an eternity to them, Kyle finally showed up.

"Sorry about the delay, a colleague needed some info on a case we're working on together," he looked at Ashley and sheepishly smiled. "Hi Ashley, you look very nice tonight."

Ashley blushed a bit and straightened her dress. "Thank you, Kyle. That's very sweet of you to say. You look quite sharp yourself."

Maddy, Rick, and Tasha stared at her. All three

were surprised at her overly sweet behavior, especially given that Kyle was only wearing worn jeans and a t-shirt.

"Hi Kyle," Rick cut in, extending his hand. "I'm Rick and this is my wife, Tasha. I think we may have met once or twice before." They all shook hands.

"Oh yeah, I remember meeting you at SOHO when Ashley and I went there to have drinks and watch an Oilers game."

"That's right, that's right. Good memory," Rick remarked.

Thanks for coming to meet us here after work hours," Tash interrupted. "Something very upsetting happened to Maddy tonight and we were wondering if you could help. It was quite scary for her. To be honest, it shook us all up."

"Let's move out of the lobby and stand by the stairs here. It will give us a bit more privacy." Kyle turned towards Maddy as they walked out of earshot, "Were you alone or was everyone here with you when this 'scary' thing happened?"

"It was just me. I swear Kyle, I didn't kill him... or her. I didn't check, so I'm not sure!"

"What??? You didn't kill who???"

"A goose! You didn't kill a goose." Ashley jumped in, pointing at the box, "Kyle, she's talking about a goose, not a person. Someone left a dead Canada Goose in front of her apartment door."

Kyle, taken aback, hesitantly peered into the box, and quickly closed the flaps.

"And what brought this on?" he asked.

"What do you mean, what brought this on?" Maddy did not like the direction this conversation was going.

"Well, you do get yourselves in… how can I put this delicately…?"

"Don't go there, man," Rick cut in, "Trust me, you don't want to go there."

"Yeah, good point." Kyle side whispered, appreciating the reminder not to point out the many misadventures of the Maddy-Ashley duo. "That's not important right now. Maddy, I'll need you to please come with me so I can take your statement and write a report. Unfortunately," he said turning towards her friends, "because the three of you weren't witnesses to the arrival of the dead goose, I'll have to ask you to wait for Maddy either here or outside." He pointed to the benches back in the lobby. "On second thought. I'd rather you wait in your cars, especially since Ashley and Tasha are looking, erm…, are quite lovely tonight. They might get some unwanted attention here." "Good call, they've already had more attention than I like." Rick gave another side-eye glance at the desk officer as the three of them started to make their way to the door. "Maddy, this way, please. Are you good to take the stairs or do you want to take the elevator?"

"The stairs are fine." She hadn't taken the stairs enough times today. Nothing was going to get in the way of her new exercise 'program', not even a dead fowl.

Kyle signed Maddy in at his floor's reception, gave her a visitor's badge, and walked her to his desk.

"Okay, why don't you put the box down here on the floor and have a seat? You're lucky that this falls under my department or else I'd have had to pass your file over to someone else."

"I thought all crimes were investigated by the Vice Department. That's how it usually is in the movies."

"That's in the movies. In real life, we have several different sections that deal with specific types of crimes. Vice isn't all fun and games, it's often boring and there's lots of paperwork."

"Learn something new every day."

"Alright, let's take it from the beginning. You were home alone when that bird was left at your door?"

"It's a goose, a Canada Goose."

"Okay, when the Canada Goose was left at your door?"

"Yes, it had been a very long day and I was looking forward to watching some Netflix. Hey, did Ash ever mention my ex, Chad? You won't believe what he did!"

"Do you suspect that Chad had anything to do with the dead goose?"

"Chad? Ha! No way. That guy doesn't have a violent bone in his body."

"Maddy, let's stick to the facts right now so we don't get sidetracked, okay?"

"Fine, but you need to hear what he had the nerve to do..."

Just then a tall, salt-and-pepper-haired man knocked on Kyle's cubicle wall, interrupting Maddy midway through her retelling of the Netflix fiasco. He had a serious "let's get to business" look on his face as he looked at Maddy.

"Excuse me, Detective O'Brady?" "Yes, Sarge. How can I help you?" "I'm looking for Maddy Whitman."

"I am Maddy Whitman. Why? Did something happen to my friends? Did Rick get into a fight? Oh, no, let me guess, it was Tasha."

"This has nothing to do with your friends. Your name was flagged when Detective O'Brady signed you into the system. I need to question you about a crime that was committed last year."

"Kyle, what's your Sergeant talking about? I just want to deal with this dead Canada goose!"

"What crime do you want to question her about, Sarge?"

"It's the Jason Thomas robbery-homicide case." "What? Jason Thomas? I knew he was dead but…

killed?" Maddy couldn't believe what she was hearing. "Do you know him, Ms. Whitman?"

"Yes. Well, not really, more like sort of. I don't know him personally. What I mean is that I know 'of' him and purchased some of his things."

"Please come with me, we need to ask you a few questions."

"Maddy's a friend of mine Sarge, can I sit in on this?" "I'm afraid not O'Brady. Especially since she's your friend. Ms. Whitman, please follow me."

Maddy, somewhat in shock, obediently got up and started to follow the Sergeant when suddenly she remembered her Canada goose.

"What about my dead goose?" "Your what?"

"My goose! You have to help me with my dead Canada goose!"

Kyle grabbed the goose-in-a-box and brought it to Maddy, "I'll let your friends know what's going on and tell them they might as well go on home. Don't worry. I'll hang around until this gets cleared up, then we'll deal with the goose and I'll drive you home."

The Sergeant brought Maddy into a private room and sat her down in front of a table that had something that looked like a tape recorder on it. It reminded her of the interrogation rooms in Law and Order. *"Oh crap!"* she thought to herself. *"I'm being interrogated for Jason Thomas' murder!"*

"Thank you for agreeing to answer our questions. You understand that this conversation is being recorded?"

"Yes." Maddy nervously answered.

"I'm Sargent Rafik Kumar and this is Detective Paul Morin. Please state your name."

"Maddy Whitman."

"Ms. Whitman, are you aware that the Spanish mask that you brought in may have possibly been used in a homicide?"

"Mexican." "Pardon?"

"The mask is from Mazatlán, Mexico. It says so on the sticker under the base."

The Sergeant turned the mask over to look and nodded.

"Alright, did you know that the mask from 'Mazatlán, Mexico' was possibly used in a robbery-turned- homicide?"

"No. I don't know anything about any of that. My friend, as well as an antique dealer at Bernard's Antiques, thought that the red stain on it was blood, I thought it was ketchup or paint or something like that. Then I was robbed. That's why I came to the station, I wanted to report the robbery. I figured that it was best if I just gave the officer the mask too. Just in case it was blood."

"Well, it is blood. It's Jason Thomas' blood. How did this mask come to be in your possession and how do you know Mr. Thomas?"

"As I said before, I don't know him. I told Constable Kowalchuk when I gave him the mask, that I bought the contents of a storage locker at a storage auction. When I find personal items, I try to return them to the owners. I had to do some research until I found out who they belonged to. I can give you the name of the storage facility if you don't believe me."

"Thank you, we will need it." Sergeant Kumar leaned back in his chair and started fiddling with a pen. "It's not a case of us not believing you, Ms. Whitman, it's about finding the owner of this mask, why it was with Mr. Thomas' belongings, and who might have used it." He sat upright and placed the pen on the desk, straightening it, all the while looking at Maddy. "Mr. Thomas was hit on the head by a heavy object. This mask is a heavy object and has his blood on its base."

"Oh God. I was hit on the head two days ago too," Maddy touched her head and winced. "Someone lured me into a dark locker and bonked me."

"Ms. Whitman, I think that you may have inadvertently stumbled upon a possible murder weapon or some evidence that may lead to a suspect. The killer is still at large, and it appears that you might have something they want."

"I found other things too."

"What other things?" Sergeant Kumar leaned towards her.

"Bunches of hair tied in ribbons, a stained scarf, and women's single shoes."

"Those might or might not be of importance, but I'll send an officer home with you to collect these items. They could be evidence."

Detective Morin spoke up for the first time. "Did you report being hit on the head, Ms. Whitman?"

"No, I just wanted to go home."

"Please file a report regarding this before you leave." The detective was almost a foot shorter than the Sergeant.

He was kind-looking and soft-spoken with a slight French accent. Maddy felt more at ease with him. "What about the Canada Goose?" she asked him.

"What Canada Goose?" Morin asked.

"The dead one in this box." Maddy put the goose-in- a-box on the table and pushed it toward him.

The two detectives looked inside.

"Dear God, that thing smells foul!" Kumar gagged a bit.

Morin tried to suppress a smile but Maddy started giggling uncontrollably.

Kumar scowled at her, "It's NOT funny. This is possibly a criminal act. We will need to call in the Animal Cruelty Investigation Unit."

"I think we should add this as part of the evidence," Morin closed the box. "It has a noose around its head so I'd be taking it as a threat if I were you, Ms. Whitman. Someone is trying to send you a message."

"Ms. Whitman," Sergeant Kumar pushed his chair back and stood up, "I'll walk you to Detective O'Brady's desk. He will take a full statement from the beginning, starting with your robbery. We will also need your fingerprints and those of anyone else who might have touched the mask since it came into your possession. Please let them know to come in as soon as possible. Detective Morin, please put that dead bird on ice in the evidence room. We don't need it fouling up the air here any longer than necessary."

"Yes, Sergeant. Ms. Whitman…"

"Yes, Detective Morin?" She was dying inside. Sergeant Kumar's unintentional puns were causing her to have nervous giggles.

"I suggest that you take this situation very seriously and leave the detective work to us."

~~~

It was two hours later when Kyle drove Maddy home. A special investigator sent to gather the other items followed them. Ashley was in her apartment, waiting for her.

"Finally!" She walked quickly to the door to meet her. "Maddy, I was worried sick about you, you were supposed to be home hours ago!"

"I'm okay." Maddy hugged her, feeling relieved to finally be home.

"It took longer than I thought, Ashley. Sorry about that," Kyle approached her, he seemed to want to hug her too but at the last minute held back.

"I had to take Maddy's statement on everything that's been happening. You both should have come in sooner. This is not a game," he added.

"Kyle, we had no idea this was related to a homicide. We just thought that someone wanted their stuff back or something."

"Ashley's right. I sometimes hear from people who skipped payments on their lockers wanting their stuff back. Some of them can get pretty aggressive."

"And you should be reporting them too!" Kyle was getting frustrated. "Ladies, I know you are very independent women but there are some crazy people out there. Please, don't try to take care of things like that on your own. I worry about you Ashley. You too Maddy."

"That's very sweet of you Kyle." Ashley smiled at him. Maddy thought that her friend might just be softening up a bit where Kyle was concerned.

The constable was done collecting the items along with the box they'd come for and had left. Kyle did a quick walk through the loft, making sure nothing looked suspicious.

"Ashley, you will have to come to the station tomorrow and give us your fingerprints."

"Yes, of course, Maddy texted me from the car." "Do you want to go out for lunch or dinner afterwards, depending on when you can stop in?"

He sounded so hopeful. Maddy thought that perhaps Ashley might agree to a date. Afterall, she had flirted with him earlier.

"I'm sorry Kyle, I have a very busy day tomorrow.

Rain check on the meal?"

"Sure, sure, no worries. I'll see you whenever then." Kyle left. Maddy could see disappointment written all over his face as she closed the door behind him.

"Ashley! Why on earth would you refuse a date with Kyle? The way you were flirting with him, I thought you had changed your mind about him."

"I haven't changed my mind about him. I like him. A lot."

"Then explain to me why you keep pushing him away. He's such a great guy. Smart, nice, and obviously into you. He's also not a major loser like the guys you've been out with lately."

"I like him too much. I'm not ready to settle down. He is. You, of all people, should understand that. I just want to date more guys. It's too soon for me to get serious about anyone. Especially a nice man."

"It's not the same! I'm not against settling down and you know it. I need a guy who has his act together."

"Can we agree to just drop it? We have bigger problems to deal with here. Kyle told me over the phone about some of what was happening at the station. A homicide? Possibly even murder? I might as well move in with you until all this is over!"

"Gawd NO!" Maddy laughed. "Want a drink? I sure could use one."

"Yeah, and get the good chocolate. The stuff you hide behind the large frying pan."

Maddy went to get their drinks and chocolate. She needed to find a better hiding place for the chocolate since it appeared that Ashley intended to spend more time at her place.

Chapter 17

The next morning, once Maddy's head had cleared some, she started to reflect on the last couple of days' events. Could her concussion have led to some overreaction on her part? Was it simply a lot of conjecture and perhaps even a wee bit of hysteria in her friends' reaction to a dead bird and a thief at her storage locker? Maybe it was a nasty prank from a former client and simply a coincidence that the mask was found in that locker. And yet, the police didn't appear to think that she'd overreacted last night. They knew much better than her what should be considered worrisome, didn't they? Plus, they were removed from all of this, not emotionally involved like she and her friends were.

'Guess I should err on the side of caution and heed the cops' advice,' she finally told herself.

She pushed away her doubts and decided to go on with her day as best she could, trying hard to put it all out of her mind. There wasn't much she could do now anyway. So, she vacuumed her apartment, wiped down her countertops, and piled her bills up on her desk. There, her housework for the day was done. Whenever she wondered if she should be at a different point in her life, like having a husband and kids, she stopped and reflected on how simpler her life was now compared to others she knew. Did she seriously want to give all this up? And yet, Rick and Tasha were so happy together, still madly in love, with two kids, and a house.

She sipped on her second cup of freshly brewed coffee of the day, pleased with her newest purchase, a high-end espresso machine. Thanks to all the items she had been able to sell online, she had splurged on a coffee machine that not only made fabulous espresso but also ground the coffee just before making it so it could be as fresh as possible. All while she slept!

"Nope," she smiled and quietly watched the cars come and go on the street below her apartment. She had just concluded that she wasn't ready to give up this peacefulness when her phone rang. The caller ID showed Kyle's office number at the police station.

"Hi Kyle," she answered, trying to sound chipper. "How's crime-busting going today?"

"It's going just great, Maddy," Kyle responded without a hint of humor, sounding somewhat impersonal.

Crap, she had hoped that things wouldn't get awkward after Ashley had turned his date down last night. It was handy having Kyle to call when she needed police input on something.

"Good to hear," she decided to pretend she didn't notice the distant tone in his voice.

"Look, we ran the fingerprints on the mask and your dead goose, there was a hit," he informed her.

"Really? Whose were they?"

"Well, the hit didn't quite tell us who the fingerprints belonged to, only that the same ones were found at Jason Thomas' home and other crime scenes," he explained. "Unsolved murder crime scenes. This means that the Jason Thomas homicide might not be the only murder case."

Maddy sat in silence, taking it all in and trying to formulate a somewhat coherent response. What the hell does one say when told that they purchased a storage unit that was not only attached to an unsolved murder but was potentially involved in several more?

After about a minute Kyle, sounding concerned, asked if she was alright.

"I really don't know, Kyle," she said. "I don't know what to think of all this right now."

"You don't need to think anything, Maddy, let the police handle this,'" Kyle's voice softened a little more as he heard the shock in hers. "Go about your day as you would any other. Just be very aware of your surroundings. Find something to distract you. We'll deal with this."

"Yeah, okay," Maddy said. Quietly sighing she added, "I guess I don't have much of a choice."

~~~

Maddy wandered aimlessly around her loft, uncertain what to do with herself. She knew she should just let it go but she couldn't stop thinking about the mask. That ugly, blood-stained, demon mask. Ashley had been right all along about it having bad juju. She needed to start listening to her friends more.

Maddy had to get out of her place, or she would go stir crazy, or even worse, she might DO something crazy. She had to take her mind off things. Going for a drive might do the trick.

Maddy went down to the parkade and approached her car hesitantly. Her heart was racing, she looked around several times during the short walk between the elevator and her parking stall. As soon as she was in the car, she hit the locks, finally able to take a deep breath.

Pulling out of the garage, she headed in the direction of her storage locker. That should distract her for a while. She needed to go through the stuff stored there and come up with a plan that would allow her to sell as much of it as possible. The unit wasn't that large, she needed to make sure things kept moving so she could maintain a positive cash flow to cover, at minimum, her living expenses. The ultimate goal was to earn more than that so she could increase her little nest egg.

She switched lanes to make a left-hand turn from 104th Avenue onto 97th Street. She frowned in her rear-view mirror, noticing that the vehicle behind her made a lane change shortly after she did. Was that car following her? She drove along, alternating between looking in her mirror and looking at the road. She was so busy keeping an eye on the car behind her that she almost rear-ended the one in front of her when a light turned red.

"Get it together Maddy!" she thought out loud. "Enough paranoia or you'll end up in an accident." She couldn't afford any more surprise repairs to Bugsy. Not if she wanted to save more money for her business plans. She ran her hand through her hair, stopping mid-head.

Oh no, after all these years, did she pick up one of Rick's nervous tics? This whole situation was getting to her.

Refusing to allow herself to look in the rear-view mirror any longer unless it was to do a shoulder check, she managed to arrive at her storage unit in one piece.

She was driving by the Triple A's office when Squiggy, aka Rod, came running out to meet her. Did he have nothing else to do but greet each and every person as they came through the gates? She pulled the car over and parked it next to the office.

"Hi Rod," she said unenthusiastically. "How are you today?"

"I'm great, just great," he sounded tickled pink to have an audience. "Been pretty busy around here, I've been running some new campaigns and I think it's working. I'm used to running my own business, so I have lots of experience."

"Yeah? What kind of business?"

"Well, you know, I did some import/export trading for a while until I got tired of it and decided to move on," he answered rather vaguely.

"Oh? What kind of import/export?" Maddy neither wanted nor cared to find out more about Squiggy, except that she needed to focus on something else than the events of the last week. As far as distractions went, he fit the bill.

"Collectibles," he responded.

"Oh, do you by any chance know my friend Ashley Mueller? She's in that business too."

"Name isn't familiar, but I was in a very specialized area."

"Oh, what area?" Maddy knew that it was wiser to let it go and get to her unit, but she just couldn't help herself. She was a sucker for punishment and was very aware that she'd pay for it in the end. Squiggy was the type of person who would see it as an invitation to talk her ear off every time she would show up there.

"Graphic novels" "Comics?" she asked.

"Graphic novels are NOT comics," he drew himself up as straight as he could and would have looked down his nose at Maddy had he not been a good three inches shorter than her.

"Oh, okay," she didn't want to push the issue by explaining she didn't know the difference. "Well, anyway, I better get to my unit."

"Okay, make sure you shut the gate on your way out, the automatic system has been wonky today and I want to maintain tight security," he sounded more than a little put out with her, "Plus Engelbert keeps running away from the office. I don't want to lose him; Aunt Shirley would kill me."

"Where is Bert?" Maddy asked, looking around for the cute little mutt.

"Aw crap! Not again! Engelbert? Come here little Bertie. Where the hell did he go?"

Maddy shrugged her shoulders.

"Come on you mutt, I've got treats for you!" Rod took off running down a row of lockers, searching for the dog. Maddy took advantage of Squiggy being momentarily distracted and left. Walking towards her unit, it felt like someone was staring at her. She glanced over her shoulder, expecting to see Squiggy standing there with Bert but they weren't there.

She unlocked her unit and reached in to turn the light on before entering. There was no way she was going to enter a storage unit in the dark ever again, for a long, long time.

She caught herself looking around the unit suspiciously, as though she expected to find something out of place or someone hiding behind a box. Realizing what she was doing, she laughed out loud. The sound bounced off and around the tin walls. She needed to get a grip!

The next hour or so was spent going through the items in her unit, documenting and taking pictures of them. She needed good pictures and exhaustive descriptions to be able to list them for sale and knowledgeably talk to her buyers. She took note of any wear and tear, scrapes, or scratches. She prided herself on being honest, building a reputation for being up-front about the stuff she was selling. If it was damaged, she took pictures and priced it accordingly.

Once she was finished, she locked up and headed back to her car. Again, she felt as though she was being watched. She could feel eyes on her back. Could it be Squiggy, staring at her from one of the windows? She wouldn't put it past him. He seemed like he would be the type to spy on people's comings and goings.

Pulling away after making sure the lot's gate had closed behind her, she turned up the music and listened to her favorite station. Her car stereo was conking out so she didn't turn it on very often, but it was all she had. Sometimes a girl just needed the sound of music. Her station was CJSR, a local university community FM radio station. She liked the idea of supporting a radio station that wasn't run by some big corporation. Maddy tried to focus on what was on the radio, but she kept finding herself looking over her shoulder, expecting to see someone following her.

At the sight of her building, she felt overwhelming relief and was looking forward to being safe inside her own home. She hoped the police would figure out what was going on soon, she couldn't live like this forever.

~~~

In her apartment, she opened her laptop to see if she had any new messages. Her heart had quit trying to beat its way out of her chest and her nerves had almost settled down. Now that she was in the quiet comfort of her own home, she scoffed at the anxiety she had felt earlier.

After reading her emails, she opened Facebook and was excited to see that Brigitte had responded to her message.

"Oh my, what a name from my very distant past! Yes, I am the Brigitte that knew Robert Ozinski. By all means, pass along my contact information to him."

The email, while short, was enough to lift Maddy's spirits and she quickly forwarded the contact information that Brigitte had left her to Robert.

Chapter 18

To think I might be responsible for uniting two long-lost lovers!" Maddy squealed as she told Ashley about the message from Brigitte.

"I forwarded him her contact info and he responded right away saying he was going to call her."

"How cute!" Ashley responded, encouraged that Maddy was thinking of something else for a change.

The two were sitting in Ashley's posh but cozy living room, staring out at the vast panoramic view of the Edmonton skyline through her condo's floor-to-ceiling windows. While Maddy was content living in her little loft off Jasper Avenue, she had to admit that there were benefits to owning an apartment in a more upscale building like Ashley's. For one thing, it was much quieter as the windows and walls were considerably newer and had better soundproofing than her older apartment building. Ashley had blended the new-age architectural look and stylish design of her condo with sleek appliances, various pieces she had collected while traveling the world, and unique items she'd fallen in love with while shopping for others in her import/export work.

Ashley's phone rang, interrupting their conversation. She picked it up off the coffee table to check the caller ID, then looked over at Maddy with an icy glare and pursed her lips, making it clear that this call was all her fault.

"Hi Kyle," she listened for a few seconds, then told him she was going to put the phone on speaker as Maddy was with her.

"Hi, Kyle!" Maddy said while grinning at Ashley.

"Hi Maddy, how are you hanging in there?" he asked. "Feeling a wee bit paranoid, but other than that, just peachy."

"Oh, sorry to hear that. Well then, umm, I'm not sure this news is going to help much," he began. "We received the results back from the hair that was in that bundle of stuff you gave us."

There was a pregnant pause as the women waited for him to continue. He hesitated as though this conversation wasn't one he wanted to be having.

"The lab found matches for the hair's DNA, we know who they belonged to..." He seemed to be stalling.

"And?" both Maddy and Ash asked as one.

"The hair belongs to three different women," he continued.

There was another pause and finally, Ashley interjected.

"Enough Kyle, we're grown women, just tell us what you found out already!"

Maddy looked over at Ashley with a scowl. What was it about men that made them think they should tiptoe around women?

"The hair belongs to three women," Kyle said. "Murdered women."

There was a heavy silence as the friends digested what he had just told them. Ashley looked at Maddy. This new turn of events increased the level of worry she had already been carrying for her friend.

Conflicting emotions ran through Maddy, she was surprised, but not shocked. There was something about that collection that sat wrong with all of them. They suspected something wasn't right from the get-go. But at the same time, having it confirmed was unsettling.

Kyle was silent, as though he could tell that his news had upset them. Maddy knew it was a part of his job that he didn't enjoy. Giving people unpleasant news. It was especially upsetting when that news was shared with someone he cared about.

"Talk to me ladies," Kyle finally said.

Both Ashley and Maddy bombarded him with questions as what he had just told them sunk in and their need to know kicked into overdrive.

"What murdered women?"

"Are they the same murdered people that were linked to the fingerprints on the mask?"

"Were they killed in Edmonton?" "Are they also unsolved murders?" "How did they die?"

"How long ago were they murdered? "Did they know each other?"

"Okay, okay, slow down. I'll do my best to answer you," Kyle replied. "We don't know a whole lot. I'm limited in what I can share because it involves unsolved murders which means that they're still open, active cases."

"How many women were killed?" Maddy asked quietly.

"Three."

"Were they from Edmonton?" Ashley asked.

"Yes, Edmonton or the immediate surrounding area. The murders happened over the last year or so, that's when the first of the three women was discovered. There could be more, but no other bodies have surfaced that can be linked to the same killer."

All three were quiet as the seriousness of the situation hung over them. These were lives they were talking about, lives that ended too soon and not from natural causes.

"How were they killed?" Maddy asked the question and looked over at Ashley. Their eyes met and she knew they were both thinking the same thing; what if one of those murdered women had been one of them? They reached across the coffee table almost at the same time and touched each other's hands. Maddy couldn't imagine if something ever happened to Ashley.

"That's something I can't talk about just yet," Kyle said reluctantly. "Sorry, but my hands are tied."

"Don't worry Kyle, we completely understand," Ashley said. "But can you at least tell us if the shoes are part of all of this?"

"I can tell you that we're actively investigating how they could be tied to this case," Kyle responded, sounding very official.

"We get it," Maddy bit her lower lip. The mood in the room had become somber and the conversation tense. Not just because he couldn't tell them everything they wanted to know, but because everything suddenly became very real and serious. It was one thing to think you were being paranoid and over-worried, it was another thing altogether to realize that you had good reason to be.

"Look ladies, I don't want to sound patronizing or like I'm trying to brush you off, but I'm concerned about your involvement in this case. I highly recommend that you stay as far away from anything related to this as possible. I consider you both friends and I want you to be safe."

"Don't worry, we don't want to be any more involved in this than we already are," Ashley reassured him. "Right Maddy?"

"Yes, of course."

"Well, I must get back to work now. If anything comes up or you have any questions whatsoever, if you have any more car break-ins, dead ducks, or knocks on the head, let me know. Please be careful, I'll be in touch soon."

After Kyle hung up, the friends stared at each other in silence. Eventually, Maddy got up to look out the window and whispered to no one in particular, "It was a dead Canada goose, not a duck."

Chapter 19

M urders, several murders.

What a living nightmare. Those poor people. She had touched their hair. She'd looked at their shoes and tossed them aside. Maddy felt terribly guilty about it. It's true that at the time she had no idea these things belonged to three dead women, but still... And now what? She was supposed to "behave' and just forget about it? Let the police handle everything? How does one do that?

Last night she tossed and turned for hours, finally falling asleep by focusing on the unrequited love in Robert's letters. Once asleep though, she dreamt of dead Canada Geese. More specifically, Canada Geese with long auburn hair, tied in ribbons, dive-bombing the Demon from Mazatlán. She kept trying to chase them away by waving the love letters. Instead of scaring them, one grabbed the pack of letters and flew away with them. Maddy ran and ran after them, calling for them to come back. They never did. They kept flying away, honking louder and louder. She would never find out why Brigitte hadn't written back to lovestruck Robert.

When she woke up in the morning, she was worn out but determined not to waste another minute on last night's disturbing turn of events. She might not like it, but Kyle had been right. Let the police handle this, it's their job. Instead, she decided to concentrate on listing some of her remaining coins online, hoping that someone in the numerous coin-collecting groups on Facebook might be interested. Within minutes, several people had responded; proving once more that one person's junk is another's treasure.

Maddy agreed to meet two of them that same afternoon at a small café-roastery she liked to frequent in her neighborhood. It had a tree-lined, sunken courtyard and was in a cool building that used to be an old telephone exchange. In it now was a brewery, a cute little boutique, a meals-to-go place, and the café- roastery. Safer to meet unknown buyers in a busy public setting. She could use the time between meetings to do some research on which vintage items were the latest 'in' things and such. But before that, some long overdue laundry was calling her name.

While tossing wet clothes into the dryer, her cell rang, it was Ashley. She wasn't in the mood to chat right this minute, so she clicked 'Ignore' and kept right on transferring her laundry. That didn't deter Ashley who was intent on speaking with her and called her again. Twice more. Maddy knew that by continuing to ignore her friend's calls, Ashley would be knocking at her door in less than 15 minutes. If that attempt was also ignored, she would use her own set of emergency keys and let herself in. There was no escaping a determined Ashley Mueller. Sighing, Maddy answered.

"Ash, I'm surrounded by wet clothes that need to dry, please make it quick."

"Easy girlfriend. Just checking up on you. How'd you sleep?"

"Meh. You?"

"Me too, Meh. Are you staying clear of that locker of yours?"

"Yes, I have enough stuff here to keep me busy for a week or so between doing research, listing items, meeting people, and actually selling things."

"You're being a good girl then?"

"Yes, Moooom, I'm being a good girl. I'm even doing my laundry before I go meet potential buyers."

"Good. I have noticed that you've been wearing the same clothes several times in a row lately."

"I have not! And for your information, I always smell the armpits first and check for stains before wearing anything twice."

"Mmm Hmm… Where are you meeting these potential buyers?"

"The café in the old telephone exchange. Hey, wanna come over for supper? I really don't want to be alone tonight. I can pick something up from the to-go place next door while I'm there."

"Sure! I've been craving their roast dinner for so long. Hint, hint."

"Message received," and with that, Maddy ended the conversation, plopped the rest of her now clean clothes in the dryer, and left for her appointments.

Chapter 20

"I can't believe you're selling a 'W' one cent silver coin!" I've been wanting to add one of these to my collection forever, other people are asking $99 or more on eBay. Are you sure you just want seventy-five dollars?"

The older, cardigan-wearing gentleman sitting across from her, a certain Mister Abboud, reminded her so much of PopPop. He was cute and so excited about the coin. She had listed the shiny 'Farewell to the Penny' Canadian silver coin at a much lower price than they were being sold on online auction sites. She knew if she listed it at its current value, it'd be just one of many. But if she listed it below the average resale price, people would want to swoop it up quickly and it'd be off her hands. It wasn't a rare coin; she had called Bob first to make sure. He had lots of them and wasn't interested in the coin itself. Maddy didn't want to sell it for its silver value, she wanted to sell it for its collectible value. Thanks to PopPop she was sentimental when it came to coins.

"Yes, I know, but I have so many coins and no place to store them," Maddy had told a little white lie, but it was a better-sounding excuse than wanting to be competitive. "I found them in a storage unit I purchased and have no use for them."

"Oh, I see, I see," Mister Abboud nodded, blowing on his cup before taking a sip of coffee. "I wanted to make sure that you knew this penny's worth. Cheating people is not something I aim to do during these kinds of transactions, even if it is a great deal for me."

"That's very thoughtful of you. I don't usually run into many honest people when I sell things. They usually buy and run, afraid that I might realize my mistake and jack up the price."

He laughed, handed her an envelope with the cash in exchange for the silver penny, and thanked her as he stood up. Leaning on his red walker, he unlocked the brakes and waved goodbye as he walked away. Why was it that sweet men were usually old guys? Where were the sweet men her age? Someone like Brigitte's Robert even. Then again, Robert was probably a sweet old man by now too.

The meeting with Mister Abboud had taken a bit longer than she had anticipated.

Maddy had barely read a couple of articles on the waning popularity of old Mason glass jars when the next potential buyer showed up. She was a tall and very well-dressed woman in her mid-thirties. As she approached the table, Maddy got a weird vibe from her, goosebumps prickled up on her arms. If Ashley had been there, she would have left the café without looking back. It was that kind of heebie-jeebies.

148

"I presume you're Maddy?" the woman asked, lowering her Gucci sunglasses just enough to peer at her. "Yes, I am. And you must be Paris Andrews?" she extended her hand out. The woman ignored it.

"Yes," she replied, looking Maddy up and down, glaringly appraising her.

"Here are the coins you were interested in," Maddy said, sliding them across the table.

"You mentioned in your message that you found them in a storage unit with items you purchased in an auction?"

"That's correct."

"And where's that storage unit?" Paris demanded to know.

"I don't see why its location matters." Who the hell did this woman think she was?

"I certainly wouldn't want to purchase stolen goods. The resale of these coins could be affected," she said derisively.

"They're NOT stolen. I am a professional with a good reputation to protect. If you don't want them, I have other potential buyers." What a nerve to accuse her of selling stolen goods! Who did this Paris person think she was to judge her so? The Queen of Sheba?

"I never said that I didn't want to buy them," she replied with a sneer. "Only that they might be difficult to sell at a later date. What else did you find in that locker? Were there other types of collectibles? What was the value of all the items you found?"

This woman's pushy attitude and Holy Inquisition style were grating on her nerves. She hadn't expected to be questioned to the nth degree.

"I'm sorry, I don't understand why you're asking me all these questions."

"I collect and sell all sorts of valuable items, I'm always on the lookout for anything unusual." Paris looked amused.

"Such as?"

"Oh, you know, coins, sports cards, unique objects such as vases and masks…"

At the mere mention of masks, Maddy froze.

"No, there were no vases or masks. Just coins and clothes. And I already got rid of the clothes. Do you want these coins or not?" If truth be told, she wanted to conclude the meeting with this Paris woman as soon as possible.

"Yes, you were asking for $300 for all five coins?"

"That's correct."

"They appear to be in good condition. Not mint though. I can see a few imperfections just with the naked eye." She pushed them closer to Maddy, "Would you take $250?"

Wanting to get rid of her, Maddy immediately agreed. "Fine, you can have them," She pushed the coins back towards Paris.

"I figured you would see reason. Here you go, $250," she handed Maddy five $50 bills and stood up. "If you ever find any unique objets d'art or more coins, please message me directly before posting on any Facebook groups. I'm always on the hunt for such things."

"Erm… sure. Thanks."

Paris picked up her Louis Vuitton purse and gingerly placed the coins in it. She gave Maddy a tilted, almost- knowing smile. Maddy could have sworn that she cackled before vanishing in a puff of smoke.

Chapter 21

"Come on, Maddy, she did not cackle and vanish into thin air," Ashley said mid-bite, gesturing at her with a forkful of roast. "You're always making fun of me, saying I'm so dramatic. Who's exaggerating now, eh?"

"Not in thin air, in a puff of smoke." "Maddy…"

"Okay, okay, maybe she didn't cackle and vanish. But she did look at me funny, and you must admit that mentioning the mask was pretty suspicious."

"She mentioned masks, not the mask. There's a difference." Ashley took another bite of the melt-in-your- mouth roast dinner and closed her eyes in appreciation. She was enjoying the meal immensely. "I'll admit that this Paris woman seems a bit odd. Look, to be quite honest here, those would be the kind of questions that I would ask. If she's a buyer, like me, those are legitimate questions. I'll admit though, that her bedside manners might be lacking," Ashley took another bite. "Mmm, this is so good!"

"'Lacking' is an understatement. She wouldn't be that obvious if she was involved with the Demon of Mazatlán, right?" Maddy still wasn't quite convinced.

"Look, nobody followed you today. Nobody attacked you. All's good. Just forget about her. You made $325 on four coins. That's good, right?"

"Yeah, it's okay, and I have a few other potential buyers lined up for next week too. That's just for the coins. I dropped off some vintage clothes at the second-hand boutique on High Street. The rest I'll probably donate to a thrift shop. I also still have to list those sports cards and the furniture. Rick promised to look at the cards next week."

"That's great! By the way, before I forget, I may have a potential buyer for that bedroom set you purchased three weeks ago. His dad worked for Gibbard in Napanee, Ontario, before they shut down. He's got a sentimental attachment for furniture made by them. It's not worth a lot though, but it'll get it off your hands."

"Thanks, Ash, I really appreciate it."

Ashley nodded as she dipped her last bit of roast in the thick, velvety gravy.

"My god, this roast is as delectable as ever! Thank you, darling. And, might I add, it's so nice sitting at a real dining room table too."

Maddy smiled. She did love her new table.

"Feeding you is the least I can do. You're such a good friend to me Ash."

"Don't you start getting all sentimental on me Mads," Ashley laughed.

"Want to watch a show?" Ashley nodded yes.

Maddy went to the couch and picked up the remote. "Persuasion or Jane Eyre? I'm in a 19.-century mood."

"Jane Eyre. I can relate to her a bit more these days."

~~~

They were happily munching on microwave popcorn when Maddy's cell vibrated. Ashley reached for the remote and pressed pause as Maddy looked at her phone.

"It says 'unknown number'."

"Just ignore it then," Ashley said as she went for the remote once more.

"No, I can't. It could be another buyer."

"Wouldn't their name show up on the screen?"

"Not always," Maddy pressed the green answer button. "Hello?"

"Hurry, there are more…" a muffled voice whispered on the other end of the line.

Taken aback, Maddy put the phone on speaker. "More what?"

"There're more," the muffled voice continued. "Hurry or they'll die."

"Who'll die?" she demanded to know. "Check your emails."

The line went dead. The caller had hung up. Maddy and Ashley stared at each other. "Get your laptop, Mads."

Maddy grabbed it and pressed the 'on' button. She clicked on Gmail and looked in her inbox.

"There's an email with the subject line 'More Will Die!!!' Who puts that as a subject line?!" She clicked on it. Ashley leaned over her shoulder to look at the screen.

"What the hell is that?" "I think it's a crate, Ash."

"I know it's a crate! But what's it supposed to be?" "No idea. This is weird. Why would someone send me a picture of a crate?"

"Mads, I think someone is trying to mess with your head."

"What a dipshidiot!"

"I've had enough. I'm done with this," Ashley took out her cell phone and called Kyle.

"Hi, it's me, Ashley. Yes, umm, no it's not about dinner." She looked across the couch at her friend. "It's about Maddy. We were just watching a movie on TV, distracting ourselves, as you told us to when her phone rang."

Maddy gestured for her to put the phone on speaker. "Hold on, I'm putting you on speakerphone."

"Can you both hear me now?" "Yes," they both replied.

"Okay, Maddy, why don't you, instead of Ashley, tell me what the caller said."

"The voice was muffled, so I couldn't distinguish if it was a man or a woman. Could you tell, Ash?"

"No, I couldn't."

"Anyway," Maddy continued. "The voice said that there were more and that I should hurry."

"More what?" Kyle asked impatiently.

"More people who would die. They also sent me an email with a picture of a huge crate." Maddy replied, trying to keep her emotions in check.

You could almost hear Kyle immediately straighten up in his chair. "I'm sending an officer over in an unmarked car, they'll watch your building tonight. I'll try to trace the call. Please forward me any emails you got, or get, if you receive any more of them. It might take a few hours, maybe more to track these down, and that's only if they're trackable. Ashley, please go home when the officer calls to let you know they're downstairs. Maddy, go to bed and try to get some sleep. We need the caller to think that everything is normal. We're on it, okay?"

"Normal?" Maddy cried out. "Ashley, try to calm her down."

"That's a bit condescending, Kyle." Ashley curtly replied.

Kyle sighed. "Please, Ashley?"

"Fine, we'll do as you ask." It was Ashley's turn to let out a sigh as she hung up.

Chapter 22

M addy had a sleepless night. She kept getting out of bed, tiptoeing carefully in the dark to look out her window, checking to see if the unmarked police car was still there. It was every time. It wasn't until around four o'clock that she finally fell asleep out of sheer exhaustion.

The next day, she got up, took a shower, got dressed, and made herself a double espresso. She would need that extra jolt of caffeine if there was any way she was going to function today.

Kyle had called around 10:30 am, saying the department had been able to trace last night's call but unfortunately, it had been made from a burner phone near the location of her storage unit. He added that she could go about her day as she normally would. The police would keep investigating. Kyle promised he would check in on her from time to time throughout the day.

Maddy figured there wasn't much she could do at this point and decided she might as well get some work done from home. Picking up her laptop, she walked to her dining room table and set it on the new-to-her tablecloth. It was a morning that called for instant oatmeal to settle her stomach. Once finished with her breakfast, she pulled open the curtains covering the window next to the table, letting the morning sunshine into the room. She loved summer, there was always so much more outdoor activity in her neighborhood at this time of year. Looking down onto the street below, she watched the city come to life; people going about their daily routines, stopping at the corner coffee shop to grab a cup of coffee, buying a newspaper from the corner box, catching the bus to work, hopping on a rental scooter. She felt almost nostalgic for a time in the not-so-distant past - a week ago - when she too could go about her days without a care in the world. She left the people to their wanderings, shuffled over to the counter, and poured herself a second cup of coffee.

Ready to face the day, or as ready as she felt she could ever be, she took a sip of java and scrolled through her emails. A smile spread across her face when she saw a message from Robert. Maddy immediately opened the message from Robert. A smile spread across her face as she read about the phone conversation Robert and Brigitte had for hours last night. Robert said that after the initial awkwardness, it was as though no time had passed. They were planning to meet for coffee. He sounded like a giddy schoolboy as he shared his excitement with Maddy.

Maddy still had a smile on her face as she pressed delete on the next message that was promising to cure her hair loss. The next ones were a phone bill, an electric company bill, two LinkedIn notifications, a warning, three Kijiji notifications, a grocery store advertisement, and a discount coupon for glasses.

Wait, what? She scrolled back to the email with the subject line 'A Warning.' She was hesitant to click on anything with that as the subject line. Her hand hovered for a moment over her mouse. Often those types of emails were best ignored and quickly deleted as they tended to be click-bait. But with all the odd things happening as of late, maybe she shouldn't ignore it. She warily clicked open the message.

I told you that there would be others, but you didn't believe me. Click on the link for proof. You have until Monday at 8 am to find her or she DIES. And don't even think of going to the police. The moment you do, she's DEAD.

Time is running out. Tick Tock Tick Tock. BOOM!

Like a zombie in a trance, she clicked on the link.

A ball of ice formed in the pit of her stomach and her blood went cold as Maddy gazed at the horrifying scene unfolding before her eyes.

Chapter 23

No, no, no, no… this wasn't happening. This COULDN'T be happening. It wasn't real. It had to be a fake video. It's like Ashley said, someone was messing with her head.

And yet, what Maddy saw on her computer screen looked alarmingly real.

A woman, close to Maddy's age, was lying on her back. Her hands and feet were tied, and she appeared to be chained to a wall. Maddy wasn't sure because the chain disappeared between two wooden slats, she couldn't see where it went beyond the crate. The woman was imprisoned in a large box, a huge wooden crate like the ones used to transport giant dinosaur skeletons. Her eyes were bound shut with a dark Louis Vuitton scarf. On her stomach was a water backpack with a tube that led to her mouth like a straw, the kind long-distance runners wore strapped to their backs. Every so often she'd twitch and would attempt to sit up.

Maddy ran to the bathroom and threw up her breakfast. This was becoming too common of an occurrence these days. Her stomach wasn't made for this stuff. Why was she being targeted? She didn't have the mask anymore or any of the evidence. Why didn't they stop harassing her? Maybe this was a sick joke some disturbed, former buyer was playing on her, some kind of stupid revenge.

Once her stomach settled, she made her way back to the dining room table to check her computer screen one more time, hoping that when she looked at it, a skeletal ghost would jump out, screaming 'Gotcha' and frighten the heck out of her. It wasn't beyond the realm of possibility. She had previously received emails from the odd dissatisfied buyer who had been quite angry with her when she'd refused to give them a refund. Maddy always included, in every single one of her ads, a notice clearly stating that all sales were final. No refunds whatsoever. Potential buyers could take all the time they wanted to inspect the items they were interested in buying. But once the money had exchanged hands, the deal was done. Her business wasn't a 'satisfaction guaranteed' brick-and- mortar shop.

When Maddy took another look at the screen, the woman was still struggling and any thoughts that it might have been a disgruntled client quickly dissipated. She was now violently thrashing her feet, her whole body shaking from what Maddy imagined to be uncontrollable sobbing.

There was blood streaking the crate's slat floor, probably from the cuts on her wrists that appeared rubbed raw by her trying to loosen the zip tie holding them together.

Maddy couldn't deal with what she was seeing anymore. Sitting there and waiting for the other shoe to drop was not her style. Something needed to be done to figure out if this was real or a hoax. She did a Google search on fake videos and came upon 'How to tell if a video is looped or not.' Sometimes a small video clip could be overlaid with audio and looped to appear longer. The first thing was to try and see if the video was continuously repeating the same piece, or several different ones, over and over. One of the websites she found suggested that she listen for three seconds long stretches of audio that seemed to be duplicated. Clicking back to the live stream, she closed her eyes so the image wouldn't distract her and interfere with her listening. She listened for 10 minutes. The woman wasn't making much noise. Maddy did notice some occasional traffic sounds. There was music that had played for a few seconds, maybe a car going by? She listened again, paying closer attention. There was music again, but it wasn't the same song as before. Okay, this wasn't a loop. It still didn't mean that it wasn't a hoax. *'Think, Maddy, think.'*

There was a second link in the email that Maddy hadn't clicked on yet. She moved her cursor to it and pressed enter. It was another live stream, this one appeared to be from a second camera, mounted somewhere outside the crate, giving the viewer a shot of the room the crate was in. Seeing what was in the room was difficult. Only a little blurred light shone through what appeared to be a window, making it difficult to see what was inside. She couldn't quite make things out. It was too dark to observe any details. Ah ha! That meant that either the room was facing west or that there was another building next door, shading it from the sun. Okay, that's one clue, but a clue to what? What was she hoping to find out? If it was a hoax, this room could be anywhere. But, if it wasn't, this might help.

Maddy did some more research on loops just in case she was wrong. Then, for the heck of it, she googled 'How to fake a kidnapping.' Lots of weird stuff came up. She found out that it wasn't illegal to fake your own kidnapping if it was only a joke and didn't involve the authorities or some kind of ransom. Like, come on, who would go to that much trouble and not expect others to contact the authorities… she ignored the fact that she hadn't made a call yet. There was also this guy that people actually paid to kidnap them. Some kind of sick adrenaline rush experience. A person could even pick the type of kidnapper they wanted. Maddy would never understand people. Other than weirdos and TV storylines, there wasn't anything online that could help her determine if what she was seeing on her screen was real or not.

Switching back to the email with the live stream, she clicked on the link for the camera inside the crate. The woman's wrists looked even more raw. She looked like she was trying to settle herself down, taking in deep breaths and slowly exhaling. She tried to scoot herself up into a sitting position. That turned out to be impossible because of the water pack on her chest. Rolling onto her side instead, she brought her knees as far as she could towards her chest in a fetal position. Other than her chest rising up and down, she remained very still. Maddy had to admire her. There's no way she could have gotten herself to calm down in this situation. No bloody way. She would be in hysterics right now.

One way or another, something had to be done about this. If it was a hoax, Maddy had had enough of this dipshidiot yanking her chain. If it wasn't, she couldn't let this woman continue to suffer. A queasy feeling in the pit of her stomach told her that this wasn't a hoax. What now?

Ashley's was the first number she dialed.

"Ash, I just opened another email. I don't think someone is trying to mess with my head. I think they're really going to kill someone."

"What are you talking about, Maddy?" She sounded disoriented by Maddy jumping into a topic without any context. "Can you forward me whatever it is they sent you?"

"I'll send it now. Call me back when you get it, okay?" "Okay, bye."

Maddy paced back and forth in front of her window, waiting impatiently. What was taking her so long? She was just about to dial her number again when Ashley called back.

"Mads, I don't think it's real. This is way too disturbing, hun."

"I disagree. I did some research. It doesn't appear to be a loop. This is live"

"It doesn't make sense. If it IS live, then it's some dark and twisted joke. Someone has gone to great lengths to mess with you. Why would anyone want to play mind games like that with you? Why involve you at all? Who have you ticked off so badly that they'd have it in this much for you?"

"I don't know…"

"Exactly! Leave it alone for a couple of hours." "What?? How?? You've got to be kidding me! I can't just ignore it."

"You're not going to ignore it. You're going to leave the live link alone for a little while, let the sender think that you're ignoring it. Do some more research on coins or whatever. That should distract you for a bit. Then, in two or three hours, open the link again. If it still looks live and if nothing has changed, we'll contact the police.

"So, you believe ignoring it will tell us if it's real or not? Okay, I'll try but I can't promise. What if they contact me again?"

"Then call me. We'll figure it out IF it happens. Until then, concentrate on all the stuff you must sell."

Ashley was right, reading up on the items left in her storage locker that still needed to be sold had helped pass the time. She then checked on the ones she'd listed on Facebook's Marketplace. Her posts on some more coins and an old mirror had interested a few buyers. Thank goodness for Marketplace, it certainly made things easier for her. She connected with them, and all sales went through without a hitch. She arranged to meet with them next week at Iconoclast to deliver the items. She hoped none of them would end up being like that Paris woman. 'That Paris woman... What if she was a psycho? What if she was the one messing with her? But why? She hadn't done business with her before. Unless she was a friend or a relative of someone who was angry with Maddy? Enough!' She had to stop thinking like this. Her imagination was getting the best of her. And yet, what if...

Her rumbling stomach interrupted her wild imagination, reminding her that she'd skipped lunch and shouldn't be skipping supper. She pulled out a plastic container from the freezer and popped it in the microwave. While the leftover roast from the to-go deli was reheating, she grabbed a beer and poured it into a Belgian ale glass. Might as well try to be classy tonight. When the microwave dinged, she pulled her dinner out of the container and plated it. Classy wouldn't end with the beer glass. She brought her roast dinner and beer to the living room and turned on Netflix. The new password worked like magic. Good, that meant Chad hadn't figured out her ruse from the other night. She was in bad need of more distraction. Distraction that wasn't on the computer.

It was around eight-thirty when she finished watching Persuasion and decided to check her emails one last time before heading for bed. And there it was, another one from that psycho.

This latest email was the creepiest yet.

"I'm watching you just like I'm watching her. She's still in the crate. Tied down and chained, no hope of escaping unless you help her. Don't even think about calling the cops. I have friends at the station. One call and she dies."

She re-read it twice. She was being watched?

This was too much. She forwarded the new email to Ashley. Then she remembered that Rick and Tasha didn't know about the links yet, so she immediately sent them the links and the email, telling them to please check them out and get back to her.

Rick was the first to call her.

"Rick? Did you see the live stream?"

"What the hell Maddy? Check around your place for any tiny holes in the wall. If there are any and you can't remember if they were there before, dig around them. There might be a hidden camera."

"Okay, I will. Should I look for hidden bugs? Like under tables and such?"

"Yeah, you should absolutely…" "Hold on, Tasha is calling me."

"What?! Why? She's sitting in the basement." Rick pulled the phone away from his ear, "Tasha, what the heck? Why are you trying to call Maddy when I'm on the phone with her?"

"I need to talk to Maddy too. And don't you yell at me!" she hollered back.

"Wait a sec. I'm going to put you on hold Rick and talk with your wife."

"Tasha? Did you look at the link?"

"This is Ashley, Maddy…"

"Hold on Ash, I have to answer Tasha's call, she called first."

"Tasha?"

"It's Rick. Tasha's still calling you." "Oh crap, okay, hold on again." "Ash?"

"No, it's Tasha…"

"Yeah, sorry, that's who I meant. Did you see the link? What do you think?"

"I most certainly did. Dio mio, Maddy, call the cops, NOW!"

"Should I? Oh, dang it! I forgot to ask Rick about the bugs. Just a minute."

"Rick, how small could those bugs be? Like could they be on one of my planters?"

"What bugs? Why the hell are you worried about insects right now?"

"Ash? Shoot! I need to ask Rick something first. I'll be back in less than a minute."

"About those bugs, how small could they be?" "Please don't tell me you have bed bugs on top of everything else?"

"Tasha? I thought I was talking to Rick. Just a sec."

"Rick?"

"Yeah?"

"How small can bugs be?"

"You haven't looked yet? What are you waiting for? This crazy lunatic could still be watching you right now!" "I've been on the phone with you! All three of you!!"

"Habibi! You'd better start looking. Yalla, now!" "Okay, okay. How small could they be?"

"Pretty small. They could be anywhere, so look very carefully."

"Could they be in the electrical outlets?" "Absolutely! Have you not watched CSI?" "That small? How on earth will I see them?"

"Use the flashlight on your cell. That's what they do."

"Good idea! Oh no! I forgot about Ashley. She must have hung up. She's calling again. I better take it. Okay?

"Sure" "Ashley?"

"What took you so long? I bet you just forgot about me. Girlfriend, this is cray-cray stuff."

"Sorry, Rick called. Tasha called. You called. They're both on hold. I don't know what to do. This is… Wait, what? Tasha is calling me via Messenger."

"Yeah, me too. She's doing a group video call. Smart woman."

All four faces popped up on the Messenger group call. "Bella, that was way more complicated than necessary. Now we can all see and talk to each other. Does that work for you, Maddy?" Tasha gave them her sweetest 'I-know-best' mom smile.

"Much better, thanks."

"Tasha, you've got smarts girlfriend. Rick, don't you dare ever leave that woman! Now Mads," Ashley continued, "this seems too insane to be real. I say it's a nasty hoax. Just ignore it."

Rick shook his head. "That doesn't look like a hoax to me. There's been too much thought put into this to be a fake. The cameras, the crate, the water backpack."

"My husband's right. I don't care what that email says, you have to call the cops. This isn't TV Lalaland. This is reality. Call. The. Cops."

"What if it's real and that psycho's watching me? I can't risk getting poor Juliette killed," Maddy responded. "Juliette?" Tasha and Ashley, confused, asked simultaneously.

"How do you know her name?" Rick added.

"I named her Juliette. I just couldn't keep calling her 'That woman'. It's too impersonal."

Her friends rolled their eyes.

"What? She's a real person and deserves a name!" "Come on you guys, it's not real! Look, the one thing

I agree with Tasha on is that this isn't TV land. Nobody does this stuff in real life. Rick, you still don't think it's fake?"

Rick shook his head.

"Really? I disagree, all the thought that's been put into it makes it look like a movie set," Ashley was sure it was a hoax.

"No Ash, it's real. And I agree with some of what Maddy said. We can't call the cops in case that wom… sorry, I mean in case Juliette and Maddy are being watched."

"Rick!! You can't be serious! The cops MUST get involved." Tasha looked none too pleased with them. "Especially if that…, especially if Juliette's truly in danger."

"Listen, everyone," Maddy's head was hurting from all this back and forth. "This conversation is going nowhere fast. I need to figure out what to do, I'm terrified that this is real. I'm not ready to risk her life. We need to come up with something and the quicker the better."

"How about this Maddy… Ashley, Tasha, and I will continue to watch the feed on and off throughout the evening and see if anything changes. You look for those bugs, cameras, and such, then go about your routine, acting as if nothing is going on. If you haven't found any monitoring devices and that nutcase is watching you, they will think that you've just given up. They won't see you monitoring the link and will think that you didn't take the bait. Maybe then, they will expose more of themselves, perhaps even send more hints. Oh, and cover the camera on your laptop. You can do all other group calls through your phone."

"What about the cops, Rick?" Tasha's concern was growing.

"Let's sleep on that," Ashley piped in. "If anything else happens, or things seem to be getting worse, we can call Kyle in the morning. This gives us the rest of the night. Does that work for you, Tasha?"

"I don't know, doing nothing concerns me but I guess I'm outnumbered. Maddy, are you okay with Rick and Ashley's plan?"

"I guess… The psycho did say that I had until Monday. Hopefully, Juliette doesn't injure herself. She must be going out of her mind."

"Maddy, try to put it out of your mind for now. It's probably fake," Ashley tried to convince her but was pretty sure her attempt was wasted and not quite as successful as her friend was letting on.

"Alright then, I'll look for bugs and all that stuff, and keep working on my sales."

"And Maddy…"

"Yes, Rick?"

"Call me if you find anything at all or if you get scared.

I'll come right over, deal?"

"Deal. Thanks guys. You truly are amazing friends. Love you."

"Love you too," each replied.

Chapter 24

Lying in bed, Maddy's heart wouldn't stop racing. She had a lump in her throat. It was impossible to get Juliette out of her mind. As she reflected on what she'd seen in the video, it was becoming more and more difficult to convince herself it was all a hoax. Yet, how could it not be? There was just no other explanation. What possible reason could anyone have for doing something like this? Maddy didn't recognize the woman, so this ruled out a kidnapping for a ransom situation, and it was much too twisted to be a joke. If indeed it was a joke, she was more than confident that none of the friends would think this was a funny one to pull on her.

She flipped over onto her belly and sighed deeply as she squeezed her eyes shut. There was something about Juliette in that video. Something oddly familiar. It wasn't anyone she was well acquainted with or she would have figured who it was by now. It was like watching a show, recognizing an actor from some role they played in a movie years ago, but you just can't place them.

Maddy dug deep into her memories, calling to mind the woman behind the till at the grocery store. The face of the barista at the coffee shop floated through her mind, as did the homeless woman who hung out on the corner by her apartment. It wasn't any of them. This was going to drive her insane. Who was doing this and why? And who was Juliette?

~~~

A blaring noise filled her head, bringing her out of a deep sleep and crashing right back down into reality. She groaned as she stretched her arm to reach the alarm clock. About a year ago, she'd given up using her cell to wake up, she'd slept in one too many times after shutting it off while in a deep slumber, completely unaware that it had gone off. On a mission, she'd gone out to Value Village, found herself an old-fashioned alarm clock, and set it up just out of arm's reach. While it significantly cut down on missed morning appointments, it hadn't improved her overall morning disposition much. Pulling her upper body off the bed, she inched close enough to smack the off switch and stop the annoying clanging alarm. Why couldn't she be one of those people who jumped out of bed, bright-eyed and bushy-tailed, ready to face the world? Or better yet, one that woke up without an alarm. Of course, those people generally were asleep by nine at night, so there was a trade-off. '*Bah, not worth it,*' she thought.

These thoughts had been running aimlessly through her mind when the horrifying memories of last night came flooding in and reality hit. The woman. Juliette.

She immediately jumped out of bed and rushed to get her laptop off the dining table. Grabbing it, she plopped down on the couch and pulled it onto her lap. She clicked on last night's link, staring in renewed horror. Seeing Juliette still tied up there, moving slightly to flex a leg or an arm, made it impossible for Maddy to believe that what she saw on her screen wasn't real. Unless this was somehow a high-quality, very long looped recording, then this woman was real, still alive, and terrified.

The exhaustion of an almost sleepless night and the sheer heinousness of what she was looking at was taking a physical toll on her; she began to shake as feelings of helplessness and anger overwhelmed her. Tears started rolling down her cheeks. What the hell was going on? What was she supposed to do now? Who sent this to her? *'Why me?'* she thought repeatedly. *'Why me?'*

"Why me?" she yelled out loud.

The insanity of hearing her words out loud made her stop. She stepped back and took a hard look at herself.

'Why me? Are you kidding Maddy?' She realized that her thoughts had been incredibly selfish. 'What's wrong with you? Why ME? You're not the one who's tied up and kept captive. You're not the one in that video. Why me indeed!' She was ashamed of herself. 'Get a grip on yourself. This isn't about you anymore, Maddy Whitman, this is about that frightened woman.'

She picked herself up, wiped her tears, and quickly changed into some clean clothes. It was time to stop sitting around and doing nothing but feeling sorry for herself. She needed to take control of things. Maddy was no hapless weakling.

Once ready and with a clearer mind, she sat down at her laptop and began typing up a list of what had occurred over the last few days. It started with the purchase of the locker, discovering the mask with blood on it, searching for the owner, her car being broken into, getting knocked on the head, the dead Canada goose, and the information they had gathered from the police.

She paused after a while and leaned back, staring at what she had typed. Looking back on the last few days, a lot had happened. When it was all put together like this, it was unmistakable that she'd stumbled upon something she shouldn't have. It was no longer deniable.

Taking a much-needed mental health break to be able to focus better later, she checked on the remainder of her items still up for sale on Marketplace. She logged in and looked at her notifications. There were a few comments asking questions that she quickly replied to. Guilty thoughts kept creeping into her conscience, thoughts about being on her computer and checking in on her business when she knew there was a poor, frightened woman lying bound in a wooden box. Yet she knew she'd thought about nothing else since that email had arrived. If there would be any hope of figuring this out, she needed to clear her mind. A diversion from the drama that was happening around her was needed. Scrolling through her emails and Facebook was mindless and fit the bill. She liked memes posted by friends and photos of their dogs and cats. Some relative's baby had taken her first step.

Noticing there was a notification from one of the missing person's groups she'd joined last night, she clicked on it. Joining those had paid off when she was looking for Jason, but Maddy no longer needed to be part of them anymore, she figured she could unjoin now. That's when she saw a new post. Someone had posted about their missing cousin.

Please help my family. My cousin Sally has been missing since Thursday night. She was last seen with a bunch of friends at the Brewery Hall. It's too early for the police to do anything, but we're really worried. It's not like her to just disappear. The police won't do anything yet. Please, if you have seen her or know anything about her whereabouts, let us know. We miss her!

Maddy zoomed in on the picture attached to the post. It was of a smiling woman, her arms entwined with a group of women. They were smiling at the camera, some making faces, others preening. Maddy felt a ripple of shock course through her body. Could that be her? She quickly searched for the name of the woman who had led her to Jason Thomas' sister.

"Holy shit," Maddy murmured to herself. Were her eyes playing tricks on her? The same picture that was posted of the missing woman was on this woman's profile as well. The missing woman was the same woman who had given her the contact information for Jason! Oh my God, could it be? Could it be the same woman who was in the box?

Maddy quickly switched over to the tab with the live stream. Was Juliette the same woman or was she imagining it? The hair appeared to be the same length and color. As far as she could tell, the woman also had the same skin tone. True, she'd never seen either of these women face to face so she couldn't be 100 percent positive.

What did this mean? Maddy closed her eyes as though trying to see in her head and find the missing piece. No such luck. There had to be something that she was missing. It was like she had a bunch of puzzle pieces, but she had no idea how they fit together. What was she overlooking? She had so many thoughts twirling in her head, each one vying for attention, not allowing her to focus on a single one at a time. The first thing needed to do was organize these thoughts on paper. She needed something tangible to look at. Her brain couldn't focus on everything at the same time while it was still in her head. She decided to turn to her years of study at the schools of CSI and Law and Order; years spent engrossed in mindless entertainment had prepared her for just this moment. What she needed was Post-it Notes, a map, and some string.

"Dollar Store, here I come!"

Chapter 25

On her walk back from the dollar store, Maddy came up with a plan to solve the kidnapping and put a stop to this heinous situation. She'd allowed herself too many emotional and panicky moments. But no more. She was no delicate flower so why was she acting like one? Shock? Nerves? Continuing to think with her heart would lead to messing things up, big time. It was time to get into Law and Order's Detective Benson's head. What would she do if this was happening to her? No more sobbing hysterics allowed. That psycho wasn't threatening to harm her, they were threatening to kill Juliette, or Sally, or whatever her name was. Benson would try to get in the kidnapper's head. She would attempt to think like them. Why kidnap Juliette? Why a crate? How did she get her there? Could anyone have seen them? Maddy had so many questions. These would need to be added to her list when she got home.

She stopped at the café by her place to pick up an iced latte. A clear and focused mind was needed. Just as she was stepping out, she thought she heard someone call her name. Looking up, she saw Jason Thomas' ex-wife waving at her.

"Hey, Maddy! Fancy meeting you here!" "Lauren? Hi! What are you doing here?"

"I'm working on a new project nearby and remembered that this place made a pretty good cappuccino. Thought I'd pick one up on my way home. Are you in a rush? Want to join me?"

She hesitated, as much as she would love to get to know Lauren a bit better, she needed to stay focused on saving Juliette.

"Is this a bad time?" Lauren asked.

"I'm a bit swamped with things and I really should be getting back," Maddy said, regret evident in her tone of voice.

"That is the best time to take a break, regroup and you will be able to tackle things with a clear mind," Lauren insisted. "We won't be long."

"I don't know, I have a lot of things on the go right now," Maddy wanted more than anything to tell Lauren what was happening, but she knew it would take more time to tell her the story than it would take to grab a quick coffee.

"Okay, I already have my coffee so I might as well drink it here," Maddy agreed. "But I can only spare ten minutes."

With a big smile, Lauren opened up the coffee shop door and the two women entered. Maddy kept Lauren company in line as they waited to place her order.

"You look tired, Maddy. Everything okay?" Lauren asked, her face lined with concern.

"Just haven't been able to sleep well."

"Have you tried taking some melatonin? Works wonders for me when I can't get any sleep," Lauren suggested.

"I'll have to give it a try. Thanks for the suggestion."

It was their turn at the counter, and Lauren placed her order. When her coffee was ready, they sat at a table by the window.

Before long, the talk turned to politics and complaining about the cost of living going up. Lauren mentioned her tight finances with a shrug and grimaced when mentioning her late husband.

"He didn't leave me anything in his will. When an ex dies, the alimony payments die too. I've had to pick up an extra contract. It's taking up my free time." Lauren smiled sardonically.

"That sucks."

"By the way, the police gave me a call a couple of days ago. They wanted to know if I knew anyone who might have wanted to hurt Jason. I told them that I didn't and asked why. They said that it looked like he could have been murdered. What the hell? Murdered! Did they call you too? Did you know anything about this?"

"Yes. Kinda. They think the mask I was telling you about last time might have been used to kill him."

"Oh my God! That's insane! Poor Jason. What happened to the mask? I hope you got rid of it."

"I gave it to them as evidence."

"Good riddance! Having that thing around would freak me out. I hate these things," she said with a shudder. "Eyeless faces that seem to be staring into your soul. Yuck!"

"That's what my girlfriend, Ashley, thinks too."
"Smart friend."

"I won't tell her that, she already thinks she knows everything."

They both laughed.

"Anyway, changing the subject here, I hate to ask but, do you know anyone who might be looking for someone good at research?" Lauren took a slow sip from her cappuccino.

"Not really. I'll keep my ears open though. Lauren, do you even have time for another contract?"

"No, but sleep is overrated. I need to make ends meet. It's been tough finding contracts that pay enough lately. You gotta do what you gotta do in life to survive. No choice."

"I hear ya! Stupid, dumbass exes."

"Hey, did you ever get that Netflix password from your ex?"

"YES! Speaking about having to do what you have to do, let me tell you what I did to get it back…"

Chapter 26

Coffee with Lauren had lasted more than the 10 minutes she had intended it to, but it was exactly what Maddy had needed. She felt refreshed and determined. Once home, she immediately got to work transforming her guest room into a war room. Taking down two paintings off the largest wall, she envisioned what she wanted it to end up looking like. She then pushed her larger chest of drawers close to the window to make more room; she'd created the perfect blank slate to put up a map. Unrolling and straightening the city map that she'd just picked up from Maps R Us, she wondered if she should use pins or tacky poster gum. Pins would mark the wall up and she would have to repair the holes. Add to those the holes from the strings she would have to push in with thumbtacks, that would leave too many holes in the wall. Then again, tacky gum would peel the paint. Enough debating, she had to get to work on this!

Thumbtacks went decidedly into all four corners of the map and in the middle of each side border. Taking a step back, she admired her handiwork so far.

'*Not bad,*' she thought. '*Now to get my timeline list and the info that Juliette's cousin posted on Facebook.*'

After an hour, the map was covered with Post-it notes. Yellow notes showing where Maddy had been and when, pink ones for whom she'd met, blue ones with events that occurred to her, and green notes with Juliette's movements. All these notes were connected with different colored strings. It looked nothing like the maps on the TV shows. Disappointed, she leaned back on the bed and stared at the map. She removed some of the strings, leaving only the ones linking related or important events, and took a step back again. That hadn't helped much. Anything that had happened to her didn't seem to link to Juliette. She took all the sticky notes down and put them on the wall beside the map. Each was grouped according to specific events. She had to rethink her approach.

Maddy went to the dining table and sat at her laptop. Time to check if there were any updates from Juliette's cousin. Nothing, just a bunch of random people 'Sending prayers for Sally's safe return'. She just couldn't call her 'Sally'. That woman had been given the wrong name at birth.

'What's this?' She had come across an interesting post. One of her friends mentioned that she had left in an Uber after the bar and had waved at Juliette from the car window while going down Jasper Avenue. She remembered seeing her walking past the General Hospital and crossing 112 Street. That gave Maddy an idea. Instead of including everything that happened to her, she would only put on the map the information she had on Juliette. That made more sense. It was Juliette who needed rescuing first. Then she could work on figuring out who the psycho was.

After rearranging the Post-it notes, she took a closer look to see if anything interesting popped out at her. She frowned, realizing she was no further ahead. Detective Benson made things look so easy. Trying to decide what to do next, she thought about reaching out to Ashley. She immediately thought better of it. The last time she texted her, Ashley had told her that there'd been nothing to update. Juliette seemed to have slept the rest of the night. "This makes my hoax theory more probable by the hour," Ashley had insisted. She could be right, but Maddy didn't want to take any chances. She needed something tangible to show Kyle if and when they decided to contact the police, or else they wouldn't believe them.

Maddy wasn't ready to tell her or the others about the Facebook post. She wanted to avoid another Messenger conversation until she had more information or had reached a dead end. Perhaps 'dead' wasn't the best choice of words.

"Wait a minute! That's it! Dead end!" In that odd way, the brain can connect thoughts, she had gone from dead end to cul-de-sac to street. She would walk the area where Juliette had last been seen!

Chapter 27

The first place to start was at the Brewery Hall. Maddy showed Juliette's picture to several staff members. None of them remembered seeing her.

A waiter with a five o'clock shadow and a bun suggested she speak to the assistant manager. He said that she had worked that night and maybe she would remember something. Directing Maddy to sit at a table, he went to get the manager.

"Hi, I'm Gaby, the assistant manager. Marc said that you wanted to see me?"

"Hi, yes. One of your patrons disappeared last week on her way home from here. Her name is Juliette. I'm helping her family find her. I was hoping that someone working here might remember anything odd that might have happened or that they perhaps saw where she went, or anything at all."

"Do you have a picture of her?"

Maddy was happy to see the manager was willing to talk with her. So far, part one of her plan was working. "Yes, just a sec, let me pull it up here on my phone."

Maddy showed Gaby Juliette's Facebook picture of her and her friends just outside the bar.

"I do know her! She's a regular here. I thought her name was Sally."

"She goes by both names. Depending on who she's with," damn, she had to remember to call her Sally when speaking with other people.

"Oh, okay. Well, Sally was here last week. She was hanging out with some of her friends, flirting with random guys. They had a really good time if you know what I mean."

"Can you describe what you mean by 'a really good time'?" She had an idea, but it was better to hear it from a witness than presume something and be wrong. That's what Detective Benson always did.

"There were a lot of shots being served at the table. I made sure that nobody drove home. Most in her group took cabs. She told me that she would walk home. I asked her if she was sure about that because she seemed to be a bit wobbly, and it was after 11 pm. Sally said not to worry, it was just a few blocks up on 113. Street."

"Did she say anything else?"

"No, sorry."

"You said they did a lot of shots. Is that normal for her on a Thursday night?" Who was she to judge? But tonight, she was wearing her Detective Benson hat so the question needed to be asked.

"Not really, they did mention that one of the

women in the group's divorce was final and they were celebrating. We comped a round of shots for them. It's something we do occasionally for celebrations."

"I'll have to remember that next time I celebrate something with my friends."

"Yeah, we'd love to help you have a fun night. I'm sorry, but I didn't get your name. I like to keep a record of these types of conversations. It's a liability thing."

"Oh, you don't have to worry about it. We just want to find her. I'm sure the family will be in touch with you soon. Thanks. Gotta run!"

Maddy got out of there as fast as she could without looking too suspicious. She didn't want the police at her door asking why she'd been snooping around and asking questions at the bar. To be honest, she didn't want to tick Kyle off. After everything that had happened so far, he was, surprisingly, still her friend. And she wanted to keep it that way.

Standing outside the building, Maddy took a little notepad out of her purse and wrote the information she had gathered from Gaby. The Brewery Hall was on the corner of 109 Street, which meant that Juliette had to walk westward to get to the General Hospital where her Facebook friend had last seen her. The hospital was between 111 and 112 streets. The assistant manager had said that Juliette had been kind of wobbly. How fast can a wobbly woman walk? Her own recollection of nights where she might have been tipsy-ish… okay, drunk as a skunk, and had to walk home, were of a slow stepped and meandering journey. Might Juliette have stopped somewhere along the way? Most likely. There were a couple of restaurants that would have been open between the Brewery Hall and the hospital. She likely wouldn't have stopped at any of these because you needed to walk up several steps to reach them. That would be too much of a challenge for a wobbly woman. Walking a bit further than two blocks before stopping made more sense. From 112 to 113 street, most of the stores and restaurants on that block would have been closed except for the pizza place. One tended to be hungry after a night of drinking, right? It was a well-known fact that pizza is the go-to food of choice when drunk. Going on a hunch, she went in and approached the man behind the counter.

"Hi, I'm wondering if I could talk to whoever was working on Thursday night," Maddy asked.

"Are you going to order something? No conversations with staff unless you order."

"Okay then, I'll have a Diet Coke." "We have a five bucks minimum."

"Fine," Maddy sighed loudly, "A diet Coke and a slice of ham and pineapple pizza."

"So, you're team pineapple, eh?" He handed her a can of pop and a slice of pizza.

She ignored his belated feeble attempt at small talk and paid.

"Now can I speak to the person who was working Thursday night?"

"You're a cut-to-the-chase woman, eh?" he snorted, "That'd be me, why?"

"A friend of mine has gone missing and we're worried about her. I was wondering if you might recognize her," Maddy held up her phone with Sally's picture.

"Umm, yeah, maybe?"

"You're not 100% sure?"

"Well, I think so, let me look again?" He squinted at Maddy's phone and took a closer look. "She was a bit drunk and had smudged makeup under her eyes and stuff but umm, yeah, I'm pretty sure it was her."

"Did she buy something?"

"Nah, she wanted to use the washroom but they're only for paying customers, otherwise we get a steady stream of people in and out of here who don't buy anything. Trust me, lady, you don't wanna see what people do to a washroom when they're drunk," he grimaced as though recalling a traumatic incident.

"Do you remember what time it was?"

"Probably later 'cause we weren't real busy. I know I was wanting to get home, so it was near the end of my shift. I'd say somewhere between 11 pm and when we close at midnight."

This information wasn't much help. Did it mean that Juliette was almost home if she lived somewhere down 113. Street? Based on where her friend had posted that she saw her crossing the street, she probably lived south of Jasper Avenue. She wouldn't be walking on the opposite side of the street to go home. That wouldn't make any sense. Her building would have had to be on 100 Avenue or lower because there was the Basilica and rectory on one side and parking lots on the other side between Jasper Avenue and 100th Avenue. Maddy turned down 113. Street and walked a couple of blocks before finally giving up and turning around to go home.

Back in her apartment, she started marking up the map with a yellow hi-lighter. She traced the route Juliette most likely took to go home. She would have had to have been kidnapped somewhere between the pizza place and her building, which could be anywhere on 113. Street from 100. Avenue to almost 98. avenue. The street ended somewhere between 97 and 98. avenues. Below that was the river valley.

Now that she had a bit more information, she decided to look at the live feed once more. She needed to make sure that it was Juliette in the crate. This whole thing was so insane; when she was away from the live feed for any length of time, she found herself doubting it was real.

What she saw on her computer broke her heart. It wasn't that Juliette was injured or anything like that, it was her body language. She had somehow managed to sit up. Her chin was leaning towards her chest, her shoulders were slumped forward, knees bent up. She had to position herself that way to be able to sit. She appeared resigned to her fate. Maddy couldn't see her face, it was turned away from her. But then something started to happen, Juliette lifted the shoulder that was towards the camera and started rubbing the side of her head up and down against it and the crook of her arm. She began doing that to loosen the scarf that was tied around her head and covering her eyes. Managing to get it to slide off one eye, Juliette lifted her head up and looked around, she appeared to be examining her surroundings. She spotted the camera and stared directly at it.

What Maddy saw wasn't defeat, it was resilience mixed with defiance. If Juliette wasn't giving up, neither would she.

Chapter 28

M̲addy couldn't believe that she'd gone out twice, and twice had forgotten to pick up the groceries she needed. Although why she was surprised, she didn't know. She hated shopping and today was no exception. Approaching her door for the third time today and rummaging through her purse to find her keys, she almost tripped over the medium-sized box that was sitting in front of her door. Time stood still as she stared down at the box, her heart pounding and her blood turning cold. '*Here we go again*', she thought.

Tentatively, Maddy reached out with her foot and pushed the box a couple of inches to the right. Setting her purse and groceries on the floor, she squatted to get a closer look at it. Leaning forward, she gave a tentative sniff. It didn't smell foul or fowl. Cautiously, she picked it up and gave it a light shake. It wasn't heavy but something shifted inside.

Opening her apartment door, she set the box down gingerly and brought in her purse and groceries. She put away the perishables and decided to deal with the rest of her shopping later. That box was hauntingly calling her.

"Please, please don't be another goose coffin!" she muttered to herself while going in search of something to cut the tape that secured the box.

Scissors in hand, she slowly approached the box, as though she expected something to jump out at her. She cut the tape at one end of the box when a horrible thought came to her, making her stomach lurch.

"Okay, I changed my mind, a goose coffin is better than a Juliette body part."

Maybe she should call Kyle and let him open it? No, it could be completely innocent and have nothing to do with what was happening in her life right now. Wouldn't she feel stupid then? What about Rick? She thought about that option and quickly discarded it. She couldn't do that to her friend if it was something horrific. She knew that he was too sensitive to take it any better than she would. She scolded herself for wanting to resort to the gendered stereotype of having a guy rescue her from potentially gross things. Especially after lecturing him at the police station the other night. That would be counterproductive. No, she needed to do this on her own. She was a grown-ass woman, she could and would take care of things herself. She was as brave and capable as Detective Benson. Fine, not exactly as brave but still, she was no coward.

With that thought, she cut the last bit of tape off the box and quickly opened the lid.

She was met with the sight of hundreds of Styrofoam peanuts escaping from the box. Her mind quickly registered that there was no blood on the packing material, that was a good sign, right?

Head turned away from the box and her face scrunched up, she tentatively reached into the box of peanuts. Her hand came in contact with something hard and narrow. She wrapped her fingers around it, pulling it out with a flourish.

A cross.

She stared at it in confusion, barely registering what she was holding. Out of a list of all the possible things she'd imagined being in that box, this ranked, oh, not at all. There was a folded piece of paper attached by a thin string dangling from the cross. Maddy opened the note and read it. Confused, she read it a second time.

"Darkness descends amongst the broken-hearted, Lit only by slivers of broken glass.

The dark soul cries out for a savior.

- Are you getting any warmer, Maddy?"

What on earth? Was this supposed to be some kind of clue or some strange joke? She flipped the wooden cross over, hoping to find something else that might help her understand what this was about. There was a slot on the back that allowed the cross to be hung on a wall. It was a medium-stained wood, about ten inches from top to bottom. It didn't look like it was anything special and it didn't have any distinguishing marks or names on it. What could this mean? And what was the meaning behind the poem?

She was still standing there, deep in thought when someone knocked at her door. Rooted on the spot, unable to move, she held her breath. The second time there was a knock, she roused herself out of her temporary frozen state and moved to check through the peephole to see who was there.

Unlocking the door, she flung it wide open and threw herself into Rick's arms.

"Whoa!" Rick exclaimed as he stumbled backward a step. "I love you too hon, but my heart belongs to Tasha."

Maddy pulled herself away from Rick and swatted him on the shoulder.

"You should be so lucky! I'm just glad it's you." "Who else would it be?" Rick asked, perplexed.

"How'd you get in?"

"I snuck in behind a delivery guy."

"Speaking of deliveries, I received another package." "Not another goose, I hope?"

"No, this time it was this," she pulled the cross out of the box and showed him.

Rick looked quizzically at the cross. "Why aren't you crossing yourself, Rick?"

"Why should I? Is there something dead in there?" "No, but it's a cross, don't you have to do that?" "What are you talking about? Nobody crosses themselves just at the sight of a cross. You're being ridiculous!"

"I am not! You crossed yourself over a dead goose!" "Because it was DEAD!"

"So, you never cross yourself in front of a cross? Ever?"

"Only if a priest is holding it up or if it's in a holy place."

"I was holding it up." "You're not a priest."

"I will never understand your Lebanese traditions." "That's because you're not Lebanese, Habibi." "Hmmph."

"Anyway, Maddy, this cross here has probably no religious significance."

"I have no idea what it means other than it's a clue from the psycho."

Rick took the cross out of her hands and read the poem out loud.

'Darkness descends amongst the broken-hearted, Lit only by slivers of broken glass The dark soul cries out for a savior.

- Are you getting any warmer, Maddy?'

"What the hell's that supposed to mean?"

"I don't know, Rick, I was hoping you'd know. Aren't crosses your thing or something?"

Rick shook his head, turned his palms up, and rolled his eyes toward the sky, letting out a frustrated sigh.

He looked back at the note.

"This has to mean something, Maddy. They didn't just send it for no reason."

"I don't know. I wouldn't think so, I don't even know where to begin to try to figure anything out." Feeling hopeless, Maddy flopped down on her couch. "A cross and a cryptic note?"

"Can I use your laptop?" Rick asked, looking around for her computer. "I want to search and see if this is part of a poem or something. Maybe that's part of the clue."

"Sure, it's on the table."

Rick sat at the dining room table for a few minutes looking things up on her laptop before closing the lid and letting out a deep breath in frustration.

"It isn't part of any poem I can find online. It's usually quite easy to find poems through a simple Google search. Unless it's an extremely obscure one."

"Check on Juliette while you're at the computer".

"Didn't you tell us that her real name was Sally?"
"Whatever."

"I can look but I know what I'm going to see, Mads. I've been watching it on and off since we last talked. Tasha and I have agreed that it's real. What we must do now is help her."

"But how do we help her? All we know is that she's being held in a crate and it has something to do with a cross and some weird three-line poem," Maddy replied.

"There's got to be something we're missing." She groaned, annoyed at her helplessness.

Rick rubbed his forehead, closed his eyes, and mumbled something in Arabic that sounded like a swear word.

"I went for a walk and tried to retrace her steps from the restaurant she left from to the general area where I think she lives," Maddy told him about the little information she gleaned from it. "I don't know what I was hoping to find but at least it felt like I was doing something instead of just sitting around twiddling my thumbs."

"There were no arrows painted on the sidewalks or an 'x' marks the spot somewhere?" Rick teased, trying to lighten the mood.

"No, if it were only that easy," Maddy gave a rueful smile. "Except for the General Hospital, it's mainly restaurants, small shops, and some office buildings."

"How far did you say you went?"

"As far as Saint Joseph's Basilica," Maddy answered. There was a split moment of silence in the room, followed by two loud, sharp intakes of breath. It was the eureka moment they'd both been waiting for!

"The Basilica!" Rick exclaimed.

"Yes, the Basilica! That's it! It was on her route. The cross, the Basilica, they must be connected, don't they?" Maddy was certain that they were on the right path.

"I'm not 100 percent sure, Mads, but we both saw the connection at the same time and it's the only idea we've come up with so far. The question is, what do we do about it?"

They thought about it for several minutes, unable to find an answer. When Maddy couldn't sit still any longer, she stood up and went to the fridge to grab a drink. She took out a large bottle of root beer and poured some into two mugs.

"I figured you might be thirsty. Here you go."

"Thanks. Do you have any cookies? This sleuthing is making me hungry."

"Sure, I'll get you a couple. Chocolate chip good?"
"Yeah, thanks. You know, I've been thinking, perhaps

Tasha's right, it's time to contact the police. What do you say? Should we maybe call Kyle about this? Get them to go to the Basilica to take a look?"

Her mouth full of a big double-stuffed chocolate chip cookie, she shook her head no.

"Why not?"

Wiping crumbs from her lips, she handed him two cookies and sat down.

"Because what if we're wrong? Not only would we be wasting the cops' time, but we'd also look foolish."

"Okay then, what do you suggest?" he took a bite out of the cookie.

"How about we go look around the Basilica first?

Kind of a reconnaissance look-see?" "And then?"

"And then, if we find anything, we contact Kyle. If we don't, no harm done."

"Let's go! I'm getting antsy just sitting here." Rick was already standing at the door, anxious to get going.

Leaving her apartment, they headed off west on Jasper Avenue. They didn't talk much during the five minutes, they'd always been comfortable with each other, never feeling the need to fill the silence with unnecessary dialogue.

When they arrived at the Basilica, they stood on the sidewalk opposite its entrance for a minute, staring at the imposing building.

"Okay, now what?" Rick asked.

"I don't know, I was hoping you had a plan."

"Why would I have a plan? You're the one who got the cross delivery."

"I don't know…"

"Okay then, let's go in and see if anything jumps out at us," Rick responded.

People were leaving the 4:30 confession while others were beginning to arrive for the five o'clock mass.

"Who knew there was a rush hour at church?" Maddy joked.

They crossed the street and walked up the stairs that were facing north, towards Jasper Avenue. As they came close to the top, Maddy noticed what appeared to be the top of a spiky hairdo going down the opposite set of stairs. She grabbed Rick's arm, jerking him back.

"Did you see that?"

"What? Where?" Rick turned his head left and right, not sure what to look for.

"I think that was what's his name," Maddy said excitedly. "From the storage locker place." She stood on her tiptoes, trying to see him again. "Zane! Yes, that's him. That's what's his name, Zane!"

"Okay, so what?"

"I don't know, but what's he doing here, of all places?

He didn't strike me as the church-going type."

"And just what does the church-going type look like?" Rick asked her, slight indignation in his voice. He'd often been teased when they were in school about his devotion to his faith and as a result, he was still a bit touchy about the topic.

"How many guys wearing a spiky hairstyle do you usually see at Mass?" Maddy asked him.

"Okay, you may have a point," he answered, somewhat mollified.

They stopped at the top of the stairs, in front of the Basilica's entrance. They had to step to one side as people were jostling by, trying to get around them and into the building. Maddy looked back through the crowd toward the street, trying to locate the person with the spiky hair. "Right there!" she cried out. "Oh my god, he's got her!"

Chapter 29

They stood there, helplessly looking down at Zane pushing a wheelchair, heading down the street at a brisk pace. The figure in the chair was covered in a crocheted blanket, none of their features visible, not even their hair.

"We have to get him, don't let him get away!" Maddy spoke excitedly, her voice increasing to a high pitch. The more excited she became, the higher her voice got. People in the crowd had begun to stop what they were doing to look around and see what the ruckus was all about. This had the effect of slowing down the flow of people in front of them. Except for Zane, who had managed to make his way through the throng and was walking at a fast pace down the sidewalk without a glance behind him.

As the distance between them grew wider and wider, Maddy's frustration increased as well. If the person in the chair was Juliette, she had to rescue her, this could be her only chance.

They were finally able to make their way down the south-facing stairs, they dodged around the last couple of people in their way, finding themselves standing on an empty sidewalk, with not a single soul in front of them.

"Where'd he go? He was right there!" Maddy cried.

"Let's try the rectory door, maybe he snuck in there somehow."

Rick opened the heavy wooden door and Maddy rushed past him, hoping to find Zane hiding in there. It was church quiet, as a rectory would be. They had only taken a few steps onto the tiled floor of a shadow-filled hallway when they were intercepted by a very serious-looking woman.

"May I help you?" she sternly asked them.

"We're looking for our friend, ma'am," Rick replied, guilt written all over his face.

"It's Sister Gertrude, not ma'am," she said, looking suspiciously at them.

"He has a spiky hairdo and was pushing a wheelchair, Sister Gertrude," Maddy asked. "Did you perhaps see him come in through here?"

"I haven't seen a single soul come through this entrance. It was locked until five minutes ago," she pointed at the large clock on the wall above their heads.

"Are you certain?" Maddy looked back suspiciously at Sister Gertrude. Two could play at that game. She tried peeking over the nun's shoulders, but she kept being intercepted. Sister Gertrude must have played sports in college. And played them well!

"Are you questioning my capability to both look after this entrance and tell time young lady?"

"No, sister. Not at all. Thank you for your time. Maddy, let's go. Zane's not here," Rick led her away by the elbow, out the door, and back onto the sidewalk.

"Rick! What the hell?!"

"Maddy, he obviously couldn't have gotten past Sister 'Guardian of the Realm' Gertrude. Let's try elsewhere. I'll look down this alleyway and you go through the parking lot across the street, but be careful," Rick said as he sprinted in front of the three-story red brick building that used to be an Oblates monastery.

Maddy quickly looked both ways then, dashed out across the street. There were a few people in the parking lot who she assumed were more parishioners leaving the Basilica after confession. She darted up and down the rows, looking for Zane. When she came upon a large family, she stopped them and asked if they'd seen a man with a spiky hairdo. They looked at her with various degrees of interest from curious to bemused. But none of them had seen anyone with spiky hair.

Desperate to find out where Zane had disappeared to, she left the lot and sprinted down the sidewalk. She was looking in the windows of cars parked on the road when she spotted Rick returning from the alleyway. He motioned to her that he was going to the other parking lot just down from him, on the other side of a low-rise apartment building.

Maddy finished with the cars on that street and joined Rick just as he returned.

"Nothing," he said, puffing a bit.

"Damn!" Maddy said, her heart beating in her chest like a bass drum and sweat trickling down her back. "What happened to him?"

Rick didn't bother answering her. They stood on the sidewalk, catching their breath and looking around, as though they expected Zane to make a sudden appearance.

"Do you really think he has something to do with this? Could Juliette have been the woman in the wheelchair?" Rick asked.

"I don't know, but the more I think about it, the more I wonder. Zane was at the auction when I bid on the locker and won it. He was also the first person on the scene when I was bonked on the head and locked in the storage unit. He seems to keep showing up."

"Could be circumstantial, but it does seem odd for him to just turn up here. Especially after you received that cross."

Just then, Maddy's phone pinged with an incoming text.

"That's probably your wife asking me what happened to you," she said, smiling at him.

Looking at her phone, the smile left her face. *"I'm disappointed, you're getting colder, and you don't even know it."*

Maddy's eyes widened, and she pursed her lips. She turned around, trying to see if he was watching them from somewhere, maybe a window or the restaurant next door.

"Zane is messing with us!" she exclaimed as she showed Rick the text. Before he was able to stop her, she'd texted back.

"Who is this? Why are you doing this? What is wrong with you?"

"You shouldn't have done that Maddy, you're just going to tick him off," Rick cautioned.

Sure enough, the only response they received was short.

"Tsk, Tsk Maddy"

She knew that pressing him for answers wasn't going to get her anywhere. It was like he enjoyed teasing and playing with her. What the hell was she supposed to do now?

"Let's go back to your apartment and re-group a bit," Rick suggested, putting his arm on her back and guiding her down the street. "We need to take a look at this again. We don't know if he meant we are getting colder by looking at the Basilica, or we're getting colder because when he texted, we were walking away from it, or we could be getting colder suspecting and chasing after Zane."

~~~

Back at her apartment, Maddy tossed Rick a can of IPA beer and opened a vodka cooler for herself. They flopped down on the couch and took a long sip from their cans.

They sat in silence for a while before she reached for her laptop and began looking at Facebook. They checked Juliette's Facebook page, as well as the family member who had posted about her being missing. Nothing new had been added. Maddy assumed that if the woman had been found, the original poster would probably have updated everyone.

Reluctantly, she clicked on the link for the live feed. Juliette was still there, but she had stopped moving around as though she was trying to get out of her restraints and had begun banging on the crate with her bound feet. After a while, she gave up in exhaustion and lay there motionless. Maddy studied her closely. Had Juliette been there the whole time or had she been in the wheelchair that Zane was seen pushing? Was he changing her location? If so, why?

Maddy slammed down the top of the laptop. She couldn't watch anymore. It broke her heart a little more each time. Worse than that even, every time she watched, she felt a large bubble of panic rise and tighten her chest, threatening to overwhelm her. Helping the woman seemed impossible right now. While she hated the idea of having more contact with the kidnapper, she found herself wishing he would drop off another clue so they had something else to go on.

She looked over at Rick to find he was looking at her too.

"It's time," she said. "Yup, it is."

Chapter 30

She dreaded this but it was now or never. This was not going to be an easy conversation, but Juliette's life was at stake. That's what mattered most. Every minute of hesitation at this point meant one minute closer to her death. There was nothing left to lose, the deadline was looming over them. Taking her courage in both hands, she dialed Kyle's direct number.

"Hey Maddy, what's up? Everything okay? You haven't received any more packages or emails?"

"No, that's not why I'm calling tonight. We need to talk about some stuff."

"Is it related to the case?"

"Yeah… It's just that…" Telling him was much harder than she thought it would be.

"Just that what, Maddy? Tell me."

"It's just that I haven't told you everything that's been going on with Juliette."

"Who's Juliette?" "Sally."

"What?"

"Never mind. It's complicated."

"Maddy, spill it," Kyle's patience appeared to be wearing thin.

"Okay, promise you won't get mad?"

"Maddy!"

"The psycho who kidnapped Sally said that if I contacted the police, they would kill her. They meant it too." Maddy was talking a mile a minute. "So I didn't tell you everything because I was afraid for her. I didn't want her to be killed. I don't want anyone to be killed."

"What? Maddy, slow down and tell me everything that you've kept from me, from the beginning."

"They sent me two live links showing Sally being held captive in that crate."

Silence hung between them, feeling heavy and expanding. When Kyle finally spoke, his voice was low and quiet. He sounded as though he was having a difficult time restraining his anger.

"Are. You. Kidding. Me?! Why the hell would you not tell us something like this? Did I ever give you any reason not to trust me?" He was mad. No, he was more than mad, he was livid.

"You promised you wouldn't get mad!" Maddy protested.

"I did no such thing."

"And this is why I didn't tell you! Trust had nothing to do with it. They said they were going to kill her immediately if I did!"

"Maddy, you'd better tell me everything you know NOW! And don't skip any details."

"Fine! It started…"

"No. Stop." "But…"

"No. I'm sending a car to pick you up. Bring your laptop, cell, and everything you have received from the kidnapper. You need to come down here and make another official statement."

"Kyle… I'm really sorry."

"Don't even get me started. You could be charged with interfering with a criminal investigation! Go and get ready, they'll be there soon."

And with that, he hung up on her.

~~~

Kyle was waiting outside for Maddy, standing rigidly on the police station's back steps when the cruiser pulled up into the parking lot. He was still fuming. His anger was more than palpable. Maddy was convinced that if he had his way, she'd end up in jail.

Maddy was pleading with him, hoping he would understand why she had done what she did. Kyle would have none of it.

"I'm so sorry, really sorry. I was scared, Kyle. Please try to understand. They were going to kill her like that poor Canada goose. We're dealing with someone who is certifiably insane here!"

"Exactly! You should have come to me with this information the minute it happened. What were you thinking, Maddy? You're not qualified to run an investigation. Your safety has been threatened! You could have been hurt. Your friends could have been hurt. Ashley could have been hurt. This woman might be going through even more physical and emotional hell than necessary because of you and your Scooby-Doo Gang!"

"STOP IT! I said that I was SORRY!" Maddy cried out, "Don't you think I realize that? We all feel horrible right now."

Kyle took a deep breath and slowly exhaled, trying hard to calm himself down.

"Come here." He gave Maddy a hug.

"Maddy, some things are better left to the police," he said, softening his tone somewhat. "You're my friend, I'd hate for something to happen to you. I'm also a damn good cop. It's my job to investigate these things. We're not the Keystone Cops here. Even if some might come across as such, they're also quite qualified. Maybe jaded but qualified just the same."

"I know…"

"Now, we're going to go inside, you'll give Sergeant Kumar and Detective Morin a detailed report. Do you remember them from the other night, when you came in?"

"Yes," Maddy said sheepishly.

"And you will show us the links, alright?" "Am I going to go to jail?"

"I spoke to my Sergeant, explained there was a threat, and that you were frightened. You realized the gravity of your error and did come forward. Hopefully, you will get away with a stern lecture and slap on the hand."

Maddy let out a deep sigh of relief.

"Alright, I'm ready Kyle. Let's get this over with."

Starting from the very beginning, Maddy retold the events around the locker, demon mask, and dead Canada goose, which they already knew about. She then told them about the emails, video links, and the cross; how she and her friends first thought it was all a hoax orchestrated by a buyer to get back at her. She recalled how upsetting it was to come upon the Facebook post about Sally's disappearance. This is what helped to convince them it wasn't a hoax at all.

Hoping to earn some brownie points, she reminded them she'd called in about the Facebook post. That still didn't improve the investigators' mood. If that wasn't bad enough, they were livid when she told them that she'd gone and questioned the bar staff and the pizza parlor guy, impersonating a family friend no less.

"Do you realize, Ms. Whitman, that you may have seriously affected our investigation?" Sergeant Kumar was far from impressed with Maddy. "You may have influenced their stories and how they might answer any of our questions!" If Kyle had been fuming earlier, Sargent Kumar was a volcano on the verge of eruption. "Do you have anything else to add?" a grim-looking Detective Morin asked.

"After receiving the cross, I did go and look at the Saint Joseph Basilica with my friend Rick. That was a waste of our time though."

"Why's that?" The Sargent's curiosity was piqued.

"First of all, we couldn't find anything around the Basilica. Second, when we tried to get into the old rectory and offices, we were shooed away by staff. This means that it's not easy to get in there. I can't imagine any loon being able to circumnavigate a Mother Superior type. Third, I received a text saying that they had fooled me. That was when I decided it was worth the risk of reporting it. At this point, my friends and I can't figure out where she is and tomorrow will be too late to save her. At least now, maybe you can help before that psycho finds out we came here."

"How long have you known about this kidnapping?" "Actually, Detective Morin, I didn't know it was a kidnapping until Saturday morning. Friday is when I received the links. I thought it was a hoax from the same person who had been trying to scare me with the Canada goose. I never imagined that they had graduated from a goose-in-a-box to a Human-in-a-crate! All this time, I thought they were trying to scare me because I purchased the mask and these other things linked to Jason Thomas' death. This is Edmonton for crying out loud! We don't have serial killers here!"

"You'd be surprised at the number of deranged people in any city, Ms. Whitman, Edmonton's no exception. They're all around you, average people going about their average day as looking normal as you or me," Detective Morin said, pointing his pencil at her, "Then for whatever reason, something triggers them. It's like a fine wire snapping inside their head," he snapped his pencil in half, driving the point in. "They lose it."

This conversation shook Maddy up. It was one more stressful thing to add on top of the events of the last few days. Everything finally seemed to hit home. The gravity of it all sunk in like a dead weight.

Maddy was feeling incredibly guilty and stupid. The stress of the last few days had started to break her resolve. Maybe she was responsible for this whole mess after all. Who did she think she was? She was not Detective Benson.

"I don't know what else to say to convince you. Believe me, I'm sorry about everything, I had no idea," Maddy was trembling. "What's going to happen now? Are you going to charge me, Sergeant Kumar?"

"Trust me, I want to. There's nothing I dislike more than when an average Joe puts themselves and others at risk thinking they can do our jobs better than we can. You're lucky that Detective O'Brady's your friend. I'm willing to look the other way as a favor to him. This time."

"Thank you, sir."

They were interrupted by a knock on the Sergeant's office door. It was another Detective letting them know that the techs had uploaded the links that were on the computer Maddy had brought with her so as not to be detected by whoever was tracking it.

"You mean this person knew my friends were watching the link too?" Maddy was mortified that she may have put her friends in danger.

"There's a good possibility, yes. If they were tracking the addresses each click came from," the new detective answered. "Would you like me to set this computer up on your desk Sergeant?"

"Yes, please. That'll be all, thank you."

The Sergeant clicked on the links and immediately froze.

"How many days did you say you'd been watching this poor woman go through hell?"

"Two days, not including today, Sergeant."

"Jesus! You thought this was a hoax? Look at the woman! Does this look like a fake video to you?"

"Sergeant, we thought that if it wasn't a loop, then someone was faking it, trying to scare me."

"I've seen enough," Sergeant Kumar slammed the laptop shut. "We'll be placing a cruiser across the street from your home. Do not go anywhere. If this person contacts you again, you call us immediately, Ms. Whitman, do you understand?"

Maddy nodded yes. She didn't need to be told twice. "Detective Morin, please escort her out. I need to

figure out how we're going to try and save this woman before tomorrow morning."

Detective Morin brought Maddy down to the entrance. Kyle saw them leave the Sergeant's office and followed them out.

"Maddy, let me give you a ride home, okay?" "Thanks, Kyle, I'd appreciate that."

"Looks like they put you through the wringer."

"It could have been worse. I deserved worse. I feel like the shittiest, dumbest person on this planet right now. And I angered you. I wasn't a very good friend."

"Hey, you did do the right thing tonight. In the end, that's what counts."

"Really? I don't think that'll matter to Sally's family tomorrow morning," Maddy said, shoulders slouched and head hanging.

Chapter 31

Back at her place, Maddy was happy to see that Rick was still there waiting for her. She didn't want to be alone right now. He took one look at her face and spread his arms wide, and she fell into his hug. She had never been so happy to see a friendly face. They sat down on the couch together and Maddy shared what had happened at the police station and how it made her feel.

After a while, Rick stood up and reluctantly said he had to leave because Tasha and the twins would be expecting him home. Saturday nights were their game night and no one in the family was allowed to miss it. He'd been gone a lot this week with all this crazy business. A family break was needed.

As he was about to go, another notification pinged on Maddy's phone. When she saw who it was from, she looked up at Rick with both dread and excitement written all over her face. It was the kidnapper.

She clicked the link they had sent; it took her to a simple page that had a white background and a poem written in black, using a vintage typewriter font.

Can death be sleep, when life is but a dream, And scenes of bliss pass as a phantom by? The transient pleasures as a vision seem, And yet we think the greatest pains to die.

"This one looks familiar," Rick said as he grabbed his phone and began a Google search. "Yup, John Keats. They're going for the tried and true this time," he said.

"Does it mean anything to you?"

"Not off-hand, but I'm going to look up its meaning and see if I can figure something out from there," Rick told her as he turned his attention back towards her laptop and started typing.

Looking at her own phone's screen, Maddy struggled to make sense of the email. Usually, the clues had something tangible with them. First the goose, then the cross. Why was this just an email? Was he getting nervous about showing up at her apartment again?

"Huh," Rick said, focusing on the screen. "What? What did you find?" Maddy asked. "Hmm…."

"Come on, tell me what it says!" Maddy was getting impatient with his hemming and hawing.

"I'm not sure, I mean it is obviously a poem about death as it's the first stanza of a poem called 'On Death'. Keats wrote it to comfort his dying brother."

"Okay? How does that apply to us?"

"I don't know Maddy, I'm reading as fast as I can!" Rick said, swatting her hand away as she tried to move the laptop closer to her.

"It says here that most people agree that he's talking about real life being a dream and we wake up into death. There's also a line of thought, it's a bit radical, but it says that he may have been part of a suicide cult who felt that death was to be embraced."

"Creepy! Although it's reassuring to know there were some nutbars back then too," Maddy said sarcastically with a shiver.

"I don't know," Rick said, exasperation evident in his tone. "None of this seems to apply, maybe the whole thing is like a threat. Find her or she dies. Maybe that's all there is to his email."

Maddy's phone began to ring. She tensed up until she looked at the call display and saw that it was Ashley.

"Hi Ash."

"Maddy, I don't often say this but… I think you're right this time."

"Great, I'm glad to hear that," Maddy responded. "Now what am I right about?"

"About this not being a hoax. I've been watching that poor woman on and off all day and there's no way this can be a hoax."

"Uh-huh."

"What do you mean 'uh huh'? There's a woman out there, trapped in a box, scared out of her mind, there's a psycho on the loose, and all you can say to me is 'Uh huh'? We need to do something!" Ashley spoke rapidly and with an increasing sense of urgency. "Where are you?"

"Rick and I are at my place."

"What are you doing there? Please tell me you're working on finding her. This woman's life is on the line!"

"You don't say," Maddy responded wryly. "That's what I've been saying all along! By the way, I've received a couple more clues since we last talked." "What? And nobody told me?"

"We've been busy trying to figure things out, and you didn't seem too concerned last time we spoke," Maddy said, defending herself. "Anyway, it doesn't matter, I'm telling you now."

Maddy proceeded to fill Ashley in on the delivery of the cross, and their excursion to the Basilica.

"Well, that's ominous," Ashley said when she'd been brought up to speed.

"Unless you can make something out of these clues, we're left clueless," Maddy told her. "Wait a sec, Rick is waving at me to put you on speakerphone."

"Hi, Ash!"

"Hey Rick, sounds like you're keeping our girl safe."

"I try, but she's not making it easy, let me tell you!" Rick half-joked.

"I believe it's time to go to the police," Ashley said in a tone that suggested she'd brook no argument.

"Okay Ashley, consider it done," Maddy looked at Rick with a twinkle in her eye. He was glad to see her looking more like her usual bratty self.

"Well... okay then?" Ashley sounded cautious but uncertain.

"We already went," Rick said loudly so she could hear on the other end of the phone.

Maddy swatted at him playfully.

"You ruin all my fun," she hissed at him. "Very funny," Ashley said.

"Sorry Ash, I just got back from the police station and I'm feeling a bit beaten up, I'm just getting my fun where I can," Maddy explained.

"Well, I'm glad you went," Ashley said. "I'm sorry you feel beat up though."

"I'll live," Maddy said. "It wasn't fun, but I feel a sense of relief that at least now it isn't all on just our shoulders."

Chapter 32

Rick had finally gone home, promising to keep an eye on Juliette's video feed in case something triggered an idea or if, God forbid, anything happened. The rest of the evening felt like it stretched out in front of her. She had to find something else to do or she'd go insane. Sitting around and waiting for the other shoe to drop was not only frustrating but also annoying as hell.

Setting her computer aside, she got up and threw on her sneakers, tucked her phone in her pocket, and headed out for a walk. She went south, then took a right under the little trolley overpass that connected to the High- Level Bridge and was soon at Constable Ezio Faraone Park. This was one of her favorite parts of downtown. As she walked past the monument that had been erected in memory of the Constable, her hands trailed along the front of it, absently running her fingers along his etched name. It always saddened her a bit when she passed through here, he was so young when killed in the line of duty.

She continued walking along the top trail of the park, looking across the river at the skyline of the edge of Old Strathcona. The pent-up energy inside her wanted to get out while at the same time, she felt such melancholy and awareness of life's fragility.

Her mother's sallow face flashed before her eyes and Maddy caught her breath. It still happened this way sometimes, even after so many years had passed. This ache that was always there, cracking open like a yawning crevice, threatening to swallow her up. The pain took her back to her mother's bedside, listening to her labored breathing, holding her cold hand.

She had reached a set of steep stairs and threw herself into descending them towards the river valley. While she was going down the stairs, she put as much effort as she could into every step she took, hoping to burn off some of that energy and her frustrations. She knew though, that what went down would also have to return, and coming back, working up a sweat would be a given. She'd end up having to stop halfway through, huffing and puffing. She wasn't sure who had come up with the bright idea that what this city needed was several outdoor stairways of more than 200 steps each, but whoever it was, she was convinced, was a sadist.

She wandered along the trails for about half an hour, enjoying the smell of the woods in the city. Amid the river valley's trails, it was so easy to forget that you were in the heart of a metropolitan city. If she strained a bit, she could hear the sound of traffic in the distance, but at this moment, the smell of the trees and the vegetation underfoot were closer and more real to her than anything else. She often came here when life got too much and she needed to re-center herself. Being close to nature was good for the soul, she believed, and for whatever else was ailing you.

Eventually, she began to retrace her steps back to her apartment, feeling renewed, reenergized, and hungry for some late-night takeout.

Chapter 33

As she walked up to her building's front door, she noticed two police officers on the street walking toward her.

"Hi, Maddy?" the policewoman asked. "Yes, can I help you?"

"We're here to keep an eye on things, I believe you were informed that we would be stationed across the street?"

"Oh yes,"

"My name is Officer Sidhu and this is Officer Tom Janvier."

"Nice to meet you both, and thank you for helping keep me safe."

"No problem, Ma'am," Officer Janvier tipped his hat in her direction and his partner sent him a glare. Maddy had no doubt he would receive some ribbing when they were back in their patrol car.

"I'll go up with you and make sure everything is okay," Officer Sidhu told Maddy.

She walked her up to her apartment door and asked for her keys. She unlocked and opened the door for Maddy, then had her wait in the entryway while she did a walkthrough around the loft, checking the two bedrooms and the washroom. She even opened the front and laundry closets.

"We'll be across the street, in the strip mall parking lot, our car will be facing your building. You should be able to see us from your window. If anything happens that frightens you, just switch your lights on and off three times. We'll come right up."

"Officer Sidhu, do you think I could really be in danger?" Maddy asked nervously. Had she come that close to getting kidnapped herself?

"Look, anything's possible. If this person is watching your every move, they'll know you spoke to us. They might even try to get back at you. What's more probable though, is that they'll try to stay away from you. They know we know. Either way, it's better to play it safe. You never know the moment a person cracks what extreme measures they'll be willing to take to exact revenge."

"Oh."

"Don't worry Ms. Whitman, we're just three light flickers away. Please lock your door behind me. Try to have a good night."

"Thank you, officer."

Making sure all her locks were bolted, she slid the chain on as an added precaution. She looked through the peephole and saw that Officer Sidhu had been standing there, waiting until she had done as asked. She waved at Maddy through the peephole and left. Most of Edmonton's police officers were kind and compassionate. They made up for the few rotten apples she'd occasionally encountered.

Taking her shoes off, she went over to her front entry bench and sat down to put on her slippers. She needed comforting. These were big, pink, and fuzzy with a cute bunny nose on the tip, ears on the top, and a cottontail on the back of each foot. They felt homey.

Her cell dinged; it was a text from Ashley checking in to see how she was holding up. Before she had a chance to respond, her phone dinged again. This time, it was Rick. He was asking the same question. She went to the kitchen to grab some cookies and a tumbler before deciding how to respond. She picked up the good bottle of Scotch that was kept hidden behind a large planter, noticing that her one and only plant was in dire need of being watered. She'd be sure to water it before going to be. Wouldn't want to kill another living thing this weekend.

Balancing the plate of cookies, tumbler, and bottle of scotch, she made her way to the dining room table and sat down. She slowly poured herself some scotch, neat. Her cell dinged again. It was Tasha, asking exactly what had happened at the police station. She ignored the text, deciding instead that a messenger video call on her laptop would be better. Nobody wanted to go through the other day's cell phone circus again. Not tonight of all nights. The laptop was still in its carrying case. She'd been relieved when the police let her take it home with her. All they'd needed was the link but had still taken a look at it. Having checked for any kind of bugs, the tech guru had assured her that it was safe to use it. If that kidnapper had been watching her, it wouldn't have been through her computer. Kyle had thought that the threat of watching Maddy was most likely a bluff. The kidnapper had probably been following her comings and goings from outside her apartment. This made her feel much safer at home.

Maddy flicked her computer on and sent out a group chat invitation via Facebook Messenger. While she waited for her friends to join, she sipped on her scotch. She usually preferred drinking it on the rocks. Tonight though, she needed her drink to be a stiff one.

The scotch was smooth and velvety as it went down her throat, warming her chest and belly. Unfortunately, it didn't wash away the feeling of guilt and doom that had enveloped her since she'd left the police station. Juliette was probably going to die and Maddy had played a big role in her demise. How could she live with herself?

"Hey, Maddy! Hello?" Ashley was waving at her from the screen.

"Oh, sorry, I had zoned out for a moment." "It's that bad, eh?"

"Worse…"

"Bella, tell us what happened?" Tasha and Rick had joined in. While she had told Rick and Ashley that her trip to the police station had been difficult, she hadn't gone into many details.

"Basically, what they said is that my not coming to them sooner with all the information may result in Juliette dying," Maddy wiped a tear away. "They were very, very upset with me. I thought Kyle might never speak to me again."

"Listen, Habibi, you weren't the only one involved in this. It was impossible to tell if it was a hoax or not," Rick tried to reassure not just her, but all of them as well.

"If you'd gone to them sooner, they would have told you not to waste their time. You know that. We know that."

"Rick's right, Maddy. I was 100 percent certain it was a hoax. If anything, we're all partly to blame. It's not all on you," Ashley added.

"I agree with them, Bella," Tasha added, sympathetically. "We haven't been keeping this from the police for weeks! It's only been a few days since you received the link. You've been in touch with Kyle and the police several times."

"I know, but…"

"Mads," Ashley interrupted her. "You took the demon mask to them from the get-go, they didn't take you seriously. Then the dead goose in a box. Those were threats to you, not to anyone else. How could we not think that the links were a hoax? That a crazy former buyer wasn't trying to mess with you further? What were you supposed to do?"

"The kidnapper did say they would kill her if I went to the police!"

Maddy frowned and looked pensive. "What you're saying is that I may have delayed her getting killed?"

"Exactly!" Rick leaned closer to the screen. "You got that psycho to give us more hints. If you'd have gone to them right away, the cops wouldn't have known where to start looking."

"We know that she's probably nearby, Rick told me about the cross," Tasha added. "And about seeing Zane at the Basilica."

"You saw Zane at the Basilica?! Nobody told me about that. I knew he shouldn't be trusted. That shifty-eyed you-know-what has been showing up every time something happens. It must be him! Did you tell Kyle?" Ashley asked excitedly.

"I didn't, Ash. I'm not sure about Zane anymore. On the one hand, he did save me when I was in the locker after being hit on the head. Why do it if he wanted me out of the picture? On the other hand, he IS always around. I just don't know."

"The police are on it now, it won't make a difference if it's Zane or not," Tasha interrupted. "If it's him, he's either in hiding or is with her."

"Even so, I've learned my lesson and I'm not going to hold anything back. I'm emailing Zane's name to Kyle as we speak," Maddy said as she opened her laptop.

"Why don't we look at the links?" Rick said. "Maybe there's been some change. Maybe we can see if anyone's there with her."

"Good idea," Ashley said.

"Mio Dio! The poor woman is still chicken-tied!" exclaimed Tasha.

"Tash sweetheart, the expression is 'hog tied'."

"Whatever, Rick. You know what I mean. She's tied up like a roast chicken. What kind of animal does that to a woman?"

"She's just lying there, very still," Ashley observed. "It looks like she's focused on something. Is there any sound?"

"No, neither of the links has sound," Maddy replied. "Look! Seems like she managed to get that scarf completely off her eyes."

"Maddy, didn't you text us that you knew it was Sally in the crate because she'd somehow been able to slip the scarf off from one of her eyes?" asked Tasha.

"Yes."

Tasha disappeared from Messenger for a few seconds before getting back to the group.

"Okay, I just scrolled my texts. You sent us that text on Saturday afternoon, right?"

"Yeah, why?" Maddy had no idea where Tasha was going with this.

"Well, if she slid off one side of the scarf on Saturday afternoon, and now we see that both eyes are uncovered, that means that the kidnapper has not been back to see her since. They probably wouldn't want her to see them or where she's being kept captive. Otherwise, they would have pulled the scarf back up."

"What does that have to do with anything?" asked Rick, "I'm not following you."

"Think, you guys. The kidnapper would not want us to see the woman's face because we might be able to identify her. That might help us find her. They don't know that Maddy has seen the missing person post on Facebook, and they might not even realize she's been asking around for her. If they've been following Maddy, they just saw her go to a couple of places. Probably thinks this was based on the hints she was sent."

"Tasha, how does that have anything to do with the scarf, or how long her eyes have been uncovered?" Ashley asked, seeming to be as confused as the others.

"It's obvious!" Tasha exclaimed. "The kidnapper has been too busy following Maddy around, they haven't checked in on Juliette. She's in all likelihood almost out of water, I presume that's what's in the water pack on her chest. Look at it, that pack is almost flat! This means that they'll have to stop by and check on her soon. Had they already checked in on her, they would have pulled up the scarf and tightened it."

"And? Tasha, you're not making any sense." Maddy still had no idea what Tasha was getting to.

"Guys! Come on! This means her water needs to be replenished. They'll probably do it during the night when they think we're all sleeping," Tasha looked from blank face to blank face, getting more and more exasperated. "If we take turns staying up, one of us might catch them in the act and see who the kidnapper is!"

"OH!" the three others exclaimed in unison. "Uff! Finally!" Tasha sighed.

Ashley raised an eyebrow. "Tasha, you're one of my dearest friends, but darling, you need to know when to cut to the chase."

"Yeah!" Both Rick and Maddy nodded in agreement. Maddy had been letting everything Tasha said sink in.

She realized they didn't have any other options.

"Tasha's idea is a good one," Maddy agreed, "We don't have any other choices at this point. The police don't want us roaming around looking for her. This way, if we do see the kidnapper, we can call the police and give them a heads up, maybe even a description."

"I'll take the first shift, from now until midnight," Ashley offered. "I need my sleep or else I'll be useless for the rest of the day."

Maddy volunteered from midnight to four and Tasha would take the next shift until eight in the morning. Rick usually did his shop's invoicing from home on Mondays so he would keep an eye on it from eight onward, in case the kidnapper showed up to follow through on their eight am deadline threat. After that, well, they didn't want to think about 'after'.

"Alright, I've got to get some shut eye so I can do my shift. Goodnight everyone and good luck!" Tasha signed off, followed by the others.

Maddy sat there, wondering what she should do next. She decided to check her emails, this time she was hoping that she'd received another clue from the kidnapper. There was a new email, but it wasn't the one she'd been wanting to get.

Hello Maddy,

I must say that I am very, very disappointed in you. If you recall, I had asked you to please let me know before you listed anything new online. Imagine my surprise when I came across a listing for a couple of coins and noticed that it was one of your posts! This isn't how someone who would like to have regular buyers, should be acting. It is not professional. Your reputation should be something to be concerned about. I'm not sure if I should even give you another chance. Reflect on THAT.

Paris

Was that a threat? Could Paris possibly be the kidnapper? She was certainly disagreeable enough to have an evil side, Maddy thought. If she wasn't the kidnapper, she certainly wasn't a very nice person. Throbbing pain began to spread between Maddy's eyes. This constant looking over her shoulders and not trusting anyone was not a great way to live your life. She thought for a few moments and then wrote what she hoped was a neutral- sounding email. She didn't want to anger Paris, in case she was the kidnapper, but she also didn't want to grovel, in case she wasn't. After typing and deleting several drafts, Maddy settled on a reply:

Hello Paris,

Please accept my sincerest apologies, my mind was elsewhere, and I completely forgot about our conversation. I will let you know of any other potential sales prior to making them publicly available. I've attached some pictures of other coins and some collector cards that you might be interested in. I will be posting these in a couple of days.

Regards, Maddy

Hopefully, this would satisfy Paris' nasty, giant ego and perhaps, if she was the kidnapper, buy them a bit more time. She wasn't sure if she should let Kyle know about this or not. There weren't any physical threats made to her or Juliette.

Ding! A text had just come in.

'You told the police! What a shame. Here I thought I could trust you. Why can't people just do what they're asked? Is that too much to be expected? You're lucky that I'm in a forgiving mood tonight. As you can tell, I'm not too worried about the cops. They won't find me. I'll still give you until tomorrow morning to figure things out. Then, it's goodnight to your crated little chickadee. Tick Tock, Maddy, Tick Tock.'

This message she would definitely forward to the police, and she would also forward along Paris'. She had learned her lesson; let the police figure out if the messages meant anything. She sent both on to Kyle. Then Maddy updated her friends. They agreed with her. The best thing to do was keep with their original plan of watching the links and forward any communication to the authorities. If the kidnapper was Paris or Zane, they would see them check in on Juliette. All they needed to do was take a screenshot and the proof the police needed would be in their hands. Patience is what they needed. They would catch her, or him, in the act.

~~~

Maddy was woken from her brief nap on the couch by the sound of her alarm going off letting her know it was time for her shift. Ashley needed to be relieved, and it was Maddy's turn to watch the link for the next four hours. Firing off a text to her friend to let her know she was ready for her watch, she waited impatiently for a reply. Ashley finally texted back that her shift had been uneventful. Juliette hadn't even twitched. She was probably asleep which is what Ashley herself intended to do now.

For the next four hours, Maddy stared at her laptop screen. After the first hour, her eyes had become heavy and she had to stand up and stretch. She felt uncomfortable watching someone sleep, knowing that they were unaware that they were being spied on. It felt voyeuristic. She rolled her shoulders, stretched her head, first to one side, then the other, and did a few yoga Sun Salutations.

"Come on baby, come to Momma!" she murmured, hoping against hope that the kidnapper would make an appearance while she was watching the live feed. No such luck.

She passed the baton over to Tasha at four in the morning and immediately collapsed on her bed. The day's excitement, her guilty conscience, and worry over Juliette had exhausted her and she quickly fell into a deep sleep. She woke with a start to hear a persistent ringing.

What was that noise? It took her groggy mind a moment to clear and realize that it was her phone ringing. Once it sunk in, it took less than a couple of seconds for her to jump up and answer.

"Tasha, talk to me. Did you see anything?"

"I KNOW WHERE SHE IS!" Tasha yelled excitedly through the phone.

Chapter 34

Tasha, talk to me. Did you see anything?"

"I KNOW WHERE SHE IS!" Tasha repeated.

Maddy could almost feel Tasha vibrating with excitement through the cell.

"Did you see Paris or Zane?"

"NO! I said I know WHERE she's being kept prisoner!" "What? Oh my God! Where? How?" Maddy jumped out of bed.

"I've never watched the live feed this early in the morning, have you?"

"No, I haven't. Tasha, please don't drag this on. Tell me quickly. Juliette's life depends on it!" Maddy didn't have the patience right now for another one of Tasha's long descriptive stories.

"Easy Bella, I'm getting there. I was just trying to answer your questions."

"Sorry, I'm just very anxious and worried about Juliette." "I know. Listen, I was watching her sleep when the sun started to rise. There was a sunbeam that shone into the crate through its slats and lit it up differently. I noticed more details about Juliette. Then, it dawned on me that the room itself might also be lit up differently! I switched links to the one in the room she's being held in. That's when I noticed a shadow on the floor. I recognized it! It was from a stained-glass window."

"From Saint Joseph's Basilica? I knew it!"

"No, not from the Basilica. I used to work in a funeral home on 113th, remember?"

"Yeah, we used to meet for lunch. It's from there?" "YES! It's in my former boss's office."

"Are you sure? There are lots of stained-glass windows in the area. Half a dozen churches are in this neighborhood alone." Maddy's excitement was fading away, replacing it once again was a feeling of hopelessness. The location Juliette was being held in could be anywhere. It would take forever to search for all the possibilities.

Tasha could hear the deflation creeping into her voice. "Cara Mia, none are like this stained-glass window. Trust me. It's unique. He's a hockey fanatic. His office is on the east side of the building. Not a lot of people notice this window unless they know about it. His wife had the Oilers' logo set in the glass as a surprise gift for his fiftieth birthday. You can only see the shadow on the floor when the sunrise shines through it. I noticed it in winter because I would already be at work when that happened. And it only happened for a few weeks, after that the sunrise hits the window differently, if at all during work hours, so there's no shadow on the floor."

235

"Wouldn't anyone working there have noticed the crate?" Maddy couldn't understand how a big wooden crate containing a prisoner, no less, could go unnoticed in a funeral director's office.

"The building is condemned, that's why I lost that job."

"I thought you had quit that one." Maddy couldn't keep track of all the different jobs Tasha had had over the years. She kept quitting either because of sexual harassment, discrimination, or boredom. She was one smart lady and didn't suffer fools easily nor mindless work.

"No, this one was a good job. Unfortunately, there was lots of black mold, asbestos, and other dangerous stuff in the walls and attic. It's much cheaper to knock it down and rebuild a new funeral home than repair this one. They told me that they would rehire me once the new building was up and back in operation. But all that's not important, SHE'S THERE!!"

"We've got to go save her!! Do we call the cops?"

"You're the closest, go right away. It's about four blocks from the Brewery Hall. I called Ashley before you, she's on her way to meet you there."

"Smart thinking!" Maddy was pulling on her pants as she was talking. "But what about the police? Should I call Kyle?"

"Don't worry about it. I'll call him while Rick and I are driving over. I just need to wake the twins up to let them know we're leaving. They'll just have to feed themselves."

"Okay, I'm on my way."

Chapter 35

Officer Giani Sidhu had just started her shift watching Maddy's building. Her partner, Officer Tom Janvier, had finished his watch and was now snoring away like a steam engine next to her. So far, this assignment had been easy. Maddy Whitman seemed like a regular civilian. Maybe a bit on edge but nothing to make her think that she was asking for trouble. According to what she'd been reading in the file, it just appeared that trouble had found her.

Officer Sidhu loved her job. Helping people was a part of her job that she enjoyed the most. She found it to be quite rewarding. Tonight was probably going to be an easy night for doing just that. Making sure that Maddy Whitman was safe in her condo. It looked secure. They only had to watch for anyone trying to sneak in that hadn't been buzzed in. Easy.

Half an hour later, Officer Sidhu noticed movement in the lobby of the building she'd been watching. Something looked suspicious. It couldn't be. Could it?

"Oh, for crying out loud!" She shook Officer Janvier awake.

"Tom, wake up."

"Huh? Is it my turn already?"

"No, Tom, look across the street. Someone just came out of the building. They're standing at the light. Am I imagining things or is that Whitman?"

Officer Janvier wiped the sleep from his eyes and peered through his window at the shadowy figure standing at the stop light, maniacally hopping from one foot to the other. Just then the lights changed.

"Holy crap, Giani, it IS Whitman. What the hell is she doing? Is she jogging at this time of the morning?"

"Aw, man! I told her to stay home."

"Guess we better follow her. Do it from a distance. We don't want to spook her." Officer Sidhu said. "I'll call it in."

"What the hell? Are those fuzzy slippers she's wearing on her feet?"

"What? Erm, I think so." She leaned forward, squinting her eyes in an attempt to get a better look. "Yes, I... I think they're... bunny slippers?"

Chapter 36

M addy hadn't been aware that the officers were trying to follow her. She had completely forgotten about them. The only thing on her mind was to get to Juliette the fastest way possible before anything terrible happened. The funeral home was six city blocks away from her place but if she took a couple of back alleys, she would save at least five minutes.

As she turned another corner, the funeral home came into view. Doubling her speed, running on pure adrenaline, and dodging debris strewn all over the back alley, she finally reached the parking lot. Out of breath, she doubled over, gasping. Damn it, she was so out of shape. She had to cut back on those cookies... and climb even more stairs. Breathing hard, Maddy leaned against one of the old oak trees that lined the parking lot. But there was no time to rest. Still puffing, she circled the old building, attempting to see if she could make out the Oilers' logo on any of the windows, all the while hoping to get her bearings. Many of the windows in the back glinted in the early morning sunlight making it almost impossible to see which one had the Oilers logo. She quickly returned to the parking lot to wait for Ashley and to try and come up with a plan. You can't just run in like a mad woman. What if the kidnapper was lurking in those shadows or something? That could mean a death sentence. And not just for Juliette.

Headlights started flashing in her eyes. Between them and the rising sun, she was temporarily blinded. She started running back and away from the lot, thinking that if it was the killer, she'd better hide. Unfortunately, all she could see were the headlights imprinted on her retinas. It was impossible to see anything but spots of white light. She got disoriented, turned around, and ran straight into a light post, almost knocking herself out. In a daze, she picked herself up as quickly as her spinning head would allow, readying herself to let off a scream and put up the fight of her life.

The car's engine turned off; its lights finally began to dim. Slowly, her eyes started to focus as she recognized the voice of the tall figure running towards her.

"What the hell were you doing? Why on earth were you running around like a chicken with its head cut off," Ashley asked.

"I thought you were the killer coming to get me! And why were you flashing your lights at me?!"

"I was flashing the lights so you would know that it was me! Are you okay?" Ashley looked quite concerned. "You can't afford another concussion!"

"Other than a bruised ego and a slight headache, I'm fine. I was just momentarily stunned. My eyes can focus now."

"Good. Now what should we do? Do we go in and look around?"

"You stay here and keep watch. You can direct the police and tell Rick and Tasha where I am. Text me if you see anything. I'll go in and try to find Juliette."

"Alright but put your phone on vibrate. Wouldn't want to announce your presence to anyone that might be in there."

"Good call. I'm going to try the back door and see if it's unlocked."

Maddy stuck to the shadows to reach the backdoor. It was one of those heavy metal fire doors. She tried its brass handle, rattling it a couple of times. Locked. Maddy cursed under her breath. Looking around for another possible entrance to the funeral home, she saw an open window situated just above her head. Unable to reach it, she texted Ashley to come and give her a boost, all the while watching out for anyone who could be lurking around. Good thing Ashley was a tall woman who, unlike Maddy, liked to work out. Hoisting Maddy up to the window of the old stone building hadn't been too much of a challenge for her. Maddy sat on the dusty window ledge, swung her legs over, and jumped down, landing in a room that looked like it had probably been used as a chapel. Standing in place for a few minutes, waiting for her eyes to adjust to the dim filtering light, Maddy took in the space around her. Not much was left of the chapel, other than the stained-glass windows and an altar. They must have removed all the benches and anything else that was in good enough shape to be reused in the new building. There were cobwebs everywhere. Strewn on the floor were the odd pieces of broken furniture and half- melted cream-colored candles Maddy assumed were relics of prior services. The chapel had an almost spooky or haunted look. Carefully, she tried to avoid the debris, walking around or over it, not wanting to make noise by accidentally stepping on something. She picked up a heavy-looking discarded wooden leg, just in case she needed a weapon. It must have belonged to a chair or some kind of bench, one of those ornate types that are usually found on the perimeters of all funeral homes' viewing rooms. Her back pocket suddenly vibrated causing Maddy to nearly leap out of her skin. She'd forgotten all about her cell phone. It was a text from Ashley. That woman had zero patience.

'*Have you found any clues yet? Do you want me to come in?*'

'*No. Stay put.*' Maddy texted back.

She didn't want anyone else coming in here. The more footsteps, the greater the likelihood they would reveal their presence before they were ready. And she needed Ashley to stay out there so she could direct the cavalry when they arrived.

'*Fine!*' Ashley responded. '*But please call me now and leave the phone on so I can hear what's going on, okay?*'

Maddy did as asked then made her way out of the chapel, turning at the first door on her right. Thankfully it was open, no worries about making noise. From what she could see through the few early morning sun rays coming into the room, it looked like one of the viewing chambers. It was bare but the dusty rose carpet and matching satin-like curtains gave it away. They both had seen better days and the curtain was worn by the sun's rays. The curtain barely hung by threads in some spots. The carpet was noticeably worn in what were probably high-traffic areas. The second room was much the same except in shades of antique blue. She went through four more rooms, not much thought had been given to interior decorating here, they were identical in style but varied in the color of their decor. She would be willing to bet that they'd been named something related to their color such as the 'Peaceful Sky' room or 'Eternal Rose'. Soon she found herself in the foyer. This meant she was at the front of the funeral home. There'd been no traces of anyone having recently occupied any of these rooms. The dust hadn't even been disturbed until Maddy had walked through. This left the second floor.

Taking the center stairs carefully on the tip of her shoes, Maddy strained to listen for any sounds that might have come from the floor above her. She felt like a sitting duck out here in the open but there hadn't seemed to be any other set of stairs for her to take. She made her way up the stairs quietly until she was at the very top step. The creaking it made when her foot landed on it sounded ten times louder in the empty space than it should have. Someone heard it and started yelling.

"Help me! Please don't leave me alone again. I need more water. Please, please give me more water."

It had to be Juliette! Not thinking, Maddy started to run from room to room, not caring if she made any noise. In the furthest room from the stairs, she spotted the crate, it was in the far corner opposite the window. And there it was, the Edmonton Oilers' logo as plain as day, although there wasn't a shadow as the sun had risen. Such an odd thing to have in a funeral home, Maddy thought, only in Edmonton. She turned her attention to the rest of the room, making sure it wasn't booby-trapped. There was a desk near the window. A computer sat on top of it. She looked up to the four corners of the room and spotted the camera, it was facing away from the window, looking towards the crate. That would explain why the kidnapper hadn't realized the window would cast such a distinctive shadow in the early morning. They probably hadn't even looked at that link at that time of the day. There was plastic sheeting on three sides of the crate and some partially covered the top, as though the crate was part of a photoshoot. She did a second scan of the room, more carefully this time. Maddy felt safe enough to enter, so she walked towards the crate.

"Hello? Hello?"

"I'm over here, help! Oh my God, help me! Please!" "I'm going to help you. I just need to figure out how to open this thing."

"Oh, thank you! Thank you!" The woman could barely speak through her sobbing, she was on the verge of hysteria.

The crate had one of those slide-down doors, like a gate on a cage. There wasn't even a lock on it, just a piece of wire thread through the clasp and then twisted. The kidnapper had apparently been confident that the woman, being bound and unable to see, posed little risk of escaping. She dropped the wooden leg she'd been holding with a death grip since picking it up in the chapel, grabbed hold of the wire, and untwisted it until it was straight. She put both hands on the bottom slat and tried to pull it up. It was heavier than it looked and awkward. She knelt and tried to get her fingers under the bottom slat instead, there was no give. Try as she might, it was impossible. There must be something to open it. How else did the kidnapper do it? Looking around the room for something that might do the trick, Maddy glimpsed behind the crate and saw a crowbar leaning against one of the walls. That might be how the door could have been lifted up slightly, but how to open it all the way? She grabbed the crowbar and tried to slide it under the door. It wouldn't budge.

'The hell with this! Think! Stay calm. Don't panic. Think!' Maddy told herself.

"What's going on? I can't see what you're doing through the slats," the woman sounded panicky.

"Give me a minute. I need to think."

Hearing what was going on through the cell phone, Ashley couldn't wait any longer. Neither the police nor Rick and Tasha had arrived yet. She texted Tasha and Kyle, telling them she was going in after Maddy. She then pressed "record conversation" to tape what was happening on the other end of the line with Maddy. Satisfied that it was working, she looked around for a garbage can or box to give her the extra foot she needed to reach the window. Ashley ventured behind the funeral home. It looked like the demolition process had already started. The storage building was now a pile of bricks. The main building's demolition was probably going to happen any day now. There were several construction vehicles parked and beside them was a large scrap bin. Maybe something in there would help. As she circled it, she spied something red next to an excavator. BINGO! It was a large cooler. Thank goodness for one construction worker's big appetite.

Quickly, she carried it over and positioned it under the window. From there on, getting into the funeral home was a piece of cake.

~~~

Maddy had a sudden flashback and recalled seeing someone at an auction open a crate using a crowbar. There had been no door. They just pried the slats open. That's what she would do! Positioning the crowbar between the bottom horizontal slat and the perpendicular side one, she started to pop the nails up, one by one, then pulled the horizontal slat off. Steadily working, she was able to remove five slats in no time. Thankfully, the crate was poorly constructed, obviously made of cheap materials. Once those five slats had been discarded, she bent down to look inside. The poor woman was lying on her side. Her wrists were raw. She must have tried to get out of the zip ties again. The hose leading to the water backpack on her chest had slipped out of her mouth. Not that it mattered, the pack was completely flat, drained of all water. The blindfold that had once been around her eyes, rendering her blind to her surroundings, was now hanging around her neck, like the fancy neck scarf it was meant to be. The irony didn't escape Maddy.

"Do I know you?" A look of bewilderment crossed her face as she looked at Maddy.

"Kind of…" she answered sheepishly, "We messaged on Facebook. My name's Maddy Whitman. I was looking for Jason Thomas. You gave me his sister's contact information."

"How did you find me?" She looked scared and relieved at the same time.

"It's a long story. Once we get out of here, I'll give you all the details." Maddy wished she didn't have to. Guilt was resurfacing once again. She needed to concentrate on getting her out of this life-threatening situation or else they both might end up dead. Maddy did not want to end up dead. "Let me look around for something I can use to cut the zip ties, then I'll see how we can get you unchained."

"No! Don't leave me here alone!" Juliette was terrified.

"I promise I'll come back! I just need to find something to cut you free. We need to get out of here."

Maddy looked around, eyeing the desk under the Oilers' stained-glass window. This was as good a place as any to start looking. She quickly rummaged through its three drawers. Nothing.

"Maddy? Are you still here?"

"Yes, just trying to find something to use. There's nothing in these drawers!"

"Why don't you try using the crowbar and get me out of these chains first?"

"Okay, let's do that," it was such an obvious solution; she couldn't believe she hadn't thought of it. She assumed that being scared enough to want to pee her pants had hindered logical thinking.

Maddy crawled back into the crate and looked around for where the chain led. It was attached somewhere outside the crate. She would have to go back out to try and dislodge it. This was taking too long. The kidnapper could show up any minute. She had to work faster.

Maddy stared at the chain, trying to figure out what her next move should be. The chain was made of thick, heavy links. It was wound through the zip ties on Juliette's wrists then hung down to her ankles and wound through the zip ties that bound those. Midway down, like a "T", the chain extended three feet away and disappeared between two of the crate's slats. Trying to break the chain was not a realistic option. She had to go for the zip ties.

"Let me try to cut the zip tie around your ankles. There's more room there. Then, I'll work on the chain. This way, maybe you can shuffle around with my help, and we can get you out of here."

"Alright, do whatever you want. Just get me out. I don't care how you do it or if you hurt me while trying. Just. Get. Me. Out!" Juliette was starting to lose her composure. All the days of being locked up in a wooden prison had taken their toll on her.

Maddy carefully wedged the crowbar between Juliette's ankles, setting the flat edge on top of the ties, trying to avoid the chain. She was grateful for the daylight that was starting to come in brighter through the slats. This wasn't going to be an easy task. The light helped some and she managed to slide the crowbar in between the woman's ankles and the chain by angling the bar just a bit. Using all her strength and weight, she shoved the crowbar down as hard as possible. There was a "pop" followed by the sound of chains falling and a piercing scream. Maddy jumped back startled.

"Oh my God! Did I hurt you?"

"It scared me more than hurt. The tie scraped my skin, it looks worse than it feels."

"I'm so sorry!" Maddy looked down at the bloody ankles and felt terrible. Not only was this woman kidnapped and stuck in a crate because of her, but she had now added injuring her to the list.

"Honestly, I don't care. You're my savior. Let's not worry about my ankles right now. Look! The chains came off my ankles!" She kicked aside the chains that had fallen to the floor. They had only been slipped through the zip ties so the chains fell off as soon as they had been cut.

All that was left were her zip-tied wrists, the chain was still wound through them. There wasn't enough space between the wrists to slip the crowbar in without severely injuring her.

Emboldened by the successful ankle release, Maddy grabbed the crowbar and crawled out of the crate once more.

"There's no way I'm risking amputating one of your wrists. Wait here while I try to deal with the chain."

She found the end of the chain. It had been wrapped around and through the handles of four heavy kettlebells. As luck would have it, there were no locks on that end either. Dropping the crowbar, she weaved the chain in and out of each handle, freeing it. There was no way she could break the chain just using the crowbar. She wasn't strong enough. She slipped it back through the slat it was hanging from. They would have to carry it out and wait to cut the ties around her wrists once outside.

Maddy quickly walked back around to the crate's opening, motioning the traumatized woman to come out. "There was no actual lock, it was just woven in and around itself. Since I freed your feet, the rest just needed a good pull."

"Thank you! Thank you!"

"There'll be plenty of time to thank me once we're out of this place. Come over here and I'll steady you while you step out. Then we can both carry the chain and get out of here."

As she helped her out, the look that Juliette gave her was not one of gratitude, it was one filled with terror.

Maddy quickly turned around to see what had scared Juliette and tripped backward over the slats she'd left on the floor, landing on her behind at the exact moment that the broken wooden chair leg was swung at her like a baseball bat. It missed her head as it swished barely a few inches away.

Maddy, trying to ignore the hysterical screaming coming from behind her, began to crawl away as the hooded figure, having missed its target, became unbalanced, falling forward on top of her. They rolled around. Her clothes were pulled, dust flew into her eyes and an elbow hit her nose. Maddy started kicking hard, her foot met a soft target, and she heard an "oomph" as breath was drawn in. She had probably landed a kick in her attacker's stomach. Taking advantage of having been let go, Maddy rolled away and reached for one of the slats, hoping that she could clobber the psycho with it.

Steadying herself, she rose on one knee, then pushed herself up to a squatting position, holding the slat over her head, ready to pounce, looking left and right, trying to see where her attacker might be. That's when she heard the click behind her.

Juliette's screaming became hysterical.

"Shut up you dumb bitch!" a female voice yelled. "Now Maddy, drop that useless piece of wood and turn around, slowly."

Maddy did as she was told. As she turned around, she could see a gun pointing at her, the figure slowly coming out of the shadows and into the light. She couldn't quite recognize the voice, the speaker was trying to disguise it, but it still sounded familiar. The kidnapper's identity was still hidden away from her by the dark hood. Taking one more step toward Maddy, she dramatically pulled the hood off, revealing her identity.

No, it couldn't be. Her eyes must have been playing tricks on her.

"Hello, Maddy. Surprised to see me, aren't you?" "Lauren? What the hell? Why are you doing this?"

How could she have misjudged her new friend so badly?

"Why? Did you think we were friends or something sappy like that? Ha! You were just prey on my web. And hiring those two thugs to break into your car was pure genius, wasn't it? Had you chasing them all over town," she laughed, proud of herself. "It was so much fun playing with you. So eager to have a new buddy to whine to about a devoted ex. All because of a changed Netflix password. What a pathetic, spoiled, princess! You don't even know the first thing about betrayal."

"You two know each other?" Juliette had somewhat regained her composure.

"Oh yes, we're the best of pals according to Mads here. Right BFF of mine?"

"We met not long ago, Lauren is Tom's ex-wife," Maddy answered.

"Look, I have nothing to do with whatever is going on here between you and Maddy, why don't you just let me go?"

"What?! You'd turn on me after I saved you?" Maddy stared in shock at Juliette.

"Don't think I'm not grateful, because I truly am, but you know, in the end, it's every woman for herself," she said with a shrug. "I have nothing to do with this. You got me mixed up in whatever it is that's going on here. Come to think of it, without you, I probably wouldn't be IN this mess!"

"That may be so, but you could at least pretend to be grateful!" Maddy insisted, raising her voice.

"Why? It's not like you actually saved me."

"Are you kidding me? What happened to me being your savior?"

Both women's voices were rising, they were almost yelling at each other.

"A whole lot of good you did me! Am I free? No. I'm still stuck in here…" She gestured at her surroundings. Looking around her, she realized that she'd never seen the actual room before, "Wherever 'here' may be."

"I swear, if you don't shut up and crawl back into that crate, I'll shoot you!" Lauren shouted at Juliette in exasperation. "I have a gun here, remember? And mark my words you annoying bitch, I won't hesitate."

Not needing to be told twice, like a scared animal, Juliette backed into the crate as far as she possibly could go.

"Now where were we? Oh, yes, betrayal. We were about to talk about my cheating bastard of an ex-husband," Lauren leaned casually up against the door frame, but Maddy could tell from her body language that she was tense. Her eyes betrayed her. They were darting from Juliette to Maddy, then around the room and back to the women, as though she wanted to ascertain that everyone stayed put.

"Your husband cheated on you and that's why you killed him?" Maddy decided to try and distract Lauren, even if that meant risking her anger.

"Of course, you don't think I was going to put up with him and that whore of his making a fool out of me, do you?" Lauren's upper lip lifted derisively. "I made sure they both knew who was boss. They had to pay for what they did." Lauren was slowly becoming unhinged, "Faithfulness is a joke to people nowadays, right bitch? You would know about that, wouldn't you?" she said, looking at Juliette. "There are no morals left, nobody cares who gets hurt while you rut like an animal. We're all just collateral damage."

Maddy looked from Lauren to Juliette. Maybe she wasn't the only reason Lauren had chosen Juliette as her captive. She had to keep Lauren talking so there was time for the police to rescue them.

"All that stuff in the locker, those were your trophies?"

"Some of it, yeah. When I realized he had this secret stash of stuff, I figured what a perfect hideaway, right? And it was, for a long time, until you had to come snooping around."

"There were more trophies than just your ex-husband's and his girlfriend's," Maddy commented. She might end up dying at the hands of this crazy woman, but at least she would satisfy her curiosity and Ashley would be a witness if she was still listening at the other end of the cell phone. Boy, was she hoping that she was still listening.

"Yes, there were, there definitely were, there are always more sluts out there, willing to sleep with a married man," Lauren said with a smile that turned Maddy's stomach. "They needed to be stopped, so I stopped them. Forever."

"You killed them because they made the mistake of sleeping with a married man?" Maddy asked incredulously.

"Well, that wasn't the only reason," Lauren chuckled. "You see, the thing most people don't realize is that once you taste the exhilaration and power of taking a life, the sound of breath being taken out of a living being, you want more and more of it. There's an excitement in knowing that you made the world stop for someone, you caused their heart to slowly stop beating. There's no feeling like it in the whole universe!"

"Why did you decide to play these games with me? Why not just kill me outright? And why kill an innocent Canada goose?" Maddy asked.

Lauren's mouth lifted into a half smile as she pushed herself away from the door frame and slowly walked towards Maddy until only inches separated them. Staring straight into her eyes, she took her gun and slowly ran it down along the side of Maddy's face as though it were a caress.

"It's kind of like sex my dear, it's so much better when there's some foreplay."

"Oh," Maddy shivered, her voice cracking. This woman was even crazier than she'd thought. How many people had she killed? How many lives were snuffed out because this woman's husband had cheated on her? Where the heck was the cavalry? Her friends should have been here by now. Did her cell phone accidentally turn off while she was wrestling to get away from Lauren? Had its battery run out?

Out of nowhere, a loud cracking sound reverberated in the abandoned office, and the floor beneath them began to shake. The stained glass in the window shattered and the whole room seemed to be moving. Without warning, they were flung around like toy ragdolls, each of them slamming to the ground with a bone-jarring crash.

Chapter 37

Clouds of dust were hanging heavy in the air making it difficult to see. Where once stood the Oilers' stained-glass window, there was a gaping hole. Maddy picked herself up, wiped the dust from her eyes, and checked on Juliette.

"What the hell just happened?" Juliette slid out of the crate, dragging the chain behind her.

"I'm not certain, but I think they've started tearing down the building," Maddy said, fearfully looking around for Lauren.

She spotted her lifting herself off the ground. She must've been knocked down by the force of the blow just like Maddy. It wasn't just Lauren that had ended up on the ground, she had also dropped her gun during the commotion. It was now lying in the middle of the floor, halfway between them. Both spotted it at the same time. They lunged for it. Maddy reached it first. Using her years of pitching practice playing in a softball league, she threw the gun as hard as she could toward the gaping hole. It flew right through it just as something made contact with the wall a second time. Drywall, bricks, and debris exploded in all directions. This sent all three women tumbling towards the door. Lauren was the first to get up. Seeing Maddy on her knees, she kicked her back down.

"You two are not worth it! But don't think for a second that I'm done with you, Maddy Whitman. Better keep looking over your shoulders, one day I'll be back to get you both." As she spoke those last words to them, she raced out the door, mowing down Ashley who was coming to the rescue.

"Friggin' Talus Balls!!" Ashley picked herself up and stood there, hesitating for a split second, trying to decide whether to go help Maddy or run after Lauren.

The building shook again as the funeral home a third time. It was followed by a blood-curdling scream.

Chapter 38

S top! Stop!" Rick yelled as he jumped out of his car and ran as fast as humanly possible toward the excavator that was moving toward the front of the funeral home. "There are people in there!"

The grizzled excavator's operator shook his head at Rick and continued towards the funeral home's entrance. Rick caught up to it and stood right in front of the building's door, stopping the large machinery in its tracks. The operator was not pleased. He jumped out of the cab, eyes bulging, hands balled into a fist.

"Hey, buddy! What in the bloody hell do you think you're doing?" He was now standing nose to nose with Rick, yelling in his face.

"I told you there are people in that building!"

"Bullshit! All the doors are locked. They've been locked for weeks. If some homeless people are squatting inside, I don't give a damn! They're not my problem. Now get out of my way or I'll make you. And trust me, it won't be pleasant, pal."

Tasha had been watching all this happen as she was getting out of the car. If she didn't do something right away to stop them, there was no doubt in her mind that things would get ugly. Nobody could threaten Rick and get away with it unscathed. He was usually a peaceful guy but if pushed too far, you didn't want to be anywhere near him.

It was now Rick's turn to get in the guy's face. Pulling himself up straight, he appeared much taller than his six- foot frame. Spitting his words out, he was almost chest- bumping the guy.

"If you so much as lay a finger on me, walla ya ebn el kalb, your great-grandchildren's children will feel me punch you!"

He was using Arabic which meant he was beyond pissed-off. That was all Tasha needed to hear to jump into the fray between the two red-faced men.

"Gentlemen!" using her angry mom's voice, she looked from one to the other, "I just called the police, so I strongly recommend that you wait for them to come and let them decide."

"With all due respect... 'Ma'am'..." the guy looked down at her and smirked, "My crew and I won't stop unless our boss tells us to."

Those were the wrong words to use with Tasha. "Don't you dare 'ma'am' or 'all due respect' me, you... you... condescending porco!" She started poking him hard repeatedly with her finger, pushing him backward while doing so.

"You... don't... want... to... mess... with... me.... buddy!"

"Listen, man, if you don't control that woman of yours…" A loud crash coming from the back of the building stopped him in mid-sentence.

Tasha's eyes went wide.

"What was that?" She looked at Rick.

"That's the rest of my crew doing their job. I'd like to see you try and stop all of us without a stop-work order."

"I'm going in there." Rick tried to enter the funeral home, but the door was locked. "Let me in there you idiot! My friends are inside!"

"Listen here, you…. idiot!" The guy gripped Rick by the collar. "I told you nobody's in there. It's a demolition site. No one is allowed in. You two shouldn't even be near here."

The high-pitched sirens of approaching police cars brought the dangerously escalating confrontation to an abrupt halt. Two police units, lights flashing, had driven at full speed into the parking lot, coming to a screeching stop next to Rick and Tasha's car. Kyle climbed out of his unmarked car and rapidly walked towards them with steely determination. This version of Kyle was not one you wanted to cross.

With an authoritative voice, he demanded to know what was going on.

"Will someone please explain to me why the three of you are standing here, arguing, while a building with people in it is being knocked down?"

Another crash could be heard coming from the other end of the building.

"Sir," he turned to the construction worker, "I strongly recommend that you radio your colleagues immediately and have them stop this demolition at once," Kyle was livid.

"I can't do that, officer." "That's Detective"

"Sir… I mean Detective, I need orders from my supervisor to do that."

"Consider this an order from your supervisor if you know what's good for you. And trust me, sir, it IS what's best for you."

A third crash was heard, this time coming from the west side of the building. It was followed by a blood-curdling scream.

"Now!" Kyle ordered.

"Yes, Detective sir, I'm on it."

~~~

Once the heavy-duty equipment had been shut down, an eerie silence fell over the worksite. The dust from the demolition hung heavily in the air. It took a few minutes for the onlookers to see things clearly. Rick, Tasha, and Kyle held their breath as they strained to see what was left of the building beyond the front entrance, which was still standing and still locked. Heart in her throat, Tasha began to pray to all her family saints and angels.

At that moment, she saw Ashley, Maddy and a bedraggled woman stumbling through the front door. Tasha had no idea if this dishevelled, dust covered woman was Juliette or the kidnapper. All three were coughing and trying to wipe the dust from their mouths and noses. The unknown woman squinted in the bright morning sun and looked around, trying to get her bearings.

"Oh, thank God!" Tasha exclaimed as she ran towards Maddy and Ashley. Throwing her arms around them, she hung on so tight and for so long that they couldn't breathe.

Rick and Kyle walked towards them. Rick hugged Maddy and Ashley, saying "Good to see you," in a tight, gruff voice, it was obvious to those who knew him that he was barely keeping it together. Rick was a big softy. He may have looked like a tough guy but on the inside, he was a worried mess. He felt so responsible for not having been able to get inside to save them. Kyle, on the other hand, just stood there, looking at the women with a huge grin on his face.

"Good to see you both still in one piece," he said. "You may not have caught the kidnapper, but it looks like you saved this woman."

"What do you mean we didn't catch the kidnapper?" Maddy couldn't believe what she had just heard. "Didn't you catch her when she came running out?"

"Running out? No one came running out!" Rick interjected, confused.

They all turned to look at the building just as somewhere in the interior, a wall collapsed with a loud crack, causing the ground to tremble. Looking at the rubble, the reality of what had just happened washed over them. They were not only looking at a demolished funeral home, but they could also be looking at a grave.

"Why didn't she come out?" Ashley asked in a subdued tone.

"Who knows, Ash?" Tasha said, hugging her once again, "Bella, she wasn't in her right mind."

"She was evil," the woman who they had rescued spoke up. "Pure evil."

"She certainly was, Juliette," Maddy said with a deep sigh.

"Who's Juliette?" asked Sally.

Chapter 39

Sipping an oat milk latte while sitting on a cafe's patio and letting the end of summer sun caress her face, Maddy sighed deeply, feeling the weight of the world being lifted from her shoulders. Ashley reached for her hand and smiled. Words weren't needed, she completely understood her. "It's really over Mads"

"I want to believe it, but they never found her body. She might still be out there, wanting revenge."

"We all heard Lauren scream. She's gone," Ashley squeezed her hand. "Kyle did say that there was too much rubble in the back to know for sure if she was buried under the debris or not. It's not like they are going to remove everything brick by brick. They did a surface search. Anything below that is going to be removed with diggers. That may take weeks. If anyone was under there, they're long dead. It's been a few days. Nothing or no one has resurfaced. They even looked at neighboring buildings' security cameras and saw nobody leave the funeral home from the back. Okay?"

"Still..."

"Look, here come Rick and Tasha. They'll agree with me."

"Hey, you two, thanks for taking the day off to spend with me," Maddy was grateful to have friends like these three. They had seen her through thick and thin over the years. Not only did they mean the world to her, but they were also her chosen family. She might not have a blood- related family around to turn to, or one she wanted to turn to, but these three had always been there for her, whether she thought she needed it or not.

After the events of the last few weeks, all four of them had decided to take some time off to debrief and destress. And boy, they needed this more than anything.

"How are the twins?" Ashley asked.

"Oh, you know, nothing fazes them. They were quite happy not having us around much the last couple of weeks as we ran around the city chasing bad guys. Rick, what did Sophia say to you this morning?"

"Let me think. I want to quote her verbatim," he smiled widely, showing off his dimples. "Oh, yeah, she said 'Baba, we've had a taste of freedom. It cannot go back to how it was before you helped Auntie Maddy, you understand?' End of quote. The nerve of that girl. I swear if I hadn't found it so funny, she would've been grounded for life."

They all laughed.

"It's hard to believe our goddaughters are almost 13 years old, you guys," Ashley reminded them. "When the three of us met we were just two years older."

"Santa Madre di Dio!" Tasha looked up to the sky. "I only met you guys in university, and you were trouble then. I can't begin to imagine you in high school. God help us all."

Rick was watching Maddy across the table, staring pensively into her latte.

"Hey Maddy, where were you just now?" Rick said, grabbing her attention.

"Hmm… What? Sorry, my mind wandered for a minute."

"She's worried that Lauren is still alive somewhere out there," Ashley informed them. "And that she'll show up to exact revenge unexpectedly one day."

"Lauren had so much pent-up anger and lust for blood," Maddy shared with her friends the insane reasoning and details behind all the murders that had been committed. "She had such hatred towards all women who had affairs with married men. Killing her ex- husband, Jason, and his mistress was just the beginning. Once she'd tasted blood and revenge, she couldn't stop herself."

"Hey, listen to me, Bella, she's gone. Lauren. Is. Gone. Finita la musica, capisce? She's not coming back to hurt you. Body or no body." Tasha emphasized this by wiping her hands together.

"I presume you told Kyle and the other detectives all of this?" Rick hadn't asked what had happened at the station right after the police had arrived at the funeral home. He had wanted to give her some time and space but now he was dying to know.

"I did. They had seen what was going on in the funeral home's office because they were still monitoring the live feed, but there was no sound. Once the wrecking ball hit, the feed died. They found the computer in the rubble and a couple of large solar panels that had apparently been connected to a battery. The electricity to the building had been cut off a few weeks before, so that's how she managed to run the computer and video cameras undetected."

"That psycho bitch had put a lot of thought into this. It's as if she had been planning it for months," Tasha observed. "And was lying in wait for the right circumstances to occur."

"I think I fell right into it. I so wanted to be able to get past my natural distrust of people, I felt that Lauren might be a friend," Maddy lifted a hand to wipe tears from her eyes. "She played me and proved me wrong. All the friends I need are sitting right here with me."

Tasha leaned over and hugged her.

"You have made new friends. Look at Kyle. He was worried sick," Ashley looked at the three of them. "Don't look at me like that."

They laughed at her.

"No, really. He was worried about all of us. He told me he'd never had anyone he cared about in danger before. Let alone four people he considered friends."

"Ash," Rick put his arm around her shoulder. "Kyle is one of the good guys. I understand why you don't want to date anyone seriously yet. Just don't make a decision that you might regret later."

Ashley smiled when she remembered the conversation she and Kyle had at the police station when she'd gone in to have her fingerprints taken. She told her friends how she'd explained to him why she wasn't ready to date him right now, repeating how he wanted more than she wanted or was able to give at this point in her life. He understood. Kyle was willing to wait for as long as she needed. "You see," he'd told her, "I know you are THE one. I'll just have to hang around until you realize that I'm it for you too. I'm not going anywhere. I'm okay with being your friend. For now."

"Like I said," Rick winked at Ashley. "He's one of the good ones."

"I, for one, am looking forward to things going back to normal," Maddy jumped in to change the topic. She could tell that Ashley was getting tired of constantly explaining herself to them. "I want my boring life back."

"Whatever happened to Robert and Brigitte?" Ashley asked, grateful for the opportunity to change the topic away from her love life. She knew the subject of the two lost love birds would do the trick.

"Oh no, didn't I tell you? In all the drama that's been happening, I must have totally forgotten!"

"You certainly did forget, so spill it," no nonsense Tasha happened to have a soft spot for anything to do with love and romance.

"Well, it's better than a soap opera! Turns out, Brigitte didn't know anything about those letters. She didn't even know how they ended up in that estate sale. She'd never seen them before, not even the ones that were opened!"

"Get out of here!" Rick exclaimed.

"I know, right?! She'd always wondered why he hadn't written to her like he said he would. She thought he was just a player who got what he wanted and then moved on to the next gullible girl," Maddy explained. "In fact, he broke her heart!"

"How could that happen?" Tasha asked, leaning forward, and resting her chin in the palm of her hands, enthralled by the romance of the story.

"They aren't completely sure but her parents couldn't stand him, they think the letters could have been intercepted. But that isn't the coolest part," Maddy said teasingly as she sat back, waiting for them to press her for more.

"Come on Maddy, don't make us beg, what's the coolest part?" Ashley was having none of her friend's coyness.

"Oh, well, if you really want to know... It turns out that Brigitte's daughter... is also Robert's!"

"What?!" all three exclaimed in unison.

"Yup, part of the reason why her parents didn't like him was because by the time they moved, they'd found out she was pregnant. Their little love affair left a lifelong reminder."

"So, Robert has a daughter he knew nothing about?" Tasha asked.

"Not only a daughter but a granddaughter as well! They're arranging for all of them to get together and have a family reunion of sorts."

"Well, here's to a much nicer story than the psycho- killer kidnapper," Rick said, raising his coffee mug in celebration.

Chapter 40

There were two more buyers left for Maddy to meet. One was for two vases she'd found in a recent storage unit auction; the other was for the last coins she had from Jason Thomas' locker. She would finally be done with all his items. She couldn't wait to put this terrible nightmare behind her.

Unfortunately, her next meeting was with Paris Andrews. The idea of meeting that awful woman turned her stomach, but Maddy was a smart businessperson, and smart businesspeople didn't let their feelings get in the way. She dreamed of eventually having a brick-and-mortar shop where she could sell all the treasures she bought at auctions. To bring that dream to fruition, she had to develop a regular clientele, repeat customers who would keep coming back to buy at her shop. This meant finding buyers with deep pockets or who had clients with even deeper pockets. According to research and asking around Ashley had done, Paris probably fit the bill.

Maddy chose to meet her buyers at a café on 124th street so she could also run some errands. The people who worked there never rushed their customers nor made them feel like they had to leave to make room for others. She could sit there all day, sipping on their homemade Chai and working on her laptop if she felt like it. The shops she wanted to go to were nearby, she could just park her car for the day, walk to do her errands, and return to meet her buyers. It was almost back to school time, and she wanted to pick up a couple of gifts for Sophia and Chloe, Rick and Tasha's girls. These two tweens were very much into buying locally made jewelry.

There was a shop right next door to the cafés that only carried products made by local artisans. That would take care of that errand. The other one was a visit to Bernard's Antiques and Collectibles. Bob had agreed to buy the remainder of the jewelry Maddy hadn't been able to sell.

Her errands were now done. Now to wait for Paris. Paris did eventually show up. Twenty minutes late.

That woman certainly didn't try to ingratiate herself to Maddy.

"Maddy, you need to get yourself a proper office," Paris said, lowering her sunglasses to look at her.

"I have a proper office. I prefer to meet people in cafés. I find it more comfortable, it's casual, and most make better coffee than I ever could."

"I, for one, prefer a more professional setting than a casual one. Less fly by night. It would indicate to me that you were a serious seller and give people more confidence in you."

Oh, how she would love to see Paris' face if she had to meet Maddy at her 'proper' office in the Triple A storage unit. The temptation to set their next meeting there was, at this moment, quite irresistible. Yet as tempting as it was, Maddy knew better. That would most likely be the end of any future sales to her.

"I'm quite sure that you're a busy person…"

"Extremely busy."

"Yes. Well, in that case, I certainly wouldn't want to keep you here longer than necessary. Let me show you the two vases," she pulled the first one out of its bag and gingerly unwrapped it from the bubble wrap that it was rolled up in. Paris' eyes went wide. Maddy knew right then that all she had to do was reel her in. As she took the second one out, she paused for a moment.

"I was visiting a friend of mine who owns an antique shop earlier today. He wanted to see the vases that I had gushed about. You're lucky I promised you first right of refusal because he was very interested in buying them."

"No! You promised them to me!" Realizing that she had just shown her cards, Paris quickly added, "Anyway, an antique dealer would take a commission or pay you less because of his overheads. I can give you much better."

"I am selling them for $700 each," Maddy gave her a determined look.

"They're not worth that much," Paris appeared just as firm.

"Hmm, I don't agree. My friend offered me $800 each. He said that they were not only unique but that they were Japanese vases signed by Yokokira Kazan.

And if, as you say, he would be paying me less because of his overheads… then I should be selling them to you for more."

In reality, Maddy hadn't shown them to Bob. She had just googled the vases and the signature on them. There were similar ones by the same artist that had been sold by some auction houses. The starting bids on most of these had been $600.00. From Paris' reaction, the woman knew their worth. Maddy wasn't an auction house. To get those prices, she would have had to pay a commission which would put much less money in her pocket.

"You have first right of refusal, Paris. I'm honoring that, but I will not give them away."

"Hmm… $400 each."

"$600. I can always sell them to my friend."

"I am willing to pay $500 and not a penny more."

"Alright, $500 each but only because I like you,"

Maddy hoped her nose wasn't growing.

"Excellent! I'm e-transferring you the money as we speak," Paris tapped away on her cell while Maddy packed up the vases.

"You drive a hard bargain, Maddy Whitman, I respect that. I think we'll be doing business again. Preferably in an office."

"Thank you. It's been a pleasure, Paris." Maddy was holding back a victorious smile.

She knew full well from her last exchange with Paris that the woman would try to get the vases for less than their market value, a lot less. That's why she made up the story and Bob's fake offer, hoping she would end up with a fair price, one she was willing to sell the vases for. You must always leave room for negotiations. Some people were fair, others wanted the best price they could get. That's understandable but certainly not how you made money as the seller.

Paris picked up the two bags with the vases and started to walk away. She then stopped, flipped her hair back and said smugly over her shoulder, "And by the way, I know what you just did. But I like the thrill of playing the game. You're getting smarter Maddy. Today, we both walked away with a win. We'll see how it goes next time." She then winked at her, opened the door, and 'poof!' disappeared into thin air.

Okay, she didn't disappear. She walked away down the street. Still, she was a witch who had just burst Maddy's happiness bubble. '*Oh, well,*' Maddy. '*Hopefully my last buyer will be decent. He sounded like a sweet old guy on the phone.*'

Half an hour later, a sweet old guy was indeed making his way towards her, he had a big, dimpled smile on his face.

"You must be Maddy!" he said. "You look very smart just like a Maddy."

That was a good start to the meeting.

"Hello, you must be Randall." She extended her hand for a handshake.

"I sure am, buttercup!" Out came the dimples again. Instead of shaking her hand, he bent down and kissed it. "It's an honor and a pleasure to meet you."

Ooo boy! Maddy blushed. She had better be careful with this one, or she might find herself giving away those coins for free.

"Let's see those two treasures you have for me."

She took out the coins and placed them on the table in front of Randall.

He took a loupe out of his shirt pocket and examined the coin. This made Maddy smile. It also sealed the deal on her buying a loupe for herself.

He looked up at her.

"Age, you know. Nowadays, I need this to see the details," he brought the loupe back up to his eye. "These are almost scratch-free. That's good, very good."

"I was told that they were almost in mint condition.

MS60, I believe."

"You did your homework, I see," he nodded, impressed. "Bravo!" Randall stared at her for a few seconds, then tilted his head. "You know, you remind me of someone."

"And who could that be?"

"Someone I loved dearly. I was told she moved to Ontario 25 years ago. Forget it, it doesn't matter," he shook his head, wiped his loupe on his shirt, and put it back in his pocket. "Tell me, did you find out how much they're worth?"

Maddy's interest was piqued. Could this be another Brigitte and Robert? Maybe she could reconnect him with this lost love of his? She definitely had a soft spot for lost lovers. Maybe she could do this sort of thing as a side gig! She needed to get some more information about this lost love of his.

"Yes, depending on the market and the demand," she said, trying to refocus her wandering mind. "They could be worth as much as $150 and $75 respectively," Maddy felt unusually proud of herself for having done the research. It's not like she never did her research, she always did. But for some reason, she felt that she wanted to please this old man. She wanted to impress him.

"That's correct. Well done!" He leaned forward, became very serious, and pointed his finger at her. "Now comes the time to negotiate. I will offer you $175 for both."

"Okay," Maddy was doomed. This little old man was much too cute. After Paris, he was a breath of fresh air. Just what she needed. He could have them for $175.

"Wrong answer!" he sat up in his chair, looking pained. "Never agree on the first offer! I thought you said you did this for a living?"

"I do, it's just that I like you." She blushed again, embarrassed. Why on earth was she blushing? She never blushed! She was under this old guy's spell. He had to be some kind of warlock.

"That's even worse! Never develop feelings toward a buyer, good or bad. Not if you want to end up with a fair deal, young lady."

Maddy felt terrible for disappointing him. Wait a minute, she thought, why did she care what he thought? What was wrong with her

"I was just being nice. Is that so bad?"

"Yes, if negotiating a sale," softening, he looked at her with a twinkle in his eyes. "But also no. If in real life, nice is very good. I'll offer you $190, what do you think?"

"No, $200," There, Maddy thought. I'll show him how I can be a ruthless negotiator.

"Ha ha ha ha ha!" Randall roared with laughter. "Deal!

You're one smart cookie and a fast learner. $200 it is." He started counting out $20 bills and then stopped. "You wouldn't happen to be selling a 1987 first- edition Canadian dollar coin, would you?"

Maddy was surprised by the question. She had that coin on her. It was the very last coin from the Thomas collection. She'd taken it out of the coin book when she sold the rest of the coins to Bob earlier, tucking it in her purse as a memento. Maybe it was time to let go of the past, of things that could have been. Out of all the potential buyers, this sweet man would be the someone she could allow herself to sell it to.

"I just happen to have one on me. It's in mint condition."

"Oh! Wonderful!" He looked like a kid at Christmas, "May I see it please?"

Maddy took out the coin and handed it to him in its clear, plastic sleeve. Out came the loupe one more time.

"It is in mint condition. MS67. Just a couple of very small contact marks. One tiny bit more noticeable but not detracting. I will take it for $180."

Wow, Maddy thought, PopPop had been right about the Loonie's potential value.

"May I ask why you have a particular interest in the 1987 Loonie?" His inquiring about that specific coin had piqued her curiosity. She had to ask.

"Oh, it's a long story…"

"I'm in no rush. Please, I'd love to hear it."

"They're for my granddaughter. I gave her one many, many years ago. I haven't seen her in a long, long time. You see, her family kept her away from me. I've been collecting these for her ever since, hoping one day I'll see her again. Funny thing, now that I think of it," he looked up at her, his brows furrowing, he seemed to be grappling with something. "Her nickname was Maddy too, but her full name was…"

Maddy stood up quickly, cutting him off, almost upending their table, and sending her empty coffee cup crashing to the floor. People turned to look at them. Maddy's jaw hung open, she gaped at him, uncertain. He looked up at her, confusion reflecting on his face. Their eyes met and he saw the shock and excitement in hers. He felt his heart leap out of his chest. Tears welled up in his eyes as it finally dawned on him.

"You're still alive?" she asked, incredulously. "Is it really you?" he whispered.

"PopPop?!"

If you enjoyed the first of the Maddy Whitman Mystery Series please leave a review where you purchased this book.

About the Authors

Monique MacDonald

Born in Montreal to Lebanese-Egyptian parents, Monique Kerba MacDonald started writing at her grandmother's kitchen table from the moment she could scribble with a crayon. Her grandmother was passionate about the written word and encouraged her to write poetry and short stories. Monique's love of writing led her to careers in education and communications, as well as being a regular columnist for various newspapers and magazines.

With the exception of a few years living in Calgary, Fort McMurray, Saint Lucia W.I., and Cambridge, Ontario, Monique has been calling Edmonton home since she was 15. She's a proud St Joseph High School grad and University of Alberta Faculty of Education alum. This is her first novel.

Carla Howatt

Alberta-born Carla Howatt is a woman who has raised three children, two husbands, and numerous pets. She is a communications professional, former politician, an avid chocolate connoisseur, and an author who has written five fiction books and several non-fiction.

Her earliest memory is bringing home her first elementary school reader; feeling as though the entire world was opening up to her, she has never lost the sense of wonder and excitement.

Coming in the Fall of 2024!

Maddy and her friends have found themselves deep in trouble once more. Where has PopPop been all these years? Did Kyle ever win over Ashley?

Read on…

Book 2 - Excerpt

Y̶ou have until ten pm to drop off the cash or else we'll decapitate your precious David Spenser."

The ransom note was written in red crayon on a striped, yellow notepad similar to the ones that had once been used for shorthand.

"I can't believe that someone would go to such lengths. Who could do such a horrible thing? A decapitation?" Maddy shook with anger as she sat beside Rick in his truck.

"Do they still make shorthand paper? Rick asked. "Who still uses that?"

"Is that all you can think of right now, Rick?" Maddy said, exasperated. "Focus on the road."

"It's just strange, that's all."

"Could you please speed up a bit?" Fear of impending violence had her wishing she was behind the steering wheel instead of Rick. She hated not being in control. Why couldn't he drive faster?

"Mads, I would if I could. Can't you see that the traffic's backed up?" Rick sounded as irritated as she was. "We just passed the last exit before the one we will need. There's nothing much we can do right now but wait. We're stuck here just like everybody else."

They had been late due to an accident on the Yellowhead freeway. A multiple-car collision and rollover had caused several injuries and it was chaos. Ambulances and firetrucks had closed the westbound lanes. It had taken almost half an hour to free up one lane to let the mile-long-backed-up traffic through.

"I know, Rick, I'm sorry. I feel so helpless."

They had sped towards the abandoned roadside gas station as fast as they could, only to find themselves slowing to a standstill. The Yellowhead was crawling with police cars due to the crash. Maddy and Rick had been quiet so far on the drive, anxious about the threat. That woman wouldn't be so callous as to commit such a horrific act for a few minutes of tardiness, would she?

"Do you think she would actually go that far?" Rick finally broke the silence and expressed what Maddy was thinking. The worry over what they might find at their destination was consuming them.

"This person was going to bash my head in, I'm lucky to have gotten away." The memory of her barely escaping another concussion wasn't a pleasant one. "Who knows how far she's willing to go?"

"You seem to attract danger. I'm not sure I want to be friends with you anymore." Rick responded, trying to create some levity.

She grimaced back at him.

"Look!" Rick pointed to the cars in front of them. "They're finally allowing people to use the shoulder. We should be able to get there in less than ten minutes."

~~~

Maddy didn't bother to wait for him to turn off the engine before jumping out of the VW Beetle named Bugsy and racing straight to the padlocked door. There was no way of breaking the lock. Two steps behind her, Rick grabbed a brick he found laying on the ground and smashed the window. Taking off his sweatshirt, he rolled it around his hand and used it to clear off the broken glass. He then helped her climb through the window. She wasn't even gone a minute when he heard her scream.

"What's wrong? Did she decapitate him?" He feared that they were too late.

"Yes, but that's not the worst of it," she answered, her voice trembling.

"What do you mean, it's not the worst of it?" He couldn't imagine what could be worse than finding a decapitated David Spencer.

"There's a dead woman's body next to the head.

There's blood everywhere."

KEEP IN TOUCH!

To hear when the next story in the series is ready for purchase, sign up for our newsletter.

HTTPS://BIT.LY/3INJP4S

Or, follow the Maddy Whitman Mystery Series on TikTok, Facebook, Instagram and Twitter (X).